Praise for Brandon Sanderson

"Sanderson's contemporary fantasy is populated with superb characterizations (as evidenced by the multiple depictions of Legion's aspects) and is surprisingly thought-provoking." —*Kirkus Reviews*

"Readers will get drawn into the fascinating world of Stephen and his friends—real and imagined—as they work together to solve the seemingly unsolvable." —*Publishers Weekly*

"Stephen Leeds is a genius with a problem with multiple personalities. . . . This collection combines three novellas featuring this fascinating character." —*Locus*

"What sets [the Stormlight Archive novels] apart is how Mr. Sanderson raises genre stakes through detailed world-building." —*The New York Times*

"Sanderson's skill at world-building is unmatched, and in the Stormlight Archive series, he has developed an innovative magical system and combined it with rich, complex characters to create a compelling story. His eagerly awaited sequel to *The Way of Kings* exceeds expectations. This developing epic series is a must-read for all fantasy fans."
—*Library Journal* (starred review)
on *Words of Radiance*

"A very impressive continuation."
—*Booklist* (starred review)
on *Words of Radiance*

BY BRANDON SANDERSON®

THE STORMLIGHT ARCHIVE®
The Way of Kings
Words of Radiance
Oathbringer

THE MISTBORN® SAGA

THE ORIGINAL TRILOGY
Mistborn
The Well of Ascension
The Hero of Ages

THE WAX AND WAYNE SERIES
The Alloy of Law
Shadows of Self
The Bands of Mourning

Elantris
Warbreaker
Arcanum Unbounded: The Cosmere® Collection
Legion: The Many Lives of Stephen Leeds

ALCATRAZ VS. THE EVIL LIBRARIANS
Alcatraz vs. the Evil Librarians
The Scrivener's Bones
The Knights of Crystallia
The Shattered Lens
The Dark Talent

THE RECKONERS®
Steelheart
Firefight
Calamity

Skyward

The Rithmatist

LEGION

|||||||||||||||||||| |||||||||||||||||||| || |||| ||||| ||||

THE MANY LIVES OF
STEPHEN LEEDS

Brandon Sanderson

TOR

A TOM DOHERTY ASSOCIATES BOOK
NEW YORK

This is a work of fiction. All of the characters, organizations, and events portrayed in these novellas are either products of the author's imagination or are used fictitiously.

LEGION: THE MANY LIVES OF STEPHEN LEEDS

Copyright © 2018 by Dragonsteel Entertainment, LLC

Legion © 2012 by Dragonsteel Entertainment, LLC. First published in 2012 by Subterranean Press

Legion: Skin Deep © 2014 by Dragonsteel Entertainment, LLC. First published in 2014 by Subterranean Press

Lies of the Beholder © 2018 by Dragonsteel Entertainment, LLC.

Mistborn®, The Stormlight Archive®, Reckoners®, Cosmere®, and Brandon Sanderson® are registered trademarks of Dragonsteel Entertainment, LLC

All rights reserved.

A Tor Book
Published by Tom Doherty Associates
120 Broadway
New York, NY 10271

www.tor-forge.com

Tor® is a registered trademark of Macmillan Publishing Group, LLC.

ISBN 978-1-250-29782-2

Our books may be purchased in bulk for promotional, educational, or business use. Please contact your local bookseller or the Macmillan Corporate and Premium Sales Department at 1-800-221-7945, extension 5442, or by email at MacmillanSpecialMarkets@macmillan.com.

First Edition: September 2018
First Mass Market Edition: August 2020

Printed in the United States of America

0 9 8 7 6 5 4 3 2 1

For Daniel Wells and Greg Creer

CONTENTS

Preface

Psychology-as-superpower is a recurring theme in my works. I've always believed that the personality traits that make us each distinctive (the way we process information, the way we motivate ourselves, the way we shelter our psyche from the bad while learning to cherish the good) can be either our greatest strengths or our most dramatic limitations. How you see yourself, along with how you use what you have, is often more important than talents, skills, or even supernatural abilities.

That said, no series I've written has explored this idea more explicitly than the Legion stories. I began the first of what would become three novellas (all of which are collected in this volume) back in 2011. The premise was simple: What if a man's hallucinations proved beneficial to him in his life, rather than the typical distraction? What followed wasn't truly an exploration of any real psychological phenomenon, but instead a look at how different facets of our personalities influence the way we interact with the world.

It also proved to be a great deal of fun. Part action-adventure, part comedy, part near-future science fiction. Over the years, I couldn't leave Stephen Leeds alone. As of this writing, *Legion* is the only original-story novella of mine that I've ever given a sequel. There was something intoxicating about the brew you'll find in these pages. Somehow, these were both fleet and airy mysteries *and* explorations of my own psychology. They were cathartic to write—welcome breaks from other projects—and in some ways the most personal stories I've ever done. (The third one in particular.)

Though these are three separate novellas, I wrote them to create a cohesive story together—with the last of the three wrapping up the series with a complete finale. And as satisfying as they were to write, it's even more satisfying to know that they are finished, that the story is wrapped up, and that I can finally present this volume. The well and truly complete story of Stephen Leeds.

Brandon Sanderson
March 2018

Acknowledgments

As always, my wonderful wife, Emily, gets a big thumbs-up for dealing with the sometimes erratic life of a professional writer. I'd like to thank Moshe Feder, my editor at Tor, for encouraging this project from its earliest days. The Incumbent and Inscrutable Peter Ahlstrom did his usual excellent job as my editorial assistant, and my agent Joshua Bilmes is equally worthy of praise.

A special thanks to Subterranean Press for giving Stephen Leeds his first release in print. Bill Schafer, Yanni Kuznia, Morgan Schlicker, and Gail Cross were fantastic to work with.

At Tor, I'd like to thank Devi Pillai, Rachel Bass, Rafal Gibek, Patty Garcia, Lucille Rettino, and Greg Collins. The copyeditor was Terry McGarry, and the proofreaders were Kirsten Brink and Janine Barlow. The beautiful cover art was provided by Miranda Meeks.

Thanks to Isaac StewaRt for the chapter header

designs. Howard Tayler also helped me brainstorm at lunch one day, and gets a writer high five.

Anat Errel was a huge help with details about Jerusalem. Beta and alpha readers included Kaylynn Zo-Bell, Danielle & Ben Olsen, Karen & Peter Ahlstrom, Dan Wells, Alan Layton, Ethan Skarstedt, Darci & Eric James Stone, Alan Layton, Emily Sanderson, Kathleen Dorsey Sanderson, Brian T. Hill, Dominique Nolan, Mi'chelle & Josh Walker, Kalyani Poluri, Rahul Pantula, Ravi Persaud, Becca Reppert, Darci & Brandon Cole, Gary Singer, Ted Herman, Deana Covel Whitney, Ross Newberry, Mark Lindberg, Paige Vest, Sumejja Muratagic-Tadic, Jory Phillips, Anthony Pero, Tyler Patrick, Drew McCaffrey, Trae Cooper, Brian Magnant, Paige Phillips, Alice Arneson, Bao Pham, William Juan, Jacqui Hopson, Evgeni Kirilov, Megan Kanne, and K. Abigail Parsons. Gamma readers also included Chris "Gunner" McGrath, Glen Vogelaar, Richard Fife, Hillary Argyle, Nikki Ramsay, and Eric Petrie.

I couldn't do this without Adam Horne, Kara Stewart, Emily Grange, Kathleen Dorsey Sanderson, and everyone else at Dragonsteel Entertainment.

Once again, many thanks to my wonderful family, including my three very excited—and very busy—little boys.

LEGION

O N E

My name is Stephen Leeds, and I am perfectly sane. My hallucinations, however, are all quite mad.

The gunshots coming from J.C.'s room popped like firecrackers. Grumbling to myself, I grabbed the earmuffs hanging outside his door—I'd learned to keep them there—and pushed my way in. J.C. wore his own earmuffs, his handgun raised in two hands, sighting at a picture of Osama bin Laden on the wall.

Beethoven was playing. Very loudly.

"I was trying to have a conversation!" I yelled.

J.C. didn't hear me. He emptied a clip into bin Laden's face, punching an assortment of holes through the wall in the process. I didn't dare get close. He might accidentally shoot me if I surprised him.

I didn't know what would happen if one of my hallucinations shot me. How would my mind interpret that? Undoubtedly, there were a dozen psychologists who'd want to write a paper on it. I wasn't inclined to give them the opportunity.

"J.C.!" I shouted as he stopped to reload.

He glanced toward me, then grinned, taking off his earmuffs. Any grin from J.C. looks half like a scowl, but I'd long ago learned to stop being intimidated by him.

"Eh, Skinny," he said, holding up the handgun. "Care to fire off a mag or two? You could use the practice."

I took the gun from him. "We had a shooting range installed in the mansion for a purpose, J.C. *Use it.*"

"Terrorists don't usually find me in a shooting range. Well, it did happen that once. Pure coincidence."

I sighed, taking the remote from the end table, then turning down the music. J.C. reached out, pointing the tip of the gun up in the air, then moving my finger off the trigger. "Safety first, kid."

"It's an imaginary gun anyway," I said, handing it back to him.

"Yeah, sure."

J.C. doesn't believe that he's a hallucination, which is unusual. Most of them accept it, to one extent or another. Not J.C. Big without being bulky, square-faced but not distinctive, he had the eyes of a killer. Or so he claimed. Perhaps he kept them in his pocket.

He slapped a new clip into the gun, then eyed the picture of bin Laden.

"Don't," I warned.

"But—"

"He's dead anyway. They got him ages ago."

"That's a story we told the public, Skinny." J.C. holstered the gun. "I'd explain, but you don't have clearance."

"Stephen?" a voice came from the doorway.

I turned. Tobias is another hallucination—or "aspect," as I sometimes call them. Lanky and ebony-skinned, he had dark freckles on his age-wrinkled cheeks. He kept his greying hair very short, and wore a loose, informal business suit with no necktie.

"I was merely wondering," Tobias said, "how long you intend to keep that poor man waiting."

"Until he leaves," I said, joining Tobias in the hall-way. The two of us began walking away from J.C.'s room.

"He was very polite, Stephen," Tobias said.

Behind us, J.C. started shooting again. I groaned.

"I'll go speak to J.C.," Tobias said in a soothing voice. "He's just trying to keep up his skills. He wants to be of use to you."

"Fine, whatever." I left Tobias and rounded a corner in the lush mansion. I had forty-seven rooms. They were nearly all filled. At the end of the hallway, I entered a small room decorated with a Persian rug and wood panels. I threw myself down on the black leather couch in the center.

Ivy sat in her chair beside the couch. "You intend to continue through *that*?" she asked over the sound of the gunshots.

"Tobias is going to speak to him."

"I see," Ivy said, making a notation on her note-pad. She wore a dark business suit, with slacks and a jacket. Her blonde hair was up in a bun. She was in her early forties, and was one of the aspects I'd had the longest.

"How does it make you feel," she said, "that your projections are beginning to disobey you?"

"Most do obey me," I said defensively. "J.C. has *never* paid attention to what I tell him. That hasn't changed."

"You deny that it's getting worse?"

I didn't say anything.

She made a notation.

"You turned away another petitioner, didn't you?" Ivy asked. "They come to you for help."

"I'm busy."

"Doing what? Listening to gunshots? Going more mad?"

"I'm *not* going more mad," I said. "I've stabilized. I'm practically normal. Even my non-hallucinatory psychiatrist acknowledges that."

Ivy said nothing. In the distance, the gunshots finally stopped, and I sighed in relief, raising my fingers to my temples. "The formal definition of insanity," I said, "is actually quite fluid. Two people can have the exact same condition, with the exact same severity, but one can be considered *sane* by the official standards while the other is considered *insane*. You cross the line into insanity when your mental state stops you from being able to function, from being able to have a normal life. By those standards, I'm not the least bit insane."

"You call this a normal life?" she asked.

"It works well enough." I glanced to the side. Ivy had covered up the wastebasket with a clipboard, as usual.

Tobias entered a few moments later. "That petitioner is still there, Stephen."

"What?" Ivy said, giving me a glare. "You're making the poor man wait? It's been *four hours*."

"All right, fine!" I leaped off the couch. "I'll send him away." I strode out of the room and down the steps to the ground floor, into the grand entryway.

Wilson, my butler—who is a real person, not a hallucination—stood outside the closed door to the sitting room. He looked over his bifocals at me.

"You too?" I asked.

"Four hours, master?"

"I had to get myself under control, Wilson."

"You like to use that excuse, Master Leeds. One wonders if moments like this are a matter of laziness more than control."

"You're not paid to wonder things like that," I said.

He raised an eyebrow, and I felt ashamed. Wilson didn't deserve snappishness; he was an excellent servant, and an excellent person. It wasn't easy to find house staff willing to put up with my . . . particularities.

"I'm sorry," I said. "I've been feeling a little worn down lately."

"I will fetch you some lemonade, Master Leeds," he said. "For . . ."

"Three of us," I said, nodding to Tobias and Ivy—who, of course, Wilson couldn't see. "Plus the petitioner."

"No ice in mine, please," Tobias said.

"I'll have a glass of water instead," Ivy added.

"No ice for Tobias," I said, absently pushing open the door. "Water for Ivy."

Wilson nodded, off to do as requested. He *was* a good butler. Without him, I think I'd go insane.

A young man in a polo shirt and slacks waited in the sitting room. He leaped up from one of the chairs. "Master Legion?"

I winced at the nickname. That had been chosen by a particularly gifted psychologist. Gifted in dramatics, that is. Not really so much in the psychology department.

"Call me Stephen," I said, holding the door for Ivy and Tobias. "What can we do for you?"

"We?" the boy asked.

"Figure of speech," I said, walking into the room and taking one of the chairs across from the young man.

"I . . . uh . . . I hear you help people, when nobody else will." The boy swallowed. "I brought two thousand. Cash." He tossed an envelope with my name and address on it onto the table.

"That'll buy you a consultation," I said, opening it and doing a quick count.

Tobias gave me a look. He hates it when I charge people, but you don't get a mansion with enough rooms to hold all your hallucinations by working for free. Besides, judging from his clothing, this kid could afford it.

"What's the problem?" I asked.

"My fiancée," the young man said, taking something out of his pocket. "She's been cheating on me."

"My condolences," I said. "But we're *not* private investigators. We don't do surveillance."

Ivy walked through the room, not sitting down. She strolled around the young man's chair, inspecting him.

"I know," the boy said quickly. "I just . . . well, she's vanished, you see."

Tobias perked up. He likes a good mystery.

"He's not telling us everything," Ivy said, arms folded, one finger tapping her other arm.

"You sure?" I asked.

"Oh, yes," the boy said, assuming I'd spoken to him. "She's gone, though she did leave this note." He unfolded it and set it on the table. "The really strange thing is, I think there might be some kind of cipher to it. Look at these words. They don't make sense."

I picked up the paper, scanning the words he indicated. They were on the back of the sheet, scrawled quickly, like a list of notes. The same paper had later been used as a farewell letter from the fiancée. I showed it to Tobias.

"That's Plato," he said, pointing to the notes on the back. "Each is a quote from the *Phaedrus*. Ah, Plato. Remarkable man, you know. Few people are aware that he was actually a *slave* at one point, sold on the market by a tyrant who disagreed with his politics—that and the turning of the tyrant's brother into a disciple. Fortunately, Plato was purchased by someone familiar with his work, an admirer you might say, who freed him. It does pay to have loving fans, even in ancient Greece. . . ."

Tobias continued on. He had a deep, comforting voice, which I liked to listen to. I examined the note, then looked up at Ivy, who shrugged.

The door opened, and Wilson entered with the lemonade and Ivy's water. I noticed J.C. standing outside, his gun out as he peeked into the room and inspected the young man. J.C.'s eyes narrowed.

"Wilson," I said, taking my lemonade, "would you kindly send for Audrey?"

"Certainly, master," the butler said. I knew, somewhere deep within, that he had not *really* brought cups for Ivy and Tobias, though he made an act of handing something to the empty chairs. My mind filled in the rest, imagining drinks, imagining Ivy strolling over to pluck hers from Wilson's hand as he tried to give it to where he thought she was sitting. She smiled at him fondly.

Wilson left.

"Well?" the young man asked. "Can you—"

He cut off as I held up a finger. Wilson couldn't see my projections, but he knew their rooms. We had to hope that Audrey was in. She had a habit of visiting her sister in Springfield.

Fortunately, she walked into the room a few minutes

later. She was, however, wearing a bathrobe. "I assume this is important," she said, drying her hair with a towel.

I held up the note, then the envelope with the money. Audrey leaned down. She was a dark-haired woman, a little on the chunky side. She'd joined us a few years back, when I'd been working on a counterfeiting case.

She mumbled to herself for a minute or two, taking out a magnifying glass—I was amused that she kept one in her bathrobe, but that was Audrey for you—and looking from the note to the envelope and back. One had supposedly been written by the fiancée, the other by the young man.

Audrey nodded. "Definitely the same hand."

"It's not a very big sample," I said.

"It's what?" the boy asked.

"It's enough in this case," Audrey said. "The envelope has your full name and address. Line slant, word spacing, letter formation . . . all give the same answer. He also has a very distinctive *e*. If we use the longer sample as the exemplar, the envelope sample can be determined as authentic—in my estimation—at over a ninety percent reliability."

"Thanks," I said.

"I could use a new dog," she said, strolling away.

"I'm *not* imagining you a puppy, Audrey. J.C. creates enough racket! I don't want a dog running around here barking."

"Oh, come on," she said, turning at the doorway. "I'll feed it fake food and give it fake water and take it on fake walks. Everything a fake puppy could want."

"Out with you," I said, though I was smiling. She was teasing. It was nice to have some aspects who didn't mind being hallucinations. The young man regarded me with a baffled expression.

"You can drop the act," I said to him.

"Act?"

"The act that you're surprised by how 'strange' I am. This was a fairly amateur attempt. You're a grad student, I assume?"

He got a panicked look in his eyes.

"Next time, have a roommate write the note for you," I said, tossing it back to him. "Damn it, I don't have time for this." I stood up.

"You could give him an interview," Tobias said.

"After he lied to me?" I snapped.

"Please," the boy said, standing. "My girlfriend . . ."

"You called her a fiancée before," I said, turning. "You're here to try to get me to take on a 'case,' during which you will lead me around by the nose while you secretly take notes about my condition. Your real purpose is to write a dissertation or something."

His face fell. Ivy stood behind him, shaking her head in disdain.

"You think you're the first one to think of this?" I asked.

He grimaced. "You can't blame a guy for trying."

"I can and I do," I said. "Often. Wilson! We're going to need security!"

"No need," the boy said, grabbing his things. In his haste, a miniature recorder slipped out of his shirt pocket and rattled against the table.

I raised an eyebrow as he blushed, snatched the recorder, then dashed from the room.

Tobias rose and walked over to me, his hands clasped behind his back. "Poor lad. And he'll probably have to walk home too. In the rain."

"It's raining?"

"Stan says it will come soon," Tobias said. "Have you considered that they would try things like this less often if you would agree to an interview now and then?"

"I'm tired of being referenced in case studies," I said, waving a hand in annoyance. "I'm tired of being poked and prodded. I'm tired of being special."

"What?" Ivy said, amused. "You'd rather work a day job at a desk? Give up the spacious mansion?"

"I'm not saying there aren't perks," I said as Wilson walked back in, turning his head to watch the youth flee out the front door. "Make sure he actually goes, would you please, Wilson?"

"Of course, master." He handed me a tray with the day's mail on it, then left.

I looked through the mail. He'd already removed the bills and the junk mail. That left a letter from my human psychologist, which I ignored, and a nondescript white envelope, large sized.

I frowned, taking it and ripping open the top. I took out the contents.

There was only one thing in the envelope. A single photograph, five by eight, in black and white. I raised an eyebrow. It was a picture of a rocky coast where a couple of small trees clung to a rock extending out into the ocean.

"Nothing on the back," I said as Tobias and Ivy looked over my shoulder. "Nothing else in the envelope."

"It's from someone else trying to fish for an interview, I'll bet," Ivy said. "They're doing a better job than the kid."

"It doesn't look like anything special," J.C. said,

shoving his way up beside Ivy, who punched him in the shoulder. "Rocks. Trees. Boring."

"I don't know . . ." I said. "There's something about it. Tobias?"

Tobias took the photograph. At least, that was what I saw. Most likely I still had the photo in my hand, but I couldn't feel it there, now that I perceived Tobias holding it. It's strange, the way the mind can change perception.

Tobias studied the picture for a long moment. J.C. began clicking his pistol's safety off and on.

"Aren't you always talking about gun safety?" Ivy hissed at him.

"I'm being safe," he said. "Barrel's not pointed at anyone. Besides, I have keen, iron control over every muscle in my body. I could—"

"Hush, both of you," Tobias said. He held the picture closer. "My God . . ."

"Please don't use the Lord's name in vain," Ivy said. J.C. snorted.

"Stephen," Tobias said. "Computer."

I joined him at the sitting room's desktop, then sat down, Tobias leaning over my shoulder. "Do a search for the Lone Cypress."

I did so, and brought up image view. A couple dozen shots of the same rock appeared on the screen, but all of them had a larger tree growing on it. The tree in these photos was fully grown; in fact, it looked ancient.

"Okay, great," J.C. said. "Still trees. Still rocks. Still boring."

"That's the Lone Cypress, J.C.," Tobias said. "It's famous, and is believed to be *at least* two hundred and fifty years old."

"So . . . ?" Ivy asked.

I held up the photograph that had been mailed. "In this, it's no more than . . . what? Ten?"

"Likely younger," Tobias said.

"So for this to be real," I said, "it would have to have been taken in the mid to late 1700s. Decades before the camera was invented."

T W O

"Look, it's clearly a fake," Ivy said. "I don't see why you two are so bothered by this."

Tobias and I strolled the hallway of the mansion. It had been two days. I still couldn't get the image out of my head. I carried the photo in my jacket pocket.

"A hoax *would* be the most rational explanation, Stephen," Tobias said.

"Armando thinks it's real," I said.

"Armando is a complete loon," Ivy replied. Today she wore a grey business suit.

"True," I said, then raised a hand to my pocket again. Altering the photo wouldn't have taken much. What was doctoring a photo, these days? Practically any kid with Photoshop could create realistic fakes.

Armando had run it through some advanced programs, checking levels and doing a bunch of other things that were too technical for me to understand, but he admitted that didn't mean anything. A talented artist could fool the tests.

So why did this photo haunt me so?

"This smacks of someone trying to prove something," I said. "There are many trees older than the Lone Cypress, but few are in as distinctive a location. This photograph is intended to be instantly recognizable as impossible, at least to those with a good knowledge of history."

"All the more likely a hoax then, wouldn't you say?" Ivy asked.

"Perhaps."

I paced back in the other direction, my aspects growing silent. Finally, I heard the door shut below. I hurried to the landing down.

"Master?" Wilson said, climbing the steps.

"Wilson! Mail has arrived?"

He stopped at the landing, holding a silver tray. Megan, of the cleaning staff—real, of course—scurried up behind him and passed us, face down, steps quick.

"She'll quit soon," Ivy noted. "You really should try to be less strange."

"Tall order, Ivy," I mumbled, looking through the mail. "With you people around." There! Another envelope, identical to the first. I tore into it eagerly and pulled out another picture.

This one was more blurry. It was of a man standing at a washbasin, towel at his neck. His surroundings were old-fashioned. It was also in black and white.

I turned the picture to Tobias. He took it, holding it up, inspecting it with eyes lined at the corners.

"Well?" Ivy asked.

"He looks familiar," I said. "I feel I should know him."

"George Washington," Tobias said. "Having a morning shave, it appears. I'm surprised he didn't have someone to do it for him."

"He was a soldier," I said, taking the photo back. "He was probably accustomed to doing things for himself." I ran my fingers over the glossy picture. The first daguerreotype—early photographs—had been taken in the mid-1830s. Before that, nobody had been able to create permanent images of this nature. Washington had died in 1799.

"Look, this one is *obviously* a fake," Ivy said. "A picture of George Washington? We're to assume that someone went back in time, and the only thing they could think to do was grab a candid of George in the bathroom? We're being played, Steve."

"Maybe," I admitted.

"It does look *remarkably* like him," Tobias said.

"Except we don't have any photos of him," Ivy said. "So there's no way to prove it. Look, all someone would have to do is hire a look-alike actor, pose the photo, and *bam*. They wouldn't even have to do any photo editing."

"Let's see what Armando thinks," I said, turning over the photo. On the back of this one was a phone number. "Someone fetch Audrey first."

THREE

"You may approach His Majesty," Armando said. He stood at his window, which was triangular—he occupied one of the peaks of the mansion. He'd demanded the position.

"Can I shoot him?" J.C. asked me softly. "You know, in a place that's not important? A foot, maybe?"

"His Majesty heard that," Armando said in his soft Spanish accent, turning unamused eyes our direction. "Stephen Leeds. Have you fulfilled your promise to me? I must be restored to my throne."

"Working on it, Armando," I said, handing him the picture. "We've got another one."

Armando sighed, taking the photo from my fingers. He was a thin man with black hair he kept slicked back. "Armando *benevolently* agrees to consider your supplication." He held it up.

"You know, Steve," Ivy said, poking through the room, "if you're going to create hallucinations, you really should consider making them less annoying."

"Silence, woman," Armando said. "Have you considered His Majesty's request?"

"I'm not going to marry you, Armando."

"You would be queen!"

"You don't have a throne. And last I checked, Mexico has a president, not an emperor."

"Drug lords threaten my people," Armando said, inspecting the picture. "They starve, and are forced to bow to the whims of foreign powers. It is a disgrace. This picture, it is authentic." He handed it back.

"That's all?" I asked. "You don't need to do some of those computer tests?"

"Am I not the photography expert?" Armando said. "Did you not come to me with piteous supplication? I have spoken. It is real. No trickery. The photographer, however, is a buffoon. He knows nothing of the *art* of the craft. These pictures offend me in their utter pedestrian nature." He turned his back to us, looking out the window again.

"*Now* can I shoot him?" J.C. asked.

"I'm tempted to let you," I said, turning over the picture. Audrey had looked at the handwriting on the back, and hadn't been able to trace it to any of the professors, psychologists, or other groups that kept wanting to do studies on me.

I shrugged, then took out my phone. The number was local. It rang once before being picked up.

"Hello?" I said.

"May I come visit you, Mr. Leeds?" A woman's voice, with a faint Southern accent.

"Who are you?"

"The person who has been sending you puzzles."

"Well, I figured *that* part out."

"May I come visit?"

"I . . . well, I suppose. Where are you?"

"Outside your gates." The phone clicked. A moment later, chimes rang as someone buzzed the front gates.

I looked at the others. J.C. pushed his way to the window, gun out, and peeked at the front driveway. Armando scowled at him.

Ivy and I walked out of Armando's rooms toward the steps.

"You armed?" J.C. asked, jogging up to us.

"Normal people don't walk around their own homes with a gun strapped on, J.C."

"They do if they want to live. Go get your gun."

I hesitated, then sighed. "Let her in, Wilson!" I called, but redirected to my own rooms—the largest in the complex—and took my handgun out of my nightstand. I holstered it under my arm and put my jacket back on. It did feel good to be armed, but I'm a *horrible* shot.

By the time I was making my way down the steps to the front entryway, Wilson had answered the door. A dark-skinned woman in her thirties stood at the doorway, wearing a black overcoat, a business suit, and short dreadlocks. She took off her sunglasses and nodded to me.

"The sitting room, Wilson," I said, reaching the landing. He led her to it, and I entered after, waiting for J.C. and Ivy to pass. Tobias already sat inside, reading a history book.

"Lemonade?" Wilson asked.

"No, thank you," I said, pulling the door closed, Wilson outside.

The woman strolled around the room, looking over the décor. "Fancy place," she said. "You paid for all of this with money from people who ask you for help?"

"Most of it came from the government," I said.

"Word on the street says you don't work for them."

"I don't, but I used to. Anyway, a lot of this came from grant money. Professors who wanted to research me. I started charging enormous sums for the privilege, assuming it would put them off."

"And it didn't."

"Nothing does," I said, grimacing. "Have a seat."

"I'll stand," she said, inspecting my Van Gogh. "The name is Monica, by the way."

"Monica," I said, taking out the two photographs. "I have to say, it seems remarkable that you'd expect me to believe your ridiculous story."

"I haven't told you a story yet."

"You're going to," I said, tossing the photographs onto the table. "A story about time travel and, apparently, a photographer who doesn't know how to use his flash properly."

"You're a genius, Mr. Leeds," she said, not turning. "By some certifications I've read, you're the smartest man on the planet. If there had been an obvious flaw—or even one that wasn't so obvious—in those photos, you'd have thrown them away. You certainly wouldn't have called me."

"They're wrong."

"They . . . ?"

"The people who call me a genius," I said, sitting down in the chair next to Tobias's. "I'm not a genius. I'm really quite average."

"I find that hard to believe."

"Believe what you will," I said. "But I'm *not* a genius. My hallucinations are."

"Thanks," J.C. said.

"*Some* of my hallucinations are," I corrected.

"You accept that the things you see aren't real?" Monica said, turning to me.

"Yes."

"Yet you talk to them."

"I wouldn't want to hurt their feelings. Besides, they can be useful."

"Thanks," J.C. said.

"*Some* of them can be useful," I corrected. "Anyway, they're the reason you're here. You want their minds. Now tell me your story, Monica, or stop wasting my time."

She smiled, finally walking over to sit down. "It's not what you think. There's no time machine."

"Oh?"

"You don't sound surprised."

"Time travel into the past is highly, *highly* implausible," I said. "Even if it were to have occurred, I'd not know of it, as it would have created a branching path of reality of which I am not a part."

"Unless this *is* the branched reality."

"In which case," I said, "time travel into the past is still functionally irrelevant to me, as someone who traveled back would create a branching path of which— again—I would not be part."

"That's one theory at least," she said. "But it's meaningless. As I said, there is no time machine. Not in the conventional sense."

"So these pictures are fakes?" I asked. "You're starting to bore me very quickly, Monica."

She slid three more pictures onto the table.

"Shakespeare," Tobias said as I held them up one at a time. "The Colossus of Rhodes. Oh . . . now that's clever."

"Elvis?" I asked.

"Apparently the moment before death," Tobias said, pointing to the picture of the waning pop icon sitting in his bathroom, head drooping.

J.C. sniffed. "As if there isn't anyone around who looks like *that guy*."

"These are from a camera," Monica said, leaning forward, "that takes pictures of the past."

She paused for dramatic effect. J.C. yawned.

"The problem with each of these," I said, tossing the pictures onto the table, "is that they are fundamentally unverifiable. They are pictures of things that have no other visual record to prove them, so small inaccuracies would be impossible to use in debunking."

"I have seen the device work," Monica replied. "It was proven in a rigorous testing environment. We stood in a clean room we had prepared, took cards and drew on the backs of them, and held them up. Then we burned the cards. The inventor of this device entered the room and took photos. Those pictures accurately displayed us standing there, with the cards and the patterns reproduced."

"Wonderful," I said. "Now, if I only had any reason at all to trust your word."

"You can test the device yourself," she said. "Use it to answer any question from history you wish."

"We could," Ivy said, "if it hadn't been stolen."

"I could do that," I repeated, trusting what Ivy said. She had good instincts for interrogation, and sometimes fed me lines. "Except the device has been stolen, hasn't it?"

Monica leaned back in her chair, frowning.

"It wasn't difficult to guess, Steve," Ivy said. "She wouldn't be here if everything were working properly, and she'd have brought the camera—to show it off—if she really wanted to prove it to us. I could believe it's in a lab somewhere, too valuable to bring. Only in that case, she'd have invited us to her center of strength, instead of coming to ours.

"She's desperate, despite her calm exterior. See how she keeps tapping the armrest of her chair? Also, notice how she tried to remain standing in the first part of the conversation, looming as if to prop up her authority? She only sat down when she felt awkward with you seeming so relaxed."

Tobias nodded. "'Never do anything standing that you can do sitting, or anything sitting that you can do lying down.' A Chinese proverb, usually attributed to Confucius. Of course, no primary texts from Confucius remain in existence, so nearly everything we *are* sure he taught is the Golden Rule—and his quote regarding it is often misattributed to Jesus of Nazareth, who worded the same concept a different way. . . ."

I let him speak, the ebbs and flows of his calm voice washing across me like waves. What he was saying wasn't important.

"Yes," Monica finally said. "The device was stolen. And that is why I am here."

"So we have a problem," I said. "The only way to prove these pictures authentic for myself would be to have the device. And yet, I can't have the device without doing the work you want me to do—meaning I could easily reach the end of this and discover you've been playing me."

She dropped one more picture onto the table. A woman in sunglasses and a trench coat, standing in a train station. The picture had been taken from the side as she inspected a monitor above.

Sandra.

"Uh-oh," J.C. said.

"Where did you get this?" I demanded, standing up.

"I've told you—"

"We're not playing games anymore!" I slammed my hands down on the coffee table. "Where is she? What do you know?"

Monica drew back, her eyes widening. People don't know how to handle schizophrenics. They've read stories, seen films. We make them afraid, though statistically we're not any more likely to commit violent crimes than the average person.

Several people who wrote papers on me claim I'm *not* schizophrenic. Half think I'm making all this up. The other half think I've got something different, something new. Whatever I have—however it is that my brain works—only one person really ever seemed to *get* me. And that was the woman in the picture Monica had just slapped down on the table.

Sandra. In a way, she'd started all of this.

"The picture wasn't hard to get," Monica said. "When you used to do interviews, you would talk about her. Obviously, you hoped someone would read the interview and bring you information about her. Maybe you hoped that she would see what you had to say, and return to you."

I forced myself to sit back down.

"You knew she went to the train station," Monica continued. "And at what time. You didn't know which train she got on. We started taking pictures until we found her."

"There must have been a dozen women in that train station with blonde hair and the right look," I said.

Nobody really knew who she was. Not even me.

Monica took out a sheaf of pictures, a good twenty of them. Each was of a woman. "We thought the one wearing sunglasses indoors was the most likely choice, but we brought the photos of every woman near the right age that we shot in the train station that day. Just in case."

Ivy rested a hand on my shoulder.

"Calmly, Stephen," Tobias said. "A strong rudder steers the ship even in a storm."

I breathed in and out.

"Can I shoot *her*?" J.C. asked.

Ivy rolled her eyes. "Remind me why we keep him around."

"Rugged good looks," J.C. said.

"Listen," Ivy continued to me. "Monica undermined her own story. She claims to have only come to you because the camera was stolen—yet how did she get pictures of Sandra without the camera?"

I nodded, clearing my head—with difficulty—and made the accusation to Monica.

Monica smiled slyly. "We had you in mind for another project. We thought these would be . . . handy to have."

"Darn," Ivy said, standing right up in Monica's face, focusing on her irises. "I think she might be telling the truth on that one."

I stared at the picture. Sandra. It had been almost ten years now. It *still* hurt to think about how she'd left me. Left me, after showing me how to harness my mind's abilities. I ran my fingers across the picture.

"We've got to do it," J.C. said. "We've got to look into this, Skinny."

"If there's a chance . . ." Tobias said, nodding.

"The camera was probably stolen by someone on the inside," Ivy guessed. "Jobs like this one often are."

"One of your own people took it, didn't they?" I asked.

"Yes," Monica said. "But we don't have any idea where they went. We've spent tens of thousands of dollars over the last four days trying to track them. I always suggested you. Other . . . factions within our company were against bringing in someone they consider volatile."

"I'll do it," I said.

"Excellent. Shall I bring you to our labs?"

"No," I said. "Take me to the thief's house."

FOUR

"Mr. Balubal Razon," Tobias read from the sheet of facts as we climbed the stairs. I'd scanned that sheet on the drive over, but had been too deep in thought to give it much specific attention. "He's ethnically Filipino, but second-generation American. Ph.D. in physics from the University of Maine. No honors. Lives alone."

We reached the seventh floor of the apartment building. Monica was puffing. She kept walking too close to J.C., which made him scowl.

"I should add," Tobias said, lowering the sheet of facts, "Stan informs me that the rain has cleared up before reaching us. We have only sunny weather to look forward to now."

"Thank goodness," I said, turning to the door, where two men in black suits stood on guard. "Yours?" I asked Monica, nodding to them.

"Yeah," she said. She'd spent the ride over on the phone with some of her superiors.

Monica took out a key to the flat and turned it in the lock. The room inside was a complete disaster. Chinese takeout cartons stood on the windowsill in a row, as if they were planters intended to grow next year's crop of General Tso's. Books lay in piles everywhere, and the walls were hung with photographs. Not the time-traveling kind, just the ordinary photos a photography buff would take.

We had to shuffle around to get through the door and past the stacks of books. Inside, it was cramped quarters with all of us.

"Wait outside, if you will, Monica," I said. "It's kind of tight in here."

"Tight?" she asked, frowning.

"You keep walking through the middle of J.C.," I said. "It's very disturbing for him; he hates being reminded he's a hallucination."

"I'm not a hallucination," J.C. snapped. "I have state-of-the-art stealthing equipment."

Monica regarded me for a moment, then walked to the doorway, standing between the two guards, hands on hips as she regarded us.

"All right, folks," I said. "Have at it."

"Nice locks," J.C. said, flipping one of the chains on the door. "Thick wood, three deadbolts. Unless I miss my guess . . ." He poked at what appeared to be a letter box mounted on the wall by the door.

I opened it. There was a pristine handgun inside.

"Ruger Bisley, custom converted to large caliber," J.C. said with a grunt. I opened the spinning thing that held the bullets and took one out. "Chambered in .500 Linebaugh," J.C. continued. "This is a weapon for a man who knows what he's doing."

"He left it behind though," Ivy said. "Was he in too much of a hurry?"

"No," J.C. said. "This was his door gun. He would have had a different regular sidearm."

"Door gun," Ivy said. "Is that really a *thing* for you people?"

"You need something with good penetration," J.C. said, "that can shoot through the wood when people are trying to force your door. But the recoil of this weapon will do a number on your hand after not too many shots. He would have carried something with a smaller caliber on his person."

J.C. inspected the gun. "Never been fired, though. Hmm . . . There's a chance someone gave this to him. Perhaps he went to a friend, asked them how to protect himself? A true soldier knows each weapon he owns through repeated firing. No gun fires perfectly straight. Each has a personality."

"He's a scholar," Tobias said, kneeling beside the rows of books. "Historian."

"You sound surprised," I said. "He *does* have a Ph.D. I'd expect him to be smart."

"He has a Ph.D. in theoretical physics, Stephen," Tobias said. "But these are some *very* obscure historical and theological books. Deep reading. It's difficult to be a widely read scholar in more than one area. No wonder he leads a solitary life."

"Rosaries," Ivy said; she picked one up from the top of a stack of books, inspecting it. "Worn, frequently counted. Open one of those books."

I picked a book up off the floor.

"No, that one. *The God Delusion*."

"Richard Dawkins?" I said, flipping through it.

"A leading atheist," Ivy said, looking over my shoulder. "Annotated with counterarguments."

"A devout Catholic among a sea of secular scientists," Tobias said. "Yes . . . many of these works are religious or have religious connotations. Thomas Aquinas, Daniel W. Hardy, Francis Schaeffer, Pietro Alagona . . ."

"There's his badge from work," Ivy said, nodding to something hanging on the wall. It proclaimed, in large letters, *Azari Laboratories, Inc.* Monica's company.

"Call for Monica," Ivy said. "Repeat what I tell you."

"Oh Monica," I said.

"Am I allowed in now?"

"Depends," I said, repeating the words Ivy whispered to me. "Are you going to tell me the truth?"

"About what?"

"About Razon having invented the camera on his own, bringing Azari in only after he had a working prototype."

Monica narrowed her eyes at me.

"Badge is too new," I said. "Not worn or scratched at all from being used or in his pocket. The picture on it can't be more than two months old, judging by the beard he's growing in the badge photo but not in the picture of him at Mount Vernon on his mantel.

"Furthermore, this is *not* the apartment of a high-paid engineer. With a broken elevator? In the northeast quarter of town? Not only is this a rough area, it's too far from your offices. He didn't steal your camera, Monica—though I'm tempted to guess that you're trying to steal it from him. Is that why he ran?"

"He *didn't* come to us with a prototype," Monica said. "Not a working one at least. He had one photo—the one of Washington—and a lot of promises. He needed money to get a stable machine working; apparently, the one he'd built had worked for a few days, then stopped.

"We funded him for eighteen months on a limited-access pass to the labs. He received an official badge when he finally got the damn camera working. And he *did* steal it from us. The contract he signed required all equipment to remain at our laboratories. He used us as a convenient source of cash, then jumped with the prize—wiping all of his data and destroying all other prototypes—as soon as he could get away with it."

"Truth?" I asked Ivy.

"Can't tell," she said. "Sorry. If I could hear a heartbeat . . . maybe you could put your ear to her chest."

"I'm sure she'd *love* that," I said.

J.C. smiled. "I'm pretty sure *I'd* love that."

"Oh please," Ivy said. "You'd only do it to peek inside her coat and find out what kind of gun she's carrying."

"Beretta M9," J.C. said. "Already peeked."

Ivy gave me a glare.

"What?" I said, trying to act innocent. "He's the one who said it."

"Skinny," J.C. put in, "the M9 is boring, but effective. The way she carries herself says she knows her way around a gun. That puffing she did when climbing the steps? An act. She's far more fit than that. She's trying to pretend she's some kind of manager or paper pusher at the labs, but she's obviously security of some sort."

"Thanks," I told him.

"You," Monica said, "are a *very* strange man."

I focused on her. She'd heard only my parts of the exchange, of course. "I thought you read my interviews."

"I did. They don't do you justice. I imagined you as a brilliant mode shifter, slipping in and out of personalities."

"That's dissociative identity disorder," I said. "It's different."

"Very good!" Ivy piped in. She'd been schooling me on psychological disorders.

"Regardless," Monica said. "I guess I'm just surprised to find out what you really are."

"Which is?" I asked.

"A middle manager," she said, looking troubled. "Anyway, the question remains. Where is Razon?"

"Depends," I said. "Does he need to be any place specific to use the camera? Meaning, did he have to *go* to Mount Vernon to take a picture of the past in that location, or can he somehow set the camera to take pictures there?"

"He has to go to the location," Monica said. "The camera looks back through time at the exact place you are."

There were problems with that, but I let them slide for now. Razon. Where would he go? I glanced at J.C., who shrugged.

"You look to him first?" Ivy said with a flat tone. "Really."

I looked to her, and she blushed. "I . . . I actually don't have anything either."

J.C. chuckled at that.

Tobias stood up, slow and ponderous, like a distant cloud formation rising into the sky. "Jerusalem," he said softly, resting his fingers on a book. "He's gone to Jerusalem."

We all looked at him. Well, those of us who could.

"Where else would a believer go, Stephen?" Tobias asked. "After years of arguments with his colleagues, years of being thought a fool for his faith? This was what it was about all along, this is why he developed the camera. He's gone to answer a question. For us, for himself. A question that has been asked for two thousand years.

"He's gone to take a picture of Jesus of Nazareth—dubbed Christ by his devout—following his resurrection."

FIVE

I required five first-class seats. This did not sit well with Monica's superiors, many of whom did not approve of me. I met one of those at the airport, a Mr. Davenport. He smelled of pipe smoke, and Ivy critiqued his poor taste in shoes. I thought better of asking him if we could use the corporate jet.

We now sat in the first-class cabin of the plane. I flipped lazily through a thick book on my seat's fold-out tray. Behind me, J.C. bragged to Tobias about the weapons he'd managed to slip past security.

Ivy dozed by the window, with an empty seat next to her. Monica sat beside me, staring at that empty seat. "So Ivy is by the window?"

"Yes," I said, flipping a page.

"Tobias and the marine are behind us."

"J.C.'s a Navy SEAL. He'd shoot you for making that mistake."

"And the other seat?" she asked.

"Empty," I said, flipping a page.

She waited for an explanation. I didn't give one.

"So what are you going to do with this camera?" I asked. "Assuming the thing is real, a fact of which I'm not yet convinced."

"There are hundreds of applications," Monica said. "Law enforcement ... Espionage ... Creating a true account of historical events ... Watching the early formation of the planet for scientific research ..."

"Destroying ancient religions ..."

She raised an eyebrow at me. "Are you a religious man then, Mr. Leeds?"

"Part of me is." That was the honest truth.

"Well," she said. "Let us assume that Christianity is a sham. Or perhaps a movement started by well-meaning people but which has grown beyond proportion. Would it not serve the greater good to expose that?"

"That's not really an argument I'm equipped to enter," I said. "You'd need Tobias. He's the philosopher. But I think he's dozing."

"Actually, Stephen," Tobias said, leaning between our two seats, "I'm quite curious about this conversation. Stan is watching our progress, by the way. He says there might be some bumpy weather up ahead."

"You're looking at something," Monica said.

"I'm looking at Tobias," I said. "He wants to continue the conversation."

"Can I speak with him?"

"I suppose you can, through me. I'll warn you, though. Ignore anything he says about Stan."

"Who's Stan?" Monica asked.

"An astronaut that Tobias hears, supposedly orbiting the world in a satellite." I turned a page. "Stan is mostly harmless. He gives us weather forecasts, that sort of thing."

"I . . . see," she said. "Stan's another one of your special friends?"

I chuckled. "No. Stan's not real."

"I thought you said none of them were."

"Well, true. They're my hallucinations. But Stan is something special. Only Tobias hears him. Tobias is a schizophrenic."

She blinked in surprise. "Your hallucination . . ."

"Yes?"

"Your hallucination has hallucinations."

"Yes."

She settled back, looking disturbed.

"They all have their issues," I said. "Ivy is a trypophobic, though she mostly has it under control. Just don't come at her with a wasp's nest. Armando is a megalomaniac. Adoline has OCD."

"If you please, Stephen," Tobias said. "Let her know that I find Razon to be a very brave man."

I repeated the words.

"And why is that?" Monica asked.

"To be both a scientist and religious is to create an uneasy truce within a man," Tobias said. "At the heart of science is accepting only that truth which can be proven. At the heart of faith is to define Truth, at its core, as being unprovable. Razon is a brave man because of what he is doing. Regardless of his discovery, one of two things he holds very dear will be upended."

"He could be a zealot," Monica replied. "Marching blindly forward, trying to find final validation that he has been right all along."

"Perhaps," Tobias said. "But the true zealot would not need validation. The Lord would provide validation. No, I see something else here. A man seeking to meld science and faith, the first person—perhaps in the history of mankind—to *actually* find a way to apply science to the ultimate truths of religion. I find that noble."

Tobias settled back. I flipped the last few pages of the book as Monica sat in thought. Finished, I stuffed the book into the pocket of the seat in front of me.

Someone rustled the curtains, entering from economy class and coming into the first-class cabin. "Hello!" a friendly feminine voice said, coming up the aisle. "I could not help seeing that you had an extra seat up here, and I thought to myself, perhaps they would let me sit in it."

The newcomer was a round-faced, pleasant young woman in her late twenties. She had tan Indian skin and a deep red dot on her forehead. She wore clothing of intricate make, red and gold, with an Indian shawl-thingy over one shoulder and wrapping around her. I don't know what they're called.

"What's this?" J.C. said. "Hey, Achmed. You're not going to blow the plane up, are you?"

"My name is Kalyani," she said. "And I am most certainly *not* going to blow anything up."

"Huh," J.C. said. "That's disappointing." He settled back and closed his eyes—or pretended to. He kept one eye cracked toward Kalyani.

"*Why* do we keep him around?" Ivy asked, stretching, coming out of her nap.

"Your head keeps going back and forth," Monica said. "I feel like I'm missing entire conversations."

"You are," I said. "Monica, meet Kalyani. A new aspect, and the reason we needed that empty seat."

Kalyani perkily held out her hand toward Monica, a big grin on her face.

"She can't see you, Kalyani," I said.

"Oh, right!" Kalyani raised both hands to her face. "I'm so sorry, Mr. Steve. I am very new to this."

"It's okay. Monica, Kalyani will be our interpreter in Israel."

"I am a linguist," Kalyani said, bowing.

"Interpreter . . ." Monica said, glancing at the book I'd tucked away. A book of Hebrew syntax, grammar, and vocabulary. "You just learned Hebrew."

"No," I said. "I glanced through the pages enough to summon an aspect who speaks it. I'm useless with languages." I yawned, wondering if there was time left in the flight to pick up Arabic for Kalyani as well.

"Prove it," Monica said.

I raised an eyebrow toward her.

"I need to see," Monica said. "Please."

With a sigh, I turned to Kalyani. "How do you say: 'I would like to practice speaking Hebrew. Would you speak to me in your language?' "

"Hm . . . 'I would like to practice speaking Hebrew' is somewhat awkward in the language. Perhaps, 'I would like to improve my Hebrew'?"

"Sure."

"Ani rotzeh leshapher et ha'ivrit sheli," Kalyani said.

"Damn," I said. "That's a mouthful."

"Language!" Ivy called.

"It is not so hard, Mr. Steve. Here, try it. *Ani rotzeh leshapher et ha'ivrit sheli.*"

"Any rote zeele shaper hap . . . er hav . . ." I said.

"Oh my," Kalyani said. "That is . . . that is very dreadful. Perhaps I will give you one word at a time."

"Sounds good," I said, waving over one of the flight attendants, the one who had spoken Hebrew to give the safety information at the start of our flight.

She smiled at us. "Yes?"

"Uh . . ." I said.

"Ani," Kalyani said patiently.

"Ani," I repeated.

"*Rotzeh.*"

"*Rotzeh . . .*"

It took a little getting used to, but I made myself known. The attendant even congratulated me. Fortunately, translating her words into English was much easier—Kalyani gave me a running translation.

"Oh, your accent is *horrible*, Mr. Steve," Kalyani said as the flight attendant moved on. "I'm so embarrassed."

"We'll work on it," I said. "Thanks."

Kalyani smiled at me and gave me a hug, then tried to give one to Monica, who didn't notice. Finally, the Indian woman took a seat next to Ivy, and the two began chatting amicably, which was a relief. It always makes my life easier when my hallucinations get along.

"You already spoke Hebrew," Monica accused. "You knew it before we started flying, and you spent the last few hours refreshing yourself."

"Believe that if you want."

"But it's not *possible*," she continued. "A man can't learn an entirely new language in a matter of hours."

I didn't bother to correct her and say I *hadn't* learned it. If I had, my accent wouldn't have been so horrible, and Kalyani wouldn't have needed to guide me word by word.

"We're on a plane hunting a camera that can take pictures of the past," I said. "How is it harder to believe that I just learned Hebrew?"

"Okay, fine. We'll pretend you did that. But if you're capable of learning that quickly, why don't you know every language—every subject, *everything*—by now?"

"There aren't enough rooms in my house for that," I said. "The truth is, Monica, I don't *want* any of this. I'd gladly be free of it, so that I could live a more simple life. I sometimes think the lot of them will drive me insane."

"You . . . aren't insane, then?"

"Heavens no," I said. I eyed her. "You don't accept that."

"You see people who aren't there, Mr. Leeds. It's a difficult fact to get around."

"And yet, I live a good life," I said. "Tell me. Why would you consider me insane, but the man who can't hold a job, who cheats on his wife, who can't keep his temper in check? You call *him* sane?"

"Well, perhaps not completely . . ."

"Plenty of 'sane' people can't manage to keep it all under control. Their mental state—stress, anxiety, frustration—gets in the way of their ability to be happy. Compared to them, I think I'm downright stable. Though I do admit, it would be nice to be left alone. I don't want to be anyone special."

"And that's where all of this came from, isn't it?" Monica asked. "The hallucinations?"

"Oh, you're a psychologist now? Did you read a book on it while we were flying? Where's your new aspect, so I can shake hands with her?"

Monica didn't rise to the bait. "You create these delusions so that you can foist things off on them. Your brilliance, which you find a burden. Your responsibility—they have to drag you along and make you help people. This lets you pretend, Mr. Leeds. Pretend that you are normal. But that's the *real* delusion."

I found myself wishing the flight would hurry up and be finished.

"I've never heard that theory before," Tobias said softly from behind. "Perhaps she has something, Stephen. We should mention it to Ivy—"

"No!" I snapped, turning on him. "She's dug in my mind enough already."

I turned back. Monica had that look in her eyes again, the look a "sane" person gets when they deal with me. It's the look of a person forced to handle unstable dynamite while wearing oven mitts. That look . . . it hurts far more than the condition itself does.

"Tell me something," I said to change the topic. "How'd you let Razon get away with this?"

"It isn't like we didn't take precautions," Monica said dryly. "The camera was locked up tightly, but we couldn't very well keep it completely out of the hands of the man we were paying to build it."

"There's more here," I said. "No offense intended, Monica, but you're a sneaky corporate type. Ivy and J.C. figured out ages ago that you're not an engineer. You're either a slimy executive tasked with handling undesirable elements, or you're a slimy security forces leader who does the same."

"What part of that am I not supposed to take offense at?" she asked coolly.

"How did Razon have access to all of the prototypes?" I continued. "Surely you copied the design without him knowing. Surely you fed versions of the camera to satellite studios, so they could break them apart and reverse engineer them. I find it quite a stretch to believe he somehow found and destroyed all of those."

She tapped her armrest for a few minutes. "None of them work," she finally admitted.

"You copied the designs exactly?"

"Yes, but we got nothing from it. We asked Razon, and he said that there were still bugs. He always had an excuse, and Razon *did* have trouble with his own prototypes, after all. This is an area of science nobody has breached before. We're the pioneers. Things are bound to have bugs."

"All true statements," I said. "None of which you believe."

"He was doing *something* to those cameras," she said. "Something to make them stop functioning when he wasn't around. He could make any of the prototypes work, given enough time to fiddle. If we swapped in one of our copies during the night, he could make *it* function. Then we'd swap it back, and it wouldn't work for us."

"Could other people use the cameras in his presence?"

She nodded. "They could even use them for a little while when he wasn't there. Each camera would always stop working after a short time, and we'd have to bring him back in to fix it. You must understand, Mr. Leeds. We only had a few months during which the cameras were working at all. For the majority of his career at Azari, he was considered a complete quack by most."

"Not by you, I assume."

She said nothing.

"Without him, without that camera, your career is nothing," I said. "You funded him. You championed him. And then, when it finally started working . . ."

"He betrayed me," she whispered.

The look in her eyes was far from pleasant. It occurred to me that if we did find Mr. Razon, I might want to let J.C. at him first. J.C. would probably want to shoot the guy, but Monica wanted to rip him clean apart.

S I X

"Well," Ivy said, "it's a good thing we picked an out-of-the-way city. If we had to find Razon in a large urban center—home to three major world religions, one of the most popular tourist destinations in the world—this would be *really* tough."

I smiled as we walked out of the airport. One of Monica's two security goons went to track down the cars her company had ordered for us.

My smile didn't do much more than crack the corner of my lips. I hadn't gotten much study done on Arabic during the second half of the flight. I'd spent the time thinking about Sandra. That was never productive.

Ivy watched me from concerned eyes. She could be motherly sometimes. Kalyani strolled over to listen in on some people speaking in Hebrew nearby.

"Ah, Israel," J.C. said, stepping up to us. "I've always wanted to come over here, just to see if I could slip through security. They have the best in the world, you know."

He carried a black duffel on his back that I didn't recognize. "What's that?"

"M4A1 carbine," J.C. said. "With attached advanced combat optical gunsight and M203 grenade launcher."

"But—"

"I have contacts over here," he said softly. "Once a SEAL, always a SEAL."

The cars arrived, though the drivers seemed bemused at why four people insisted on two cars. As it was, they'd barely fit us all. I got into the second one, with Monica, Tobias, and Ivy—who sat between Monica and me in the back.

"Do you want to talk about it?" Ivy asked softly as she did up her seat belt.

"I don't think we'll find her, even with this," I said. "Sandra is good at avoiding attention, and the trail is too cold."

Monica looked at me, a question on her lips, obviously thinking I'd been talking to her. It died as she remembered whom she was accompanying.

"There might be a good reason why she left, you know," Ivy said. "We don't have the entire story."

"A good reason? One that explains why, in ten years, she's never contacted us?"

"It's possible," Ivy said.

I said nothing.

"You're not going to start losing us, are you?" Ivy asked. "Aspects vanishing? Changing?"

Becoming nightmares. She didn't need to add that last part.

"That won't happen again," I said. "I'm in control now."

Ivy still missed Justin and Ignacio. Honestly, I did too.

"And . . . this hunt for Sandra," Ivy said. "Is it only

about your affection for her, or is it about something else?"

"What else could it be about?"

"She was the one who taught you to control your mind." Ivy looked away. "Don't tell me you've never wondered. Maybe she has more secrets. A . . . cure, perhaps."

"Don't be stupid," I said. "I like things how they are."

Ivy didn't reply, though I could see Tobias looking at me in the car's rearview mirror. Studying me. Judging my sincerity.

In fact, I was judging my own.

What followed was a long drive to the city—the airport is quite a ways away, closer to Tel Aviv. The route was scenic between cities, and once we entered the modern part of Jerusalem, we passed several parks along one side of the road. As we approached our destination Tobias pointed out the Tower of David, its stones bearing the weight of unimaginable time. Passing through Jaffa Gate was followed by a hectic ride through the streets of the Old City. It was uneventful, save for us almost running over about seventeen tourists. When the cars stopped we piled out, entering a sea of chattering sightseers and pious pilgrims.

There was no parking at the church itself, so we had to walk through alleys and streets for a good five minutes before arriving. But finally it stood before us. Built like a box, it had an ancient, simple façade with two large arched windows on the wall above us. "The Church of the Holy Sepulchre," Tobias said. "Held by tradition to be the site of the crucifixion of Jesus of Nazareth, the structure *also* encloses one of the traditional locations of his burial. This marvelous structure was originally two buildings, constructed in the fourth century by order of Constantine the Great. It replaced a temple to Aphrodite that had occupied the same site for approximately two hundred years."

"Thank you, Wikipedia," J.C. grumbled, shouldering his assault rifle. He'd changed into combat fatigues.

"Whether tradition is correct," Tobias continued calmly, hands clasped behind his back, "and whether this is the *actual* location of the historical events, is a subject of some dispute. Though tradition has many convenient explanations for anomalies—such as reasoning that the temple to Aphrodite was constructed here to suppress early Christian worship—it has been shown that this church follows the shape of the pagan one in key areas. In addition, the fact that the church lies within the city walls makes for an excellent disputation, as the tomb of Jesus would have been outside the city."

"It doesn't matter to us whether it is authentic or not," I said, passing Tobias. "Razon would have come here. It's one of the most obvious places—if not *the* most obvious place—to start looking. Monica, a word, please."

She fell into step beside me, her goons going to check if we needed tickets to enter. The police presence here seemed very heavy—but then, the church is in the West Bank, and there had been a couple of terrorist scares lately.

"What is it you want?" Monica asked me.

"Does the camera spit out pictures immediately?" I asked. "Does it give digital results?"

"No. It takes pictures on film only. Medium format, no digital back. Razon insisted it be that way."

"Now a harder one. You do realize the problems with a camera that takes pictures of one's exact location, only farther back in time, don't you?"

"What do you mean?"

"Merely this: We're not in the same location now as we were two thousand years ago. The planet moves. One of the theoretical problems with time travel is that if you were to go back in time a hundred years to the exact point we're standing now, you'd likely find yourself in outer space. Even if you were extremely lucky—and the planet were in the exact same place in its orbit—the Earth's rotation would mean that you'd appear somewhere else on its surface. Or under its surface, or hundreds of feet in the air."

"That's ridiculous."

"It's science," I said, looking up at the face of the church. *What we're doing here is ridiculous.*

And yet . . .

"All I know," she said, "is that Razon had to go to a place to take pictures of it."

"All right," I said. "One more. What's he like? Personality?"

"Abrasive," she said immediately. "Argumentative. And he is *very* protective of his equipment. I'm sure half of the reason he got away with the camera was because he'd repeatedly convinced us he was OCD with his stuff, so we gave him too much leniency."

Eventually, our group made its way into the church. The stuffy air carried the sounds of whispering tourists and feet shuffling on the stones. It was still a functioning place of worship.

"We're missing something, Steve," Ivy said, falling into step beside me. "We're ignoring an important part of the puzzle."

"Any guesses?" I asked, looking over the highly ornamented insides of the church.

"I'm working on it."

"Wait," J.C. said, sauntering up. "Ivy, you think

we're missing something, but you don't know what it is, and have no clue what it might be?"

"Basically," Ivy said.

"Hey, Skinny," he said to me, "I think I'm missing a million dollars, but I don't know why, or have any clue as to how I might have earned it. But I'm *really* sure I'm missing it. So if you could do something about that . . ."

"You are such a buffoon," Ivy said.

"That there, that thing I said," J.C. continued, "that was a *metaphor*."

"No," she said, "it was a logical proof."

"Huh?"

"One intended to demonstrate that you're an idiot. Oh! Guess what? The proof was a success! *Quod erat demonstrandum*. We can accurately say, without equivocation, that you are indeed an idiot."

The two of them walked off, continuing the argument. I shook my head, moving deeper into the church. The place where the crucifixion had supposedly taken place was marked by a gilded alcove, congested with both tourists and the devout. I folded my arms, displeased. Many of the tourists were taking photographs.

"What?" Monica asked me.

"I'd hoped they'd forbid flash photography," I said. "Most places like this do." If Razon had tried to use his, it would have made it more likely that someone had spotted him.

Perhaps it was forbidden, but the police officers standing nearby didn't seem to care what people did.

"We'll start looking," Monica said, gesturing curtly to her men. The three of them moved through the crowd, going about our fragile plan—which was to try

to find someone at one of the holy sites who remembered seeing Razon.

I waited, noticing that a couple of the police officers nearby were chatting in Hebrew. One waved to
the other, apparently going off duty, and began to walk
away.

"Kalyani," I said. "With me."

"Of course, of course, Mr. Steve." She joined me
with a hop in her step as we walked up to the depart-
ing officer.

The officer gave me a tired look.

"*Hello,*" I said in Hebrew with Kalyani's help. I'd
first mutter under my breath what I wanted to say, so
she could translate it for me. "*I apologize for my terrible Hebrew!*"

He paused, then smiled. "*It's not so bad.*"

"*It's dreadful.*"

"*You are Jewish?*" he guessed. "*From the States?*"

"*Actually, I'm not Jewish, though I am from the
States. I just think a man should try to learn a country's language before he visits.*"

The officer smiled. He seemed an amiable enough
fellow; of course, most people were. And they liked to
see foreigners trying their own language. We chatted
some more as he walked, and I found that he was indeed going off duty. Someone was coming to pick him
up, but he didn't seem to mind talking to me while
he waited. I tried to make it obvious that I wanted to
practice my language by speaking with a native.

His name was Moshe, and he worked this same shift
almost every day. His job was to watch for people doing stupid things, then stop them—though he confided
that his more important duty was to make sure no terrorist strikes happened in the church. His usual police
beat was elsewhere in the city, but he'd been moved

here for the holidays, when the government worried about violence and wanted a more visible presence in tourist sites. This church was, after all, in contested territory.

A few minutes in, I started moving the conversation toward Razon. *"I'm sure you must see some interesting things,"* I said. *"Before we came here, we were at the Garden Tomb. There was this crazy Asian guy there, yelling at everybody."*

"Yeah?" Moshe asked.

"Yeah. Pretty sure he was American from his accent, but he had Asian features. Anyway, he had this big camera set up on a tripod—as if he were the most important person around, and nobody else deserved to take pictures. Got in this big argument with a police officer who didn't want him using his flash."

Moshe laughed. *"He was here too."*

Kalyani chuckled after translating that. "Oh, you're good, Mr. Steve."

"Really?" I asked, casually.

"Sure was," Moshe said. *"Must be the same guy. He was here . . . oh, two days back. Kept cursing out everyone who jostled him, tried to bribe me to move them all away and give him space. Thing is, when he started taking pictures, he didn't mind if anyone stepped in front of him. And he took shots all over the church, even outside, pointed at the dumbest locations!"*

"Real loon, eh?"

"Yes," the officer said, chuckling. *"I see tourists like him all the time. Big fancy cameras that they spent a ridiculous amount on, but they don't have a bit of photography training. This guy, he didn't know when to turn off his flash, you know? Used it on every shot— even out in the sun, and on the altar over there, with all the lights on it!"*

I laughed.

"*I know!*" he said. "*Americans!*" Then he hesitated. "*Oh, uh, no offense meant.*"

"*None taken,*" I said, relaying immediately what Kalyani said in response. "*I'm Indian.*"

He hesitated, then cocked his head at me.

"Oh!" Kalyani said. "Oh, I'm sorry, Mr. Steve! I wasn't thinking."

"It's all right."

The officer laughed. "*You are good at Hebrew, but I do not think that means what you think!*"

I laughed as well, and noticed a woman moving toward him, waving. I thanked him for the conversation, then inspected the church some more. Monica and her flunkies eventually found me, one of them tucking away some photos of Razon. "Nobody here has seen him, Leeds," she said. "This is a dead end."

"Is that so?" I asked, strolling toward the exit.

Tobias joined us, hands clasped behind his back. "Such a marvel, Stephen," he said to me. He nodded toward an armed police officer at the doorway. "Jerusalem, a city whose name literally means 'peace.' It is filled with islands of serenity like this one, which have seen the solemn worship of men for longer than most countries have existed. Yet here, violence is never more than a few steps away."

Violence . . .

"Monica," I said, frowning. "You said you'd searched for Razon on your own, before you came to me. Did that include checking to see if he was on any flights out of the States?"

"Yeah," she said. "We have some contacts in Homeland Security. Nobody by Razon's name flew out of the country, but false IDs aren't *that* hard to find."

"Could a fake passport get you into Israel? One of the most secure countries on the planet?"

She frowned. "I hadn't thought of that."

"It seems risky," I said.

"Well, this is a fine time to bring it up, Leeds. Are you saying he's not here after all? We've wasted—"

"Oh, he's here," I said absently. "I found a policeman who spoke to him. Razon took pictures all over the place."

"Nobody we talked to saw him."

"The police and clergy in this place see *thousands* of visitors a day, Monica. You can't show them a picture and expect them to remember. You have to focus on something memorable."

"But—"

"Hush for a moment," I said, holding up my hand. *He got into the country. A mousy little engineer with extremely valuable equipment, using a fake passport. He had a gun back at his apartment, but hadn't ever fired it. How did he get it?*

Idiot. "Can you find out when Razon bought that gun?" I asked her. "Gun laws in the state should make it traceable, right?"

"Sure. I'll look into it when we get to a hotel."

"Do it now."

"Now? Do you realize what time it is in the—"

"Do it anyway. Wake people. Get the answers."

She glared at me, but moved off and made a few phone calls. Some angry conversations followed.

"We should have seen this earlier," Tobias said, shaking his head.

"I know."

Eventually, Monica moved back, slapping closed her phone. "There is no record of Razon buying a gun,

ever. The one in his apartment isn't registered anywhere."

He had help. Of *course* he had help. He'd been planning this for years, and he had access to all those
photos to use in proving that he was legitimate.

He'd found someone to supply him. Protect him.
Someone who had given him that gun, some fake identification. They'd helped him sneak into Israel.

So whom had he approached? Who was helping
him?

"Ivy," I said. "We need . . ." I trailed off. "Where's
Ivy?"

"No idea," Tobias said. Kalyani shrugged.

"You've *lost* one of your hallucinations?" Monica
asked.

"Yes."

"Well, summon her back."

"It doesn't work that way," I said, and poked through
the church, looking around. I got some funny looks
from clergy until I finally peeked into a nook and
stopped flat.

J.C. and Ivy hastily broke apart from their kissing.
Her makeup was mussed, and—incredibly—J.C. had
set his gun to the side, ignoring it. That was a first.

"Oh, you've got to be *kidding* me," I said, raising a
hand to my face. "*You two?* What are you doing?"

"I wasn't aware we had to report the nature of our
relationship to you," Ivy said coldly.

J.C. gave me a big thumbs-up and a grin.

"Whatever," I said. "Time to go. Ivy, I don't think Razon was working alone. He came into the country on
a fake passport, and other factors don't add up. Could
he have had some sort of aid here? Maybe a local organization to help him escape suspicion and move in
the city?"

"Possible," she said, hurrying to keep up. "I would point out it's not *impossible* that he's working alone, but it does seem unlikely, upon consideration. You thought that through on your own? Nice work!"

"Thanks. And your hair is a mess."

We eventually reached the cars and climbed in, me with Monica, Ivy, and J.C. The two suits and my other aspects took the forward car.

"You could be right on this point," Monica said as the cars started off.

"Razon is a smart man," I said. "He would have wanted allies. It could be another company, perhaps an Israeli one. Do any of your rivals know about this technology?"

"Not that we know of."

"Steve," Ivy said, sitting between us. She put her lipstick away, her hair fixed. She was obviously trying to ignore what I'd seen between her and J.C.

Damn, I thought. I'd assumed the two *hated* each other. *Think about that later.* "Yes?" I asked.

"Ask Monica something for me. Did Razon ever approach her company about a project like this? Taking photos to prove Christianity?"

I relayed the question.

"No," Monica said. "If he had, I'd have told you. It would have led us here faster. He never came to us."

"That's an oddity," Ivy said. "The more we work on this case, the more we find that Razon went to incredible lengths in order to come here, to Jerusalem. Why not use the resource he already had? Azari Laboratories."

"Maybe he wanted freedom," I said. "To use his invention as he wished."

"If that's the case," Ivy said, "he wouldn't have approached a rival company, as you proposed. Doing so

would have put him back in the same situation. Prod
Monica. She looks like she's thinking about something."

"What?" I asked Monica. "You have something to
add?"

"Well," Monica said, "once we knew the camera
was working, Razon *did* ask us about some projects he
wanted to attempt. Revealing the truth of the Kennedy
assassination, debunking or verifying the Patterson-
Gimlin bigfoot video, things like that."

"And you shot him down," I guessed.

"I don't know if you've spent much time considering the ramifications of this device, Mr. Leeds," Monica said. "Your questions to me on the plane indicate
you've at least started to. Well, we have. And we're terrified.

"This thing will change the world. It's about more
than proving mysteries. It means an end to privacy as
we know it. If someone can gain access to *any* place
where you have *ever* been naked, they can take photos
of you in the nude. Imagine the ramifications for the
paparazzi.

"Our entire justice system will be upended. No
more juries, no more judges, lawyers, or courts. Law
enforcement will simply need to go to the scene of the
crime and take photos. If you're suspected, you provide an alibi—and they can prove whether or not you
were where you claim."

She shook her head, looking haunted. "And what
of history? National security? Secrets become much
harder to keep. States will have to lock down sites
where important information was once presented. You
won't be able to write things down. A courier carrying sensitive documents has passed down the street?
The next day, you can get into just the right position

and take a picture *inside* the envelope. We tested that. Imagine having such power. Now imagine every person on the planet having it."

"Dang," Ivy whispered.

"So no," Monica said. "No, we wouldn't have let Mr. Razon go and take photos to prove or disprove Christianity. Not yet. Not until we'd done a *lot* of discussion about the matter. He knew this, I think. It explains why he ran."

"That didn't stop you from preparing ways to bait me into entering into a business arrangement with you," I said. "I suspect if you did it for me, you did it for other important people as well. You've been gathering resources to get yourself some strategic allies, haven't you? Maybe some of the world's rich and elite? To help you ride this wave, once the technology goes out?"

She drew her lips into a line, eyes straight forward.

"That probably looked self-serving to Razon," I said. "You won't help him with bringing the truth to mankind, but you'll gather bribery material? Even blackmail material."

"I'm not at liberty to continue this conversation," Monica said.

Ivy sniffed. "Well, we know why he left. I still don't think he'd have gone to a rival company, but he would have gone to *someone*. The Israeli government, maybe? Or—"

Everything went black.

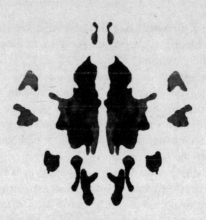

S E V E N

I awoke, dazed. My vision was blurry.

"Explosion," J.C. said. He crouched beside me. I was . . . I was tied up somewhere. In a chair. Hands bound behind me.

"Stay calm, Skinny," J.C. said. "*Calm*. They blew the car in front of us. We swerved. Hit a building at the side of the road. Do you remember?"

I barely did. It was vague.

"Monica?" I croaked, looking about.

She was tied to a chair beside me. Kalyani, Ivy, and Tobias were there as well, tied and gagged. Monica's security men weren't there.

"I managed to crawl free of the wreckage," J.C. said. "But I can't get you out."

"I know," I said. It was best not to push J.C. on the fact that he was a hallucination. I'm pretty sure he knew, deep down, exactly what he was. He just didn't like admitting it.

"Listen," J.C. said. "This is a bad situation, but you

will keep your head, and you *will* escape alive. Understand, soldier?"

"Yeah."

"Say it again."

"*Yes,*" I said, quiet but intense.

"Good man," J.C. said. "I'm going to go untie the others." He moved over, letting my other aspects free.

Monica groaned, shaking her head. "What . . ."

"I think we've made a gross miscalculation," I said. "I'm sorry."

I was surprised at how evenly that came out, considering how terrified I was. I'm an academic at heart—at least most of my aspects are. I'm not good with violence.

"What do you see?" I asked. This time, my voice quivered.

"Small room," Ivy said, rubbing her wrists. "No windows. I can hear plumbing and faint sounds of traffic outside. We're still in the city."

"Such lovely places you take us, Stephen," Tobias said, nodding in thanks as J.C. helped him to his feet. Tobias was getting on in years now.

"That's Arabic I hear outside," Kalyani said.

"Yes," Tobias said, eyes closed. "A passing train. Slowing. Stopping . . . Something about the way it's pausing there . . . Not a station, but a stop of some other sort. Cars, people talking. Church bells. Is that Yiddish? And a muezzin, sounding the call to prayer?" He snapped his eyes open. "We're somewhere along the Shivtei Israel Street, near the Old City. This is a busy area. Screaming might draw help."

"Or might get us killed," J.C. said. "Those ropes are tight, Skinny. Monica's are too."

"What's going on?" Monica asked. "What happened?"

"The pictures," Ivy said.

I looked at her.

"Monica and her goons showed off those pictures of Razon, walking around the church," Ivy said. "They probably asked every person there if they'd seen him. If he *was* working with someone . . ."

I groaned. Of course. Razon's allies would have been watching for anyone hunting him. Monica had drawn a big red bull's-eye on us.

"All right," I said. "J.C. You're going to have to get us out of this. What should—"

The door opened.

I immediately turned toward our captors. I didn't find what I'd expected. Instead of Islamic terrorists of some sort, we were faced by a group of Filipino men in suits.

"Ah . . ." Tobias said.

"Mr. Leeds," said the man in the front, speaking with an accented voice. He flipped through a folder full of papers. "By all accounts, you are a very interesting and very . . . reasonable person. We apologize for your treatment so far, and would like to see you placed in much more comfortable conditions."

"I sense a deal coming on," Ivy warned.

"I am called Salic," the man said. "I represent a certain group with interests that may align with your own. Have you heard of the MNLF, Mr. Leeds?"

"The Moro National Liberation Front," Tobias said. "It is a Filipino revolutionary group seeking to split off and create its own nation-state."

"I've heard of it," I said.

"Well," Salic said. "I have a proposal for you. We have the device for which you are searching, but we have run into some difficulties in operating it. How much would it cost us to enlist your aid?"

"One million, US," I said without missing a beat.

"Traitor!" Monica sputtered.

"You aren't even paying me, Monica," I said, amused. "You can't blame me for taking a better deal."

Salic smiled. He fully believed I'd sell out Monica. Sometimes it is very useful to have a reputation for being a reclusive, amoral jerk.

The thing is, I'm really only the reclusive part. And maybe, admittedly, the jerk part. When you have that mix, people generally assume you don't have morals either.

"The MNLF is a paramilitary organization," Tobias continued. "There hasn't been much in the way of violence on their part, however, so this is surprising to see. Their fundamental difference with the main Filipino government is over religion."

"Isn't it always?" J.C. said with a grunt, inspecting the newcomers for weapons. "This guy is packing," he said, nodding to the leader. "I think they all are."

"Indeed," Tobias said. "Think of the MNLF as the Filipino version of the IRA, or Palestine's own Hamas. The latter may be a more accurate comparison, as the MNLF is often seen as an Islamic organization. Most of the Philippines is Roman Catholic, but the Bangsamoro region—where the MNLF operates—is predominantly Islamic."

"Untie him," Salic said, gesturing toward me.

His men got to work.

"He's lying about something," Ivy said.

"Yes," Tobias said. "I think . . . Yes, he's not MNLF. He's perhaps trying to pin this on them. Stephen, the MNLF is *very much* against endangering civilians. It's really quite remarkable, if you read about them. They are freedom fighters, but they have a strict code of whom they'll hurt. They have recently been dedicated to peaceful secession."

"That must not make them terribly popular with all who would follow them," I said. "Are there splinter groups?"

"What is that?" Salic asked.

"Nothing," I said, standing up, rubbing my wrists. "Thank you. I would *very much* like to see the device."

"This way, please," Salic said.

"Bastard," Monica called after me.

"Language!" Ivy said, pursing her lips. She and my other aspects followed me out, and the guards shut the door on Monica, leaving her alone in the room.

"Yes . . ." Tobias said, walking behind the men who escorted me up the steps. "Stephen, I think this is the Abu Sayyaf. Led by a man named Khadaffy Janjalani, they split from the MNLF because the organization wasn't willing to go far enough. Janjalani died recently, and the future of the movement is somewhat in doubt, but his goal was to create a purely Islamic state in the region. He considered the killing of anyone opposed to him an . . . elegant way to achieve his goals."

"Sounds like we have a winner," J.C. said. "All right, Skinny. Here's what you need to do. Kick the guy behind you as he's taking a step. He'll fall into the fellow next to him, and you can tackle Salic. Spin him around to cover gunfire from behind, take his weapon from inside his coat, and start firing through his body at the men down there."

Ivy looked sick. "That's awful!"

"You don't think he's going to let us go, do you?" J.C. asked.

"The Abu Sayyaf," Tobias said helpfully, "has been the source of numerous killings, bombings, and kidnappings in the Philippines. They also are *very* brutal with the locals, acting as more of an organized crime family than true revolutionaries."

"So . . . that would be a no, eh?" J.C. said.

We reached the ground floor, and Salic led us into a side room. Two more men were here, outfitted as soldiers, with grenades on their belts and assault rifles in their hands.

Between them, on the table, was a medium format camera. It looked . . . ordinary.

"I need Razon here," I said, sitting down. "To ask him questions."

Salic sniffed. "He will not speak to you, Mr. Leeds. You can trust us on this count."

"So he's not working with them?" J.C. asked. "I'm confused."

"Bring him anyway," I said, and carefully began prodding at the camera.

Thing is, I had *no* idea what I was doing. *Why, WHY didn't I bring Ivans with me?* I should have known I'd need a mechanic on this trip.

But if I brought too many aspects—kept too many of them around me at once—bad things happened. That was immaterial, now. Ivans was a continent away.

"Anyone?" I asked under my breath.

"Don't look at me," Ivy said. "I can't get the remote control to work half the time."

"Cut the red wire," J.C. said. "It's always the red wire."

I gave him a flat stare, then unscrewed one part of the camera in an attempt to look like I knew what I was doing. My hands were shaking.

Salic, fortunately, sent someone to do as I requested. After that, he watched me carefully. He'd probably read about the Longway Incident, where I'd disassembled, fixed, and reassembled a complex computer system in time to stop a detonation. But that had all been Ivans, with some aid by Chin, our resident computer expert.

Without them, I was useless at this sort of thing. I tried my best to look otherwise until the soldier brought back Razon. I recognized him from the pictures Monica had shown me. Barely. His lip was cracked and bleeding, his left eye puffy, and he walked with a stumbling limp. As he sat down on a stool near me, I saw that he was missing one hand. The stump was wrapped with a bloody rag.

He coughed. "Ah. Mr. Leeds, I believe," he said with a faint Filipino accent. "I'm terribly sorry to find you here."

"Careful," Ivy said, inspecting Razon. She was standing right beside him. "They're watching. Don't act too friendly."

"Oh, I do *not* like this at all," Kalyani said. She'd moved over to some crates at the back of the room, crouching down for cover. "Is it often going to be like this around you, Mr. Steve? Because I am not very well cut out for this."

"You're *sorry* to find me here?" I said to Razon, making my voice harsh. "Sorry, but not surprised. You're the one who helped Monica and her cronies get blackmail material on me."

His unswollen eye widened a fraction. He knew it hadn't been blackmail material. Or so I hoped. Would he see? Would he realize I was here to help him?

"I did that . . . under duress," he said.

"You're still a bastard, so far as I'm concerned," I spat.

"Language!" Ivy said, hands on hips.

"Bah," I said to Razon. "It doesn't matter. You're going to show me how to make this machine work."

"I will not!" he said.

I turned a screw, my mind racing. How could I get

close enough to speak to him quietly, but not draw suspicion? "You will, or—"

"Careful, you fool!" Razon said, leaping from his chair.

One of the soldiers leveled a gun at us.

"Safety's on," J.C. said. "Nothing to be worried about. Yet."

"This is a very delicate piece of equipment," Razon said, taking the screwdriver from me. "You mustn't break it." He started screwing with his good arm. Then, speaking very softly, he continued. "You are here with Monica?"

"Yes."

"She is not to be trusted," he said. Then paused. "But she never beat me or cut my hand off. So perhaps I am not one to speak on whom to trust."

"How did they take you?" I whispered.

"I bragged to my mother," he said. "And she bragged to her family. It got to these monsters. They have contacts in Israel." He wavered, and I reached to steady him. His face was pale. This man was *not* in good shape.

"They contacted me," he said, forcing himself to keep screwing. "They claimed to be Christian fundamentalists from my country, eager to fund my operation to find proof. I did not find out the truth until two days ago. It—"

He cut off, dropping the screwdriver as Salic stepped closer to us. The terrorist waved, and one of his soldiers grabbed Razon and jerked him back by his bloodied arm. Razon cried out in pain.

The soldiers proceeded to throw him to the ground and beat him with the butts of their rifles. I watched in horror, and Kalyani began crying. Even J.C. turned away.

"I am not a monster, Mr. Leeds," Salic said, squatting down beside my chair. "I am a man with few resources. You will find that the two are quite difficult to differentiate, in most situations."

"Please stop the soldiers," I whispered.

"I am *trying* to find a peaceful solution, you see," Salic said. He did not stop the beating. "My people are condemned when we use the only methods we have—the methods of the desperate—to fight. These are the methods that every revolutionary, including the founders of your own country, has used to gain freedom. We will kill if we have to, but perhaps we do not have to. Here on this table we have peace, Mr. Leeds. Fix this machine, and you will save thousands upon thousands of lives."

"Why do you want it?" I said, frowning. "What is it to you? Power to blackmail?"

"Power to fix the world," Salic said. "We just need a few photos. Proof."

"Proof that Christianity is false, Stephen," Tobias said, walking up beside me. "That will be a difficult task for them, as Islam accepts Jesus of Nazareth as a prophet. They do not accept the resurrection, however, or many of the miracles attributed to later followers. With the right photo, they could try to undermine Catholicism— the religion followed by most Filipinos—and therefore destabilize the region."

I'll admit that, strangely, I was tempted. Oh, not tempted to help a monster like Salic. But I did see his point. Why not take this camera, prove *all* religions false?

It would cause chaos. Perhaps a great deal of death, in some parts of the world.

Or would it?

"Faith is not so easily subverted," Ivy said dismissively. "This wouldn't cause the problems he thinks it would."

"Because faith is blind?" Tobias asked. "Perhaps you are right. Many would continue to believe, despite the facts."

"What facts?" Ivy said. "Some pictures that may or may not be trustworthy? Produced by a science nobody understands?"

"Already you try to protect that which has yet to be discounted," Tobias said calmly. "You act as if you know what will happen, and need to be defensive about the proof that *may* be found. Ivy, don't you see? What facts would it take to make you look at things with rational eyes? How can you be so logical in so many areas, yet be so blind in this one?"

"Quiet!" I said to them. I raised my hands to my head. "Quiet!"

Salic frowned at me. Only then did he notice how badly his soldiers had beaten Razon.

He shouted something in Tagalog, or perhaps one of the other Filipino languages—perhaps I should have studied those instead of Hebrew. The soldiers backed away, and Salic knelt to roll over the fallen Razon.

Razon snapped his good hand into Salic's jacket, reaching for the gun. Salic jumped back, and one of the soldiers cried out. A single quiet *click* followed.

Everyone in the room grew still. One of the soldiers had taken out a handgun with a suppressor on it and shot Razon in a panic. The scientist lay back, dead eyes staring open, Salic's handgun slipping from his fingers.

"Oh, that poor man," Kalyani said, moving over to kneel beside him.

At that moment, someone tackled one of the soldiers by the door, pulling him down from behind.

Shouting began immediately. I jumped out of my chair, reaching for the camera. Salic got it first, slamming one hand down on it, then reached toward his gun on the floor.

I cursed, scrambling away, throwing myself behind the stack of crates where Kalyani had taken cover a few minutes before. Gunfire erupted in the room, and one of the crates near me threw up chips as a shot hit it.

"It's Monica!" Ivy said, taking cover beside the desk. "She got out, and she's attacking them."

I dared to peek around the crates in time to see one of the Abu Sayyaf suits fall to gunfire, toppling in the center of the room near Razon's body. The others fired at Monica, who'd taken cover in the stairwell that led down to where we'd been captive.

"Holy hell!" J.C. said, crouching beside me. "She escaped on her own. I think I might have to start liking that woman!"

Salic yelled in Tagalog. He hadn't come after me, but had taken cover near his guards. He clutched the camera close, and was joined by two other soldiers who had run down the stairs from above.

This gunfire would draw attention soon, I guessed. Not soon enough. They had Monica pinned. I could barely see her, hiding in her stairwell, trying to find a way to get out and fire on the men with the weapon she'd stolen from the guard she'd tackled. His feet stuck out of the doorway near her.

"Okay, Skinny," J.C. said. "This is your chance. Something has to be done. They'll get her before help comes, and we lose the camera. It's hero time."

"I . . ."

"You could run, Stephen," Tobias said. "There's a room right behind us. There will be windows. I'm not saying you should do it; I'm giving you the options."

Kalyani whimpered, huddled down in the corner. Ivy lay under a table, fingers in her ears, watching the firefight with calculating eyes.

Monica tried to duck out and fire, but bullets tore into the wall beside her, forcing her back. Salic was still yelling something. Several of the soldiers started firing on me, driving me back under cover.

Bullets popped against the wall above me, chips of stone dropping on my head. I breathed in and out. "I can't do this, J.C."

"You can," he said. "Look, they're carrying grenades. Did you see those on the belts of the soldiers? One will get smart, toss one of those down the stairwell, and Monica's gone. Dead."

If I let them keep the camera—that kind of power, in the hands of men like this . . .

Monica yelled.

"She's hit!" Ivy called.

I scrambled out from behind the crates and ran for the fallen soldier at the center of the room. He'd dropped a handgun. Salic noticed me as I grabbed the weapon and raised it. My hands shook, quivering.

This is never going to work. I can't do this. It's impossible.

I'm going to die.

"Don't worry, kid," J.C. said, taking my wrist in his own. "I've got this."

He pulled my arm to the side and I fired, barely looking; then he moved the gun in a series of motions, pausing just briefly for me to pull the trigger each time. It was over in moments.

Each of the armed men dropped. The room went completely still. J.C. released my wrist, and my arm fell leaden at my side.

"Did *we* do that?" I asked, looking at the fallen men.

"Damn," Ivy said, unplugging her ears. "I *knew* there was a reason we kept you around, J.C."

"Language, Ivy," he said, grinning.

I dropped the pistol—probably not the smartest thing I've ever done, but then again, I wasn't exactly in my right mind. I hurried to Razon's side. He had no pulse. I closed his eyes, but left the smile on his lips.

This was what he'd wanted. He'd wanted them to kill him so that he couldn't be forced to give up his secrets. I sighed. Then, checking a theory, I shoved my hand into his pocket.

Something pricked my fingers, and I brought them out bloodied. "What . . . ?"

I hadn't expected *that*.

"Leeds?" Monica's voice said.

I looked up. She was standing in the doorway to the room, holding her shoulder, which was bloodied. "Did *you* do this?"

"J.C. did it," I said.

"Your hallucination? Shot these men?"

"Yes. No. I . . ." I wasn't sure. I stood up and walked over to Salic, who had been hit square in the forehead. I leaned down and picked up the camera, then twisted one piece of it, my back to Monica.

"Uh . . . Mr. Steve?" Kalyani said, pointing. "I do not think that one is dead. Oh my."

I looked. One of the guards I'd shot was turning over. He held something in a bloodied hand.

A grenade.

"Out!" I yelled at Monica, grabbing her by the arm as I charged out of the room.

The detonation hit me from behind like a crashing wave.

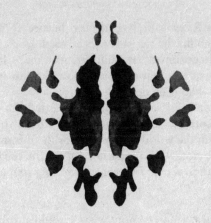

EIGHT

Exactly one month later, I sat in my mansion, drinking a cup of lemonade. My back ached, but the shrapnel wounds were healing. It hadn't been that bad.

Monica did not give the cast on her arm much notice. She held her own cup, seated in the room where I'd first met her.

Her offer today had not been unexpected.

"I'm afraid," I said, "you've come to the wrong person. I must refuse."

"I see," Monica said.

"She's been working on her scowl," J.C. said appreciatively from where he leaned against the wall. "It's getting better."

"If you would *look* at the camera . . ." Monica said.

"When I saw it last, it was in least sixteen pieces," I said. "There's just not anything to work with."

She narrowed her eyes at me. She still suspected I'd dropped it on purpose as the explosion hit. It didn't help that Razon's body had been burned to near un-recognizability in the subsequent explosions and fire that had consumed the building. Any items he'd had on him—secrets that explained how the camera *really* worked—had been destroyed.

"I'll admit," I said, leaning forward, "that I'm not terribly sorry to discover you can't fix the thing. I'm not certain the world is prepared for the information it could provide." *Or at least I'm not certain the world is prepared for people like you controlling that information.*

"But—"

"Monica, I don't know what I could do that your engineers haven't. We're simply going to have to accept the fact that this technology died with Razon. If what he did was anything other than a hoax. To be honest, I'm increasingly certain it was one. Razon was tortured beyond what a simple scientist could have endured, yet did not give the terrorists what they wanted. It was because he couldn't. It was all a sham."

She sighed and stood up. "You are passing up on greatness, Mr. Leeds."

"My dear," I said, standing, "you should know by now that I've already *had* greatness. I traded it for mediocrity and some measure of sanity."

"You should ask for a refund," she said. "Because I'm not certain I have found either in you." She took something from her pocket and dropped it on the table. A large envelope.

"And this is?" I asked, taking it.

"We found film in the camera," she said. "Only one image was recoverable."

I hesitated, then slipped the picture out. It was in black and white, like the others. It depicted a man, bearded and robed, sitting—though on what, I couldn't see. His face was striking. Not because of its shape, but because it was looking *directly* at the camera. A camera that wouldn't be there for two thousand years.

"We think it comes from the Triumphal Entry," she said. "The background looks to be the Beautiful Gate. It's hard to tell."

"My God," Ivy whispered, stepping up beside me.

Those eyes . . . I stared at the photo. Those *eyes*.

"Hey, I thought we weren't supposed to swear around you," J.C. called to Ivy.

"It wasn't a curse," she said, resting her fingers reverently on the photo. "It was an identification."

"It's meaningless, unfortunately," Monica said. "There's no way to prove who that is. Even if we could, it wouldn't do anything toward proving or disproving Christianity. This was before the man was killed. Of all the shots for Razon to get . . ." She shook her head.

"It doesn't change my mind," I said, slipping the photo back into the envelope.

"I didn't think it would," Monica said. "Consider it as payment."

"I didn't end up accomplishing much for you."

"Nor we for you," she said, walking from the room. "Good evening, Mr. Leeds."

I rubbed my finger on the envelope, listening as Wilson showed Monica to the door, then shut it. I left Ivy and J.C. having a conversation about his cursing, then walked into the entryway and up the stairs. I wound around them, hand on the banister, before reaching the upper hallway.

My study was at the end. The room was lit by a single lamp on the desk, the shades drawn against the night. I walked to my desk and sat down. Tobias sat in one of the two other chairs beside it.

I picked up a book—the last in what had been a

huge stack—and began leafing through. The picture of Sandra, the one recovered from the train station, hung tacked to the wall beside me.

"Have they figured it out?" Tobias asked.

"No," I said. "Have you?"

"It was never the camera, was it?"

I smiled, turning a page. "I searched his pockets right after he died. Something cut my fingers. Broken glass."

Tobias frowned. Then, after a moment's thought, he smiled. "Shattered lightbulbs?"

I nodded. "It wasn't the camera, it was the *flash*. When Razon took pictures at the church, he used the flash even outside in the sunlight. Even when his subject was well lit, even when he was trying to capture something that happened during the day, such as Jesus' appearance outside the tomb following his resurrection. That's a mistake a good photographer wouldn't make. And he was a good photographer, judging by the pictures hung in his apartment. He had a good eye for lighting."

I turned a page, then reached into my pocket and took something out, setting it on the table. A detachable flash, the one I'd taken off the camera just before the explosion. "I'm not sure if it's something about the flash mechanism or the bulbs, but I do know he was swapping out the bulbs in order to stop the thing from working when he didn't want it to."

"Beautiful," Tobias said.

"We'll see," I replied. "This flash doesn't work; I've tried. I don't know what's wrong with it. You know how the cameras would work for Monica's people for a while? Well, many camera flashes have multiple bulbs like this one. I suspect that only one of these had anything to do with the temporal effects. The special bulbs burned out quickly, after maybe ten shots."

I turned a few pages.

"You're changing, Stephen," Tobias finally said. "You noticed this without Ivy. Without any of us. How long before you don't need us any longer?"

"I hope that never happens," I said. "I don't want to be that man."

"And yet you chase *her*."

"And yet I do," I whispered.

One step closer. I knew what train Sandra had taken. A ticket peeked out of her coat pocket. I could make out the numbers, just barely.

She'd gone to New York. For ten years, I'd been hunting this answer—which was only a tiny fraction of a much larger hunt. The trail was a decade old, but it was *something*.

For the first time in years, I was making progress. I closed the book and sat back, looking up at Sandra's picture. She was beautiful. So very beautiful.

Something rustled in the dark room. Neither Tobias nor I stirred as a short, balding man sat down at the desk's empty chair. "My name is Arnaud," he said. "I'm a physicist specializing in temporal mechanics, causality, and quantum theories. I believe you have a job for me?"

I set the final book on the stack of those I'd read during the last month. "Yes, Arnaud," I said. "I do."

LEGION:
SKIN DEEP

PART ONE

PART ONE

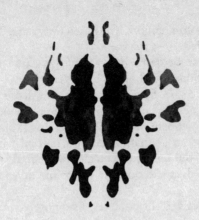

O N E

"What's her angle?" Ivy asked, walking around the table with her arms folded. Today, she wore her blonde hair in a severe bun, which was stuck through with several dangerous-looking pins.

I tried, unsuccessfully, to ignore her.

"Gold digger, perhaps?" Tobias asked. Dark-skinned and stately, he had pulled a chair over to the table so he could sit beside me. He wore his usual relaxed suit with no tie, and fit in well with this room of crystalline lighting and piano music. "Many a woman has seen only Stephen's wealth, and not his acumen."

"She's the daughter of a real estate magnate," Ivy said with a dismissive wave. "She has wealth coming out of her nose." Ivy leaned down beside the table, inspecting my dinner companion. "A nose, by the way, which seems to have had as much work done on it as her chest."

I forced out a smile, trying to keep my attention on

my dinner companion. I was used to Ivy and Tobias by
now. I relied upon them.

But it can be damn hard to enjoy a date when your
hallucinations are along.

"So . . ." said Sylvia, my date. "Malcom tells me
you're some kind of detective?" She gave me a timid
smile. Resplendent in diamonds and a tight black dress,
Sylvia was an acquaintance of a mutual friend who
worried about me far too much. I wondered how much
research Sylvia had done on me before agreeing to the
blind date.

"A detective?" I said. "Yes, I suppose you could say
that."

"I just did!" Sylvia replied with a chittering laugh.

Ivy rolled her eyes, refusing the seat Tobias pulled
over for her.

"Though honestly," I said to Sylvia, "the word 'detective' probably gives you the wrong idea. I just help
people with very specialized problems."

"Like Batman!" Sylvia said.

Tobias spat out his lemonade in a spray before him.
It spotted the tablecloth, though Sylvia—of course—
couldn't see it.

"Not . . . really like that," I said.

"I was just being silly," Sylvia said, taking another
drink of her wine. She'd had a lot of that for a meal that
she'd only just begun. "What kind of problems do you
solve? Like, computer problems? Security problems?
Logic problems?"

"Yes. All three of those, and then some."

"That . . . doesn't sound very specialized to me,"
Sylvia said.

She had a point. "It's difficult to explain. I'm a spe-
cialist, just in lots of areas."

"Like what?"

"Anything. Depends on the problem."

"She's hiding things," Ivy said, arms still folded. "I'm telling you, Steve. She's got an angle."

"Everyone does," I replied.

"What?" Sylvia asked, frowning as a server with a cloth over her arm made our salad plates vanish.

"Nothing," I said.

Sylvia shifted in her chair, then took another drink. "You were talking to *them*, weren't you?"

"So you *have* read up on me."

"A girl has to be careful, you know. There are some real psychos in the world."

"I assure you," I said, "it's all under control. I see things, but I'm completely aware of what is real and what is not."

"Be careful, Stephen," Tobias said from my side. "This is dangerous territory for a first date. Perhaps a discussion of the architecture instead?"

I realized I'd been tapping my fork against my bread plate, and stopped.

"This building is a Renton McKay design," Tobias continued in his calm, reassuring way. "Note the open nature of the room, with the movable fixtures, and geometric designs in ascending patterns. They can rebuild the interior every year or so, creating a restaurant that is half eatery, half art installation."

"My psychology really isn't that interesting," I said. "Not like this building. Did you know that it was built by Renton McKay? He—"

"So you see things," Sylvia interrupted. "Like visions?"

I sighed. "Nothing so grand. I see people who aren't there."

"Like that guy," she said. "In that movie."

"Sure. Like that. Only he was crazy, and I'm not."

"Oh, yeah," Ivy said. "What a great way to put her at ease. Explain in depth how *not* crazy you are."

"Aren't you supposed to be a therapist?" I snapped back at her. "Less sarcasm would be delightful."

That was a tall order for Ivy. Sarcasm was kind of her native tongue, though she was fluent in "stern disappointment" and "light condescension" as well. She was also a good friend. Well, imaginary friend.

She just had a thing about me and women. Ever since Sandra abandoned us, at least.

Sylvia regarded me with a stiff posture, and only then did I realize I'd spoken out loud to Ivy. As Sylvia noticed me looking at her, she plastered on a smile as fake as Red Dye No. 6. Inside, I winced. She was quite attractive, despite what Ivy claimed—and no matter how crowded my life had become, it also got terribly lonely.

"So . . ." Sylvia said, then trailed off. Entrées arrived. She had chic lettuce wraps. I'd chosen a safe-sounding chicken dish. "So, uh . . . You were speaking to one of them, just now? An imaginary person?" She obviously considered it polite to ask. Perhaps the proper lady's book of etiquette had a chapter on how to make small talk about a man's psychological disabilities.

"Yes," I said. "That was one of them. Ivy."

"A . . . lady?"

"A woman," I said. "She's only occasionally a lady."

Ivy snorted. "Your maturity is stunning, Steve."

"How many of your personalities are female?" Sylvia asked. She hadn't touched her food yet.

"They aren't personalities," I said. "They're separate from me. I don't have dissociative identity disorder. If anything, I'm schizophrenic."

That is a subject of some debate among psychologists. Despite my hallucinations, I don't fit the profile for schizophrenia. I don't fit *any* of the profiles. But why should that matter? I get along just fine. Mostly.

I smiled at Sylvia, who still hadn't started her food. "It's not a big deal. My aspects are probably just an effect of a lonely childhood, spent mostly by myself."

"Good," Tobias said. "Now transition the conversation away from your eccentricities and start talking about her."

"Yes," Ivy said. "Find out what she's hiding."

"Do you have siblings?" I asked.

Sylvia hesitated, then finally picked up her silverware. Never had I been so happy to see a fork move. "Two sisters," she said, "both older. Maria is a consultant for a marketing firm. Georgia lives in the Cayman Islands. She's an attorney. . . ."

I relaxed as she continued. Tobias raised his glass of lemonade to me in congratulations. Disaster avoided.

"You're going to have to talk about it with her eventually," Ivy said. "We aren't exactly something she can ignore."

"Yes," I said softly. "But for now, I'll settle for surviving the first date."

"What was that?" Sylvia looked at us, hesitating in her narrative.

"Nothing," I said.

"She was speaking about her father," Tobias said. "A banker. Retired."

"How long was he in banking?" I asked, glad that one of us had been paying attention.

"Forty-eight years! We kept saying he didn't need to continue on. . . ."

I smiled and began cutting my chicken as she talked.

"Perimeter clear," a voice said from behind me.

I started, looking over my shoulder. J.C. stood there, wearing a busboy's uniform and carrying a tray of dirty dishes. Lean, tough, and square-jawed, J.C. is a cold-blooded killer. Or so he claims. I think it means he likes to murder amphibians.

He was a hallucination, of course. J.C., the plates he was carrying, the handgun he had holstered inconspicuously under his white server's jacket . . . all hallucinations. Despite that, he'd saved my life several times.

That didn't mean I was pleased to see him.

"What are you doing here?" I hissed.

"Watching out for assassins," J.C. said.

"I'm on a date!"

"Which means you'll be distracted," J.C. said. "Perfect time for an assassination."

"I told you to stay home!"

"Yeah, I know. The assassins would have heard that too. That's why I had to come." He nudged me with an elbow. I felt it. He might be imaginary, but he felt perfectly real to me. "She's a looker, Skinny. Nice work!"

"Half of her is plastic," Ivy said dryly.

"Same goes for my car," J.C. said. "It still looks nice." He grinned at Ivy, then leaned down to me. "I don't suppose you could . . ." He nodded toward Ivy, then raised his hands to his chest, making a cupping motion.

"J.C.," Ivy said flatly. "Did you just try to get Steve to imagine me with a larger chest?"

J.C. shrugged.

"You," she said, "are the most loathsome non-being on the planet. Really. You should feel proud. Nobody has imagined anything more slimy, *ever*."

The two of them had an off-again, on-again relationship. Apparently, "off-again" had started when I wasn't looking. I really had no idea what to make of it—this was the first time two of my aspects had become romantically entangled.

Curiously, J.C. had been completely unable to say the words about me imagining Ivy with a different body shape. He didn't like to confront the fact that he was a hallucination. It made him uncomfortable.

J.C. continued looking the room over. Despite his obvious hang-ups, he was keen-eyed and very good with security. He'd notice things I would not, so perhaps it was good he'd decided to join us.

"What?" I asked him. "Is there something wrong?"

"He's just paranoid," Ivy said. "Remember when he thought the postman was a terrorist?"

J.C. stopped scanning, his attention focusing sharply on a woman sitting three tables over. Dark-skinned and wearing a nice pantsuit, she turned toward her window as soon as I noticed her. That window reflected back our way, and it was dark outside. She could still be watching.

"I'll check it out," J.C. said, moving away from our table.

"Stephen . . ." Tobias said.

I glanced back at our table and found Sylvia staring at me again, her fork held loosely as if forgotten, her eyes wide.

I forced myself to chuckle. "Sorry! Got distracted by something."

"By what?"

"Nothing. You were saying something about your mother—"

"What distracted you?"

"An aspect," I said, reluctant.

"A hallucination, you mean."

"Yes. I left him home. He came on his own."

Sylvia stared intently at her food. "That's interesting. Tell me more."

Being polite again. I leaned forward. "It's not what

you think, Sylvia. My aspects are just pieces of me, receptacles for my knowledge. Like . . . memories that get up and walk around."

"She's not buying it," Ivy noted. "Breathing quickly. Fingers tense . . . Steve, she knows more about you than you think. She's not acting shocked, but instead like she's been set up on a date with Jack the Ripper and is trying to keep her cool."

I nodded at the information. "It's nothing to worry about." Had I said that already? "Each of my aspects help me in some way. Ivy is a psychologist. Tobias is a historian. They—"

"What about the one that just arrived?" Sylvia asked, looking up and meeting my eyes. "The one who came when you weren't expecting?"

"Lie," Tobias said.

"Lie," Ivy said. "Tell her he's a ballet dancer or something."

"J.C.," I said instead, "is ex–Navy SEAL. He helps me with that sort of thing."

"*That* sort of thing?"

"Security situations. Covert operations. Any time I might be in danger."

"Does he tell you to kill people?"

"It's not like that. Okay, well, it is *kind* of like that. But he's usually joking."

Ivy groaned.

Sylvia stood up. "Excuse me. I need the restroom."

"Of course."

Sylvia took her purse and shawl and left.

"Not coming back?" I asked Ivy.

"Are you kidding? You just told her that an invisible man who tells you to kill people just showed up when you didn't want him to."

"Not one of our smoothest interactions," Tobias agreed.

Ivy sighed and sat down in Sylvia's seat. "Better than last time at least. She lasted . . . what? Half an hour?"

"Twenty minutes," Tobias said, glancing at the restaurant's grandfather clock.

"We're going to need to get over this," I whispered. "We can't keep going to pieces every time romance is potentially involved."

"You didn't need to say what you did about J.C.," Ivy said. "You could have made something up. Instead, you told her the truth. The frightening, embarrassing, J.C.-filled truth."

I picked up my drink. Lemonade in a fancy wineglass. I turned it about. "My life is fake, Ivy. Fake friends. Fake conversations. Often, on Wilson's day off, I don't speak to a single real person. I guess I don't want to start a relationship with lies."

The three of us sat in silence until J.C. came jogging back, dancing to the side of a real server as they passed one another.

"What?" he asked, glancing at Ivy. "You chased the chick off already?"

I raised my glass to him.

"Don't be too hard on yourself, Stephen," Tobias said, resting his hand on my shoulder. "Sandra is a difficult woman to forget, but the scars will eventually heal."

"Scars don't heal, Tobias," I said. "That's kind of the definition of the word *scar*." I turned my glass around, looking at the light on the ice.

"Yeah, great, whatever," J.C. said. "Emotions and metaphors and stuff. Look, we've got a problem."

I looked at him.

"The woman we saw earlier?" J.C. said, pointing. "She—" He cut off. The woman's seat was empty, her meal left half-eaten.

"Time to go?" I asked.

"Yeah," J.C. said. "*Now.*"

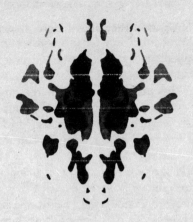

T W O

"Zen Rigby," J.C. said as we rushed from the restaurant. "Private security—and, in this case, those are fancy words for 'killer on retainer.' She has a list of suspected hits as long as your psychological profile, Skinny. No proof. She's good."

"Wait," Ivy said from my other side. "You're saying that an assassin really *did* show up at dinner?"

"Apparently," I replied. J.C. could only know what I did, so if he was saying these things, they were dredged from deep in my memory. I periodically looked over lists of operatives, spies, and professional assassins for missions I did.

"Great," Ivy said, not looking at J.C. "He's going to be insufferable to live with now."

On the way out of the restaurant, at J.C.'s prompting, I looked at the reservation list. That simple glance dumped the information there into my mind, and gave the aspects access to it.

"Carol Westminster," J.C. said, picking a name off

the list. "She's used that alias before. It was Zen for sure."

We stopped at the valet stand outside, the rainy evening making cars swish as they drove past on the wet road. The weather dampened the city's normal pungency—so instead of unwashed hobo, it smelled like recently washed hobo. A man asked for our valet ticket, but I ignored him, texting Wilson to bring our car.

"You said she's on retainer, J.C.," I said as I texted. "Whom does she work for?"

"Not sure," J.C. said. "Last I heard, she was looking for a new home. Zen isn't one of those 'hire for a random hit' assassins. Companies bring her on and keep her long term, use her to clean up messes, fix problems in legally ambiguous ways."

I knew all of this, deep down, but J.C. had to tell it to me. I'm not crazy, I'm compartmentalized. Unfortunately, my aspects . . . well, *they* tend to be a little unhinged. Tobias stood to the side, muttering that Stan—the voice he hears sometimes—hadn't warned him of the rain. Ivy pointedly did not look at the series of small wormholes in the post nearby. Had it always been this bad?

"It could just be a coincidence," Tobias said to me, shaking his head and turning away from his inspection of the sky. "Assassins go out for dinner like everyone else."

"I suppose," J.C. said. "If it is a coincidence, though, I'm gonna be annoyed."

"Looking forward to shooting someone tonight?" Ivy asked.

"Well, yeah, obviously. But that's not it. I hate coincidences. Life is much simpler when you can just assume that everyone is trying to kill you."

Wilson texted back. *Old friend called. Wanted to speak with you. He is in car. Okay?*

I texted back. *Who?*

Yol Chay.

I frowned. Yol? Was the assassin his? *Fine*, I texted.

A few minutes out, Wilson texted to me.

"Yo," J.C. said, pointing. "Scope it."

Nearby, Sylvia was getting into a car with a man in a suit. Glen, reporter for the *Mag*. He shut the door for Sylvia, then glanced at me and shrugged, tipping his antiquated fedora before climbing in the other side of the car.

"I *knew* she had an angle!" Ivy said. "It was a setup! I'll bet she was recording the entire date."

I groaned. The *Mag* was a tabloid of the worst kind—meaning that it published enough truths mixed with its fabrications that people kind of trusted it. For most of my life I'd avoided mainstream media attention, but recently the papers and news websites had latched on to me.

J.C. shook his head in annoyance, then jogged off to scout the perimeter as we waited for the car.

"I *did* warn you something was up," Ivy said, arms folded as we stood beneath the canopy with the valets, rain pattering above.

"I know."

"You're normally more suspicious than this. I'm worried that you are developing a blind spot for women."

"Noted."

"And J.C. is disobeying you again. Coming on his own when you pointedly left him at home? We haven't ever discussed what happened in Israel."

"We solved the case. That's all that happened."

"J.C. shot your gun, Steve. He—an aspect—shot *real people*."

"He moved my arm," I said. "I did the shooting."

"That's a blurring between us that has never happened before." She met my eyes. "You're trying to find Sandra again; I think you purposely sabotaged this date to have an excuse to avoid future ones."

"You're jumping to conclusions."

"I'd better be," Ivy said. "We had an equilibrium, Steve. Things were working. I don't want to start worrying about aspects vanishing again."

My limo finally pulled up, Wilson—my butler—driving. It was late evening, and the regular driver only worked a normal eight-hour shift.

"Who's that in the back?" J.C. said, jogging up and trying to get a clear view through the tinted windows.

"Yol Chay," I said.

"Huh," J.C. said, rubbing his chin.

"Think he's involved?" I asked.

"I'd bet your life on it."

Delightful. Well, a meeting with Yol was always interesting, if nothing else. The restaurant valet pulled open the door for me. I moved to step in, but J.C. put his hand on my chest and stopped me, unholstering his sidearm and peering in.

I glanced at Ivy and rolled my eyes, but she wasn't looking at me. Instead she watched J.C., smiling fondly. What was *up* with those two?

J.C. stood back and nodded, removing his hand from my chest. Yol Chay lounged inside my limo. He wore a pure white suit, a silver bow tie, and a polished set of black-and-white oxford shoes. He topped it all with sunglasses that had diamonds studding the rims—an extremely odd outfit for a fifty-year-old Korean businessman. For Yol, though, this was actually reserved.

"Steve!" he said, holding out a fist to be bumped and speaking with a moderately thick Korean accent.

He said the name *Stee-vuh*. "How are you, you crazy dog?"

"Dumped," I said, letting my aspects climb in first, so the valet didn't close the door on them. "The date didn't even last an hour."

"What? What is wrong with the women these days?"

"I don't know," I said, climbing in and sitting down as my aspects arranged themselves. "I guess they want a guy who doesn't remind them of a serial killer."

"Boring," Yol said. "Who wouldn't want to date you? You're a steal! One body, forty people. Infinite variety."

He didn't quite understand how my aspects worked, but I forgave him that. *I* wasn't always sure how they worked.

I let Yol serve me a cup of lemonade. Helping him with his problem a few years back had been some of the most fun, and least stress, I'd ever encountered on a project. Even if it *had* forced me to learn to play the saxophone.

"How many today?" Yol asked, nodding to the rest of the limo.

"Only three."

"Is the spook here?"

"I'm *not* CIA," J.C. said. "I'm special forces, you twit."

"Is he annoyed to see me?" Yol asked, grinning behind his garish sunglasses.

"You could say that," I replied.

Yol's grin deepened, then he took out his phone and tapped a few buttons. "J.C., I just donated ten grand in your name to the Brady Campaign to Prevent Gun Violence. I just thought you'd like to know."

J.C. growled. Like, *literally* growled.

I leaned back, inspecting Yol as the limo drove us.

Another followed behind, filled with Yol's people. Yol had given Wilson instructions, apparently, as this wasn't the way home. "You play along with my aspects, Yol," I said. "Most others don't. Why is that?"

"It's not play to you, is it?" he asked, lounging.

"No."

"Then it isn't to me either." His phone chirped the sound of some bird.

"That's actually the call of an eagle," Tobias said. "Most people are surprised to hear how they really sound, as the American media uses the call of the red-tailed hawk when showing an eagle. They don't think the eagle sounds regal enough. And so we lie to ourselves about the very identity of our national icon . . ."

And Yol used this as his ringtone. Interesting. The man answered the phone and began speaking in Korean.

"Do we *have* to deal with this joker?" J.C. said.

"I like him," Ivy said, sitting beside Yol. "Besides, you yourself said he was probably involved with that assassin."

"Yeah, well," J.C. said. "We could get the truth out of him. Use the old five-point persuasion method." He made a fist and pounded it into his other hand.

"You're terrible," Ivy said.

"What? He's so weird, he'd probably get off on it."

Yol hung up his phone.

"Any problems?" I asked.

"News of my latest album."

"Good news?"

Yol shrugged. He had released five music albums. All had flopped spectacularly. When you were worth 1.2 billion from a life of keen commodities investing, a little thing like poor sales on your rap albums was not going to stop you from making more.

"So . . ." Yol said. "I have an issue I might need help with."

"Finally!" J.C. said. "This had better not involve trying to make people listen to that awful music of his." He paused. "Actually, if we need a new form of torture . . ."

"Does this job involve a woman named Zen?" I asked.

"Who?" Yol frowned.

"Professional assassin," I replied. "She was watching me at dinner."

"Could be wanting a date," Yol said cheerfully.

I raised an eyebrow.

"Our problem," Yol said, "might involve some danger, and our rivals are not above hiring such . . . individuals. She's not working for me though, I promise you that."

"This job," I said. "Is it interesting?"

Yol grinned. "I need you to recover a corpse."

"Oooo . . ." J.C. said.

"Hardly worth our time," Tobias said.

"There's more," Ivy said, studying Yol's expression.

"What's the hitch?" I asked Yol.

"It's not the corpse that is important," Yol said, leaning in. "It's what the corpse knows."

THREE

"Innovation Information Incorporated," J.C. said, reading the sign outside the business campus as we pulled through the guarded gate. "Even *I* can tell that's a stupid name." He hesitated a moment. "It is a stupid name, right?"

"The name is a little obvious," I replied.

"Founded by engineers," Yol said, "run by engineers, and—unfortunately—named by engineers. They're waiting for us inside. Note, Steve, that what I'm asking you to do goes beyond friendship. Deal with this for me, and our debt will be settled, and then some."

"If a hit woman is really involved, Yol," I said reluctantly, "that's not going to be enough. I'm not going to risk my life for a favor."

"What about wealth?"

"I'm already rich," I said.

"Not riches, *wealth*. Complete financial independence."

That gave me pause. It was true; I had money. But my

delusions required a lot of space and investment. Many rooms in my mansion, multiple seats on the plane each time I fly, fleets of cars and drivers whenever I wanted to go somewhere for an extended time. Perhaps I could have bought a smaller house and forced my aspects to live in the basement or shacks on the lawn. The problem was that when they were unhappy—when the illusion of it started to break down—things got . . . bad for me.

I was finally dealing with this thing. Whatever twisted psychology made me tick, I was far more stable now than I had been at the start. I wanted to keep it that way.

"Are you in personal danger?" I asked him.

"I don't know," Yol said. "I might be." He handed me an envelope.

"Money?" I asked.

"Shares in I3," Yol said. "I purchased the company six months ago. The things this company is working on are revolutionary. That envelope gives you a ten percent stake. I've already filed the paperwork. It's yours, whether you take the job or not. A consultation fee."

I fingered the envelope. "If I don't solve your problem, this will be worthless, eh?"

Yol grinned. "You got it. But if you do solve it, that envelope could be worth tens of millions. Maybe hundreds of millions."

"Damn," J.C. said.

"Language," Ivy said, punching him in the shoulder. At this rate, those two were heading for either a full-blown screaming match or a make-out session. I could never tell.

I looked at Tobias, who sat across from me in the limo. He leaned forward, clasping his hands before him, looking me in the eye. "We could do a lot with that money," he said. "We might finally have the resources to track *her* down."

Sandra knew things about me, things about how I thought. She understood aspects. Hell, she'd taught me how they work. She'd captivated me.

And then she'd gone. In an instant.

"The camera," I said.

"The camera doesn't work," Tobias said. "Arnaud said he could be *years* away from figuring it out."

I fingered the envelope.

"She's actively blocking your efforts to find her, Stephen," Tobias said. "You can't deny that. Sandra doesn't want to be found. To get to her, we'll need resources. Freedom to ignore cases for a while, money to overcome roadblocks."

I glanced at Ivy, who shook her head. She and Tobias disagreed on what we should be doing in regard to Sandra—but she'd had her say earlier.

I looked back at Yol. "I assume that I have to agree before I can know about the technology you people are involved in?"

Yol spread his hands. "I trust you, Steve. That money is yours. Go in. Hear them out. That's all I'm asking. You can say yes or no afterward."

"All right," I said, pocketing the envelope. "Let me hear what your people have to say."

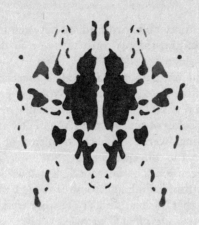

FOUR

I3 was one of those "new" technology companies, the kind decorated like a daycare, with bright walls painted in primary colors and beanbag chairs set at every intersection. Yol popped some ice cream bars out of a chest freezer and tossed one to each of his bodyguards. I declined, hands behind my back, but he then wagged one at the empty air between us.

"Sure," Ivy said, holding out her hands.

I pointed, and Yol tossed one in her direction. Which was a problem. Those who work closely with me know to just pantomime, letting my mind fill in the details. Since Yol *actually* threw the thing, my ability to imagine broke down for a moment.

The bar split into two. Ivy caught one, sidestepping the other—the real one—which hit the wall and bounced to the floor.

"I didn't need two," Ivy said, rolling her eyes. She stepped over the fallen ice cream bar and unwrapped hers, but she looked uncomfortable. Any time a flaw

appeared in my ability to mediate between my imaginary world and the real one, we were in dangerous
territory.

We went on, passing glass-walled meeting rooms.
Most of these were empty, as one would expect at this
hour, but every table was covered in small plastic bricks
in various states of construction. Apparently at I3, business meetings were supplied with plenty of Legos to
accompany the conversation.

"The receptionist at the front desk is new," Ivy noted.
"She had trouble finding the visitor name badges."

"Either that," Tobias said, "or visitors are rare here."

"Security is *awful*," J.C. growled.

I looked at him, frowning. "The doors are key
carded. That's good security."

J.C. snorted. "Key cards? Please. Look at all of these
windows. The bright colors, the inviting carpets . . .
and is that a *tire swing*? This place just screams 'hold
the door for the guy behind you.' Key cards are useless.
At least most of the computers are facing away from
windows."

I could imagine how this place might feel during
the day, with its playful atmosphere, treat bins in the
halls and catchy slogans on the walls. It was the type
of environment carefully calculated to make creative
types feel comfortable. Like a gorilla enclosure for
nerds. The lingering scents in the air spoke of an in-
house cafeteria, probably free, to keep the engineers
plump and fed—and to keep them on campus. Why go
home when you can have a meal here at six? And since
you're hanging around, you might as well get some
work done. . . .

That sense of playful creativity seemed thin, now.
We passed engineers working into the night, but they
hunched over their computers. They'd glance at us,

then shrink down farther and not look up again. The foosball table and arcade machines stood unused in the lounge. It felt like even in the evening this place should have borne a pleasant buzz of chatter. Instead, the only sounds were hushed whispers and the occasional beep from an idle game machine.

Ivy looked to me, and seemed encouraged that I'd noticed all of this. She gestured, indicating that I should go farther. *What does it mean?*

"The engineers know," I said to Yol. "There has been a security breach, and they're aware of it. They're worried that the company is in danger."

"Yeah," Yol said. "Word should never have gotten to them."

"How did it?"

"You know these IT types," Yol said from behind his sparkling sunglasses. "Freedom of information, employee involvement, all of that nonsense. The higher-ups held a meeting to explain what had happened, and they invited everyone but the damn cleaning lady."

"Language," Ivy said.

"Ivy would like you not to swear," I said.

"Did I swear?" Yol asked, genuinely confused.

"Ivy has a bit of puritan in her," I said. "Yol, what *is* this technology? What do they develop here?"

Yol stopped beside a meeting room—a more secure one, its only glass a small, square window on its door. A handful of men and women waited inside. "I'll let them tell you," Yol said as one of his security guards held open the door.

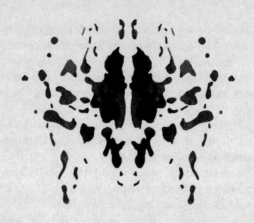

FIVE

"Every cell in your body contains seven hundred and fifty megs of data," the engineer said. "For comparison, one of your fingers holds as much information as the *entire internet*. Of course, your information is repeated and redundant, but the fact remains that cells are capable of great storage."

Garvas, the engineer, was an affable man in a button-down shirt with a pair of aviator sunglasses hanging from the pocket. He wasn't particularly overweight, but had some of the round edges that came from a life working a desk job. He was building a dinosaur out of Legos on the table as he spoke, while Yol paced outside, taking a call.

"Do you have any idea of the potential there?" Garvas continued, snapping on the head. "As the years pass, technology shrinks, and people grow tired of carrying around bulky laptops, phones, tablets. Our goal is to find a method to do away with that by using the body itself."

I glanced at my aspects. Ivy and Tobias sat at the table with us. J.C. stood by the door, yawning.

"The human body is an incredibly efficient machine," said another engineer. A thin man with an eager attitude, Laramie had built his Legos into an ever-growing tower. "It has great storage and self-replicating cells, and comes with its own power generator. The body is also very long-lived, by current manufacturing standards."

"So you were turning human bodies," I said, "into computers."

"They're *already* computers," Garvas said. "We were simply adding a few new features."

"Imagine," said the third engineer—a thin, arrow-faced woman named Loralee. "Instead of carrying a laptop, what if you made use of the organic computer already built into you? Your thumb becomes storage. Your eyes are the screen. Instead of a bulky battery, you eat an extra sandwich in the morning."

"That," J.C. said, "sounds *freakish*."

"I'm inclined to agree," I said.

"What?" Garvas asked.

"Figure of speech," I said. "So, your thumb becomes storage. It looks like, what. A . . . um . . . USB drive?"

"He was going to say 'thumb drive,'" Laramie said. "We really need to stop using thumbs as an example."

"But it's so *neat*!" Loralee said.

"Regardless," Garvas said, "what we were doing didn't change the look of the organ." He held up his thumb.

"You've had the procedure *done*?" I asked. "You're testing on yourselves?"

"Freaks," J.C. said, shifting uncomfortably. "This is going to be about zombies. I'm calling it now."

"We've done some very initial tests," Garvas said. "Most of what we just told you is just a dream, a goal.

Here, we've been working on the storage aspect exclusively, and have made good progress. We can embed information into cells, and it will stay there, reproduced by the body into new cells. My thumb doubles as backup for my laptop. As you can see, there are no adverse effects."

"We keep it in the DNA of the muscles," Laramie said, excited. "Your genetic material has tons of extraneous data anyway. We mimic that—all we have to do is add in a little extra string of information, with marks to tell the body to ignore it. Like commented-out sections of code."

"I'm sorry," J.C. said. "I don't speak supergeek. What did he just say?"

"When you 'comment out' something in computer code," Ivy explained, "you write lines, but tell the program to ignore them. That way, you can leave messages to other programmers about the code."

"Yup," J.C. said. "Gibberish. Ask him about the zombies."

"Steve," Ivy said to me, pointedly ignoring J.C., "these people are serious and excited. Their eyes light up when they talk, but there are reservations. They are being honest with you, but they *are* afraid."

"You say this is perfectly safe?" I asked the three.

"Sure," Garvas said. "People have been doing this with bacteria for years."

"The trouble is not the storage," Loralee said. "It's access. Sure, we can store all of this in our cells—but writing and reading it is very difficult. We have to inject data to get it in, and have to remove cells to retrieve it."

"One of our teammates, Panos Maheras, was working on a prototype delivery mechanism involving a virus," Garvas said. "The virus infiltrates the cells carrying a payload of genetic data, which it then splices into the DNA."

"Oh, *lovely*," Ivy said.

I grimaced.

"It's *perfectly safe*," Garvas said, a little nervous. "Panos's virus had fail-safes to prevent it from overre-producing. We have done only limited trials, and have been very careful. And note, the virus route was only *one* method we were researching."

"The world will soon change," Laramie said, ex-cited. "Eventually, we will be able to write to the ge-netic hard disk of every human body, using its own hormones to—"

I held up a hand. "What can the virus you made do *right now*?"

"Worst case?" Loralee asked.

"I'm not here to talk about ponies and flowers."

"Worst case," Loralee said, looking to the others, "the virus that Panos developed could be used to de-liver huge chunks of useless data to people's DNA—or it could cut out chunks of their DNA."

"So . . . zombies?" J.C. said.

Ivy grimaced. "Normally, I'd call him an idiot. But . . . yeah, this kind of sounds like zombies."

Not again, I thought. "I hate zombies."

The engineers all gave me baffled looks.

". . . Zombies?" Loralee asked.

"That's where this is going, isn't it?" I asked. "You turning people into zombies by accident?"

"Wow," Garvas said. "That's *way* more awesome than what we actually did."

The other two looked at him, and he shrugged.

"Mr. Leeds," Laramie said, looking back to me. "This is not science fiction. Removing chunks of someone's

DNA doesn't immediately produce some kind of zombie. It just creates an abnormal cell. One that, in our experiments, has a habit of proliferating uncontrollably."

"Not zombies," I said, feeling cold. "Cancer. You created a virus that gives people cancer."

Garvas winced. "Kind of?"

"It was an unintended result that is perfectly manageable," Laramie said, "and only dangerous if used malignly. And why would anyone want to do that?"

We all stared at him for a moment.

"Let's shoot him," J.C. said.

"Thank heavens," Tobias replied. "You hadn't suggested we shoot someone in over an hour, J.C. I was beginning to think something was wrong."

"No, listen," J.C. said. "We can shoot Pinhead McWedgy over there, and it will teach everyone in this room an important life lesson. One about not being a stupid mad scientist."

I sighed, ignoring the aspects. "You said the virus was developed by a man named Panos? I'll want to talk to him."

"You can't," Garvas said. "He's . . . kind of dead."

"How surprising," Tobias said as Ivy sighed and massaged her forehead.

"What?" I asked, turning to Ivy.

"Yol said a body was involved," Ivy said. "And their company is about storing data in human cells, so . . ."

I looked to Garvas. "He had it in him, didn't he? The way to create this virus? He stored the data for your product inside his own cells."

"Yes," Garvas said. "And somebody stole the corpse."

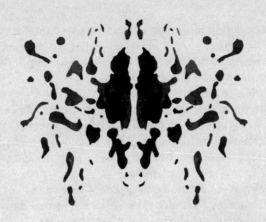

SIX

"Security nightmare," J.C. said as we made our way to the office of Panos, the deceased gene-splicer.

"So far as we can tell," Loralee said, "Panos's death was perfectly natural. We were all devastated when he had his fall, as he was a friend. But nobody thought it was anything more than a random accident on the ski slopes."

"Yeah," J.C. said, walking with my other two aspects just behind him, "because scientists working on doomsday viruses dying in freak accidents isn't *at all* suspicious."

"Occasionally, J.C.," Tobias said, "accidents *do* happen. If someone wanted his secrets, I suspect killing him and stealing his body would be low on the list of methods."

"Are you sure he's dead?" I asked Garvas, who walked on my other side. "It could be some kind of hoax, part of an espionage ploy of some sort."

"We're very sure," Garvas replied. "I saw the corpse.

The neck doesn't . . . uh . . . turn that way on someone alive."

"We'll want to corroborate that," J.C. said. "Get coroner reports, photos if possible."

I nodded absently.

"If we follow the simplest line of events," Ivy said, "this is quite logical. He dies. Someone discovers that his cells hide information. They snatch the body. I'm not saying it couldn't be something else, but I find what they're saying to be plausible."

"When did the body disappear?" I asked.

"Yesterday," Loralee said. "Which was two days after the accident. The funeral was to be today."

We stopped in the hallway beside a wall painted with cheerful groups of bubbles, and Garvas used his key card to open the next door.

"Do you have any leads?" I asked him.

"Nothing," he replied. "Or, well, too many. Our area of research is a hot one, and lots of biotech companies are involved in the race. Any one of our less scrupulous rivals could be behind the theft." He pulled open the door for me.

I took the door from Garvas and held it, much to the man's confusion. If I didn't, though, he was likely to walk through while my aspects were trying to enter. The engineers entered. Once they'd gone in, my aspects went through, and I followed. Where had Yol run off to?

"Finding out who did this should be easy," J.C. said to me. "We just have to figure out who hired that assassin to watch us. What I don't get is why everyone is so worried. So the nerds accidentally invented a cancer machine. Big deal. I've got one of those already." J.C. held up a cell phone and wiggled it.

"You have a mobile phone?" Ivy asked, exasperated.

"Sure," J.C. said. "Everyone does."

"And who are you going to call? Santa?"

J.C. stuffed the phone away, drawing his lips to a line. Ivy danced around the fact that none of them were real, but she always seemed—deep down—to be okay with it, unlike J.C. As we walked along this new hallway, Ivy fell in beside him and began saying some calming things, as if embarrassed for calling out his hallucinatory nature.

This newer area of the building was less like a kindergarten, more like a dentist's office, with individual rooms along a hallway decorated in tans with fake plants beside doorways. Garvas fished out another key card as we reached Panos's office.

"Garvas," I asked, "why didn't you go to the government with your virus?"

"They'd have just wanted to use it as a weapon."

"No," I said, putting my hand on his arm. "I doubt it. A weapon like this wouldn't serve a tactical purpose in war. Give the enemy troops cancer? It would take months or years to take effect, and even then would be of marginal value. A weapon like this would only be useful as a threat against a civilian population."

"It's not supposed to be a weapon at all."

"And gunpowder was first just used to make fireworks," I said.

"I mentioned that we were looking for other methods to read and write into our cells, right?" Garvas said. "Ones that didn't use the virus?"

I nodded.

"Let's just say that we started those projects because some of us were concerned about the virus approach. Research on Panos's project was halted as we tried to find a way to do all of this with amino acids."

"You still should have gone to the government."

"And what do you think they'd have done?" Garvas asked, looking me right in the eye. "Pat us on the heads? Thank us? Do you know what happens to laboratories that invent things like this? They vanish. Either they get consumed by the government or they get dismantled. Our research here is important . . . and, well, lucrative. We don't want to get shut down; we don't want to be the subject of a huge investigation. We just want this whole problem to go away."

He pulled open the door and revealed a small, neat office. The walls were decorated with an array of uniformly framed, autographed pictures of science fiction actors.

"Go," I said to my aspects, holding Garvas back.

The three entered the office, poking and prodding at objects on the desk and walls.

"He was of Greek descent," Ivy said, inspecting some books on the wall and a set of photos. "Second-generation, I'd say, but still spoke the language."

"What?" J.C. said. "Panos isn't a w—"

"Watch it," Ivy said.

"—Mexican name?"

"No," Tobias said. He leaned down beside the desk. "Stephen, some aid, please?"

I walked over and moved the papers on the desk so Tobias could get a good look at each of them. "Dues to a local fablab . . ." Tobias said. "Brochure for a Linux convention . . . DIY magazine . . . Our friend here was a maker."

"Speak dumb person, please," J.C. said.

"It's a subculture of technophiles and creative types, J.C.," Tobias said. "A parallel, or perhaps an outgrowth, of the open source software movement. They value hands-on craftsmanship and collaboration, particularly in the creative application of technology."

"He kept each name badge from conventions he attended," Ivy said, pointing toward a stack of them. "And each is signed not by celebrities, but by—I'd guess—people whose talks he attended. I recognize a few of the names."

"See that rubber wedge on the floor?" J.C. said with a grunt. "There's a scuff on the carpet. He often stuffed the wedge under his door to prop it open, circumventing the autolock. He liked to leave his office open for people to stop by and chat."

I poked at a few stickers stuck to the top of his desk. *Support Open Source, Information for Every Body, Words Should Be Free.*

Tobias had me sit at the computer. It wasn't password protected. J.C. raised an eyebrow.

Panos's latest website visits were forums, where he posted energetically, but politely, about information and technology issues. "He was enthusiastic," I said, scanning some of his emails, "and talkative. People genuinely liked him. He often attended nerdy conventions, and though he would be reticent to talk about them at first, if you could pry a little bit out of him, the rest would come out like a flood. He was always tinkering with things. The Legos were his idea, weren't they?"

Garvas stepped up beside me. "How . . ."

"He believed in your work," I continued, narrowing my eyes at one of Panos's posts on a Linux forum. "But he didn't like your corporate structure, did he?"

"Like a lot of us, he felt that investors were an annoying but necessary part of doing what we loved." Garvas hesitated. "He didn't sell us out, Leeds, if that's what you're wondering. He *wouldn't* have sold us out."

"I agree," I said, turning around in the chair. "If this man were going to betray his company, he'd simply have posted everything on the internet. I find it highly unlikely that he'd sell your files to some other evil corporation rather than just giving them away."

Garvas relaxed.

"I'll need that list of your rival companies," I said. "And coroner's reports, with photos of the body. Specifics on how the corpse vanished. I'll also want details about where Panos lived, his family, and any non-work friends you know about."

"So . . . you're agreeing to help us?"

"I'll find the body, Garvas," I said, standing. "But first I'm going to go strangle your employer."

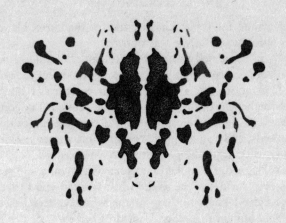

SEVEN

I found Yol sitting alone in a cafeteria, surrounded by clean white tables, chairs of green, red, yellow. Each table sported a jar filled with lemons.

Empty, yet decorated with perky colors, the room felt . . . as if it were holding its breath. Waiting for something. I waved for my aspects to wait outside, then walked in to confront Yol alone. He'd removed his garish sunglasses; without them, he looked almost like an ordinary businessman. Did he wear the glasses to pretend he was a star, or did he wear them to keep people from seeing those keen eyes of his, so certain and so wily?

"You set me up," I said, taking a seat beside him. "Ruthlessly, like a pro."

Yol said nothing.

"If this story breaks," I said, "and everything about I3 goes to hell, I'll be implicated as part owner in the company."

I waited for Ivy to chastise me for the curse, bland though it was. But she was outside.

"You could tell the truth," Yol said. "Shouldn't be too hard to prove that you only got your shares today."

"No good. I'm a story, Yol. An eccentric. I don't get the benefit of the doubt with the press. If I'm connected in any way, no protests will keep me out of the tabloids, and you know it. You gave me shares *specifically* so I'd be in the pot with you, you bastard."

Yol sighed. He looked far older when you could see his eyes. "Maybe," he said, "I just wanted you to feel like I do. I knew *nothing* of the whole cancer fiasco when I bought this place. They dropped the worst of it on me two weeks ago."

"Yol," I said, "you need to talk to the authorities. This is bigger than me or you."

"I know. And I am. The feds are sending CDC officials tonight. The engineers are going to be quarantined; I probably will be too. I haven't told anyone else yet. But Stephen, the government is wrong; they're looking at this *wrong*. This isn't about a disease, but about information."

"The corpse," I said, nodding. "How could I3 let this happen? Didn't they consider that he was *literally* a walking hard drive?"

"The body was to be cremated," Yol said. "Part of an in-house agreement. It wasn't supposed to be an issue. And even still, the information might not be easy to get. Everyone here is supposed to encrypt the data they store inside their cells. You've heard of a one-time pad?"

"Sure," I said. "Random encryption that requires a unique key to decode. Supposed to be unbreakable."

"Mathematically, it's the *only* unbreakable form of encryption," Yol said. "The process isn't very practical for everyday use, but what people were doing here wasn't about practicality, not yet. Company policy insisted on such encryption—before they put data in their bodies, they encrypt it with a unique key. To read the data, you'd need that exact key. We don't have the one Panos used, unfortunately."

"Assuming he actually followed policy and encrypted his data."

Yol grimaced. "You noticed?"

"Not the most interested in security, our deceased friend."

"Well, we have to hope he used a key—because if he did, the people who have his body won't be able to read what he stored. And we might be safe."

"Unless they find the key."

Yol pushed a thick folder toward me. "Exactly. Before we arrived, I had them print this out for you."

"And it is?"

"Panos's net interactions. Everything he's done over the last few months—every email sent, every forum post. We haven't been able to find anything in it, but I thought you should have it just in case."

"You're assuming I'm going to help you."

"You told Garvas—"

"I told him I'd find the corpse. I'm not sure I'll return it to you when I do."

"That's fine," Yol said, standing up, taking his sunglasses out of his pocket. "We have our data, Stephen. We just don't want it falling into the wrong hands. Tell me you disagree."

"I'm pretty sure that your hands *are* the wrong hands." I paused. "Did you kill him, Yol?"

"Panos? No. As far as I can tell, it really *was* an accident."

I studied him, and he met my eyes before slipping

on the ridiculous sunglasses. Trustworthy? I'd always thought so in the past. He tapped the packet of information. "I'll see that Garvas and his team get you everything else you asked for."

"If it were only your company," I said, "I'd probably just let you burn."

"I know that. But people are in danger."

Damn him. He was right. I stood up.

"You have my number," Yol said. "I'll likely be on lockdown here, but I should still be able to talk. You, however, need to make a quick exit before the feds arrive."

"Fine." I brushed past him, heading toward the door.

"Finding the decryption key isn't enough," Yol said after me. "We don't know how many copies of it there are—and that's assuming Panos even followed encryption protocol in the first place. Find that body, Stephen, and *burn it*. That's what I wish I'd done to this whole building weeks ago."

I opened the door, stepping out and waving to Ivy, Tobias, and J.C. They fell in with me as we walked.

"J.C.," I said, "use that phone of yours. Call the other aspects. Send them to the White Room. We've got work to do."

PART TWO

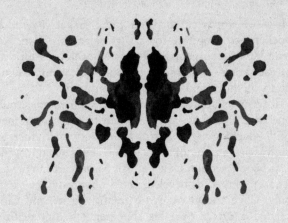

EIGHT

I've got a lot of aspects. Forty-seven, to be exact, with Arnaud being the latest to join us. I don't usually need all of them—in fact, imagining more than four or five at a time is taxing, something I can't do for long. That limitation is yet another thing that makes my psychologists salivate. A psychotic who finds it more tiring to create his fantasy world than live in the real one?

On occasion, a job comes along that requires extra effort, and I need the attention of a large number of aspects. That's why I made the White Room. Blank walls, floor, and ceiling painted the same uniform matte white; smooth, cool surfaces, unbroken save for lights in the ceiling. Soundproofed and calm, here there were no distractions—nothing to focus on but the dozens of imaginary people who flooded in through the double doors.

I don't consciously choose how my aspects look, but something about me seems to appreciate variety. Lua, a Samoan, was a beefy fellow with a vast smile.

He wore sturdy cargo pants and a jacket covered in pockets—appropriate for a survivalist. Mi Won, Korean, was our surgeon and field medic. Ngozi—forensic investigation—was a six-foot-four black woman, while Flip was short, white, fat, and often tired.

It went on and on and on. They'd joined me slowly, one case at a time, as I'd needed to learn some new skill—packing my overcrowded brain with an increasingly diverse array of proficiencies. They acted just like real people would, chatting in a variety of languages. Audrey looked disheveled; she'd obviously been napping. Clive and Owen wore golfing outfits, and Clive carried a driver over his shoulder. I hadn't realized that Owen had finally gotten him to pick up the sport. Kalyani, decked out in a bright red and gold silk sari, rolled her eyes as J.C. called her "Achmed" again, but I could tell he was growing fond of her. It was tough *not* to be fond of Kalyani.

"Mr. Steve!" Kalyani said. "How was your date? Fun, I hope?"

"It was a step forward," I said, looking around the room. "Have you seen Armando?"

"Oh! Mr. Steve." The diminutive Indian woman took me by the arm. "Some of us tried to get him to come down. He refused. He says he is on a hunger strike until his throne is returned to him."

I winced. Armando was getting worse. Nearby, Ivy gave me a pointed look.

"Mr. Steve," Kalyani said, "you should have my husband Rahul join us."

"I've explained this before, Kalyani. Your husband is not one of my aspects."

"But Rahul is *very* helpful," Kalyani said. "He's a photographer, and since Armando is so unhelpful lately . . ."

"I'll consider it," I said, which seemed to placate her. Kalyani was new, and didn't yet know how all this worked. I couldn't create new aspects at will, and though many of my aspects spoke of their lives—their families, friends, and hobbies—I never actually *saw* any of this. Good thing too. Keeping track of forty-seven hallucinations is tough enough. If I had to imagine their in-laws too, I just might end up going crazy.

Tobias cleared his throat, trying to draw everyone's attention. That proved to be futile before the jabbering horde of aspects; getting together at once was too novel, and they were enjoying it. So J.C. pulled out his sidearm and shot once into the air.

The room immediately silenced, then was filled with the sounds of aspects grousing and complaining as they rubbed their ears. Tobias stepped out of the way of a small trail of dust that floated down from above.

I glared at J.C. "You realize, genius, that now I'm going to have to imagine a *hole* in the ceiling every time we come in here?"

J.C. gave a little shrug, holstering his weapon. He at least had the decency to look embarrassed.

Tobias patted me on the arm. "I'll patch the hole," he told me, then turned to the now-silenced crowd. "A corpse has been stolen. We have been employed to recover it."

Ivy walked among the aspects, delivering sheets of paper.

"You'll find the details explained here," Tobias continued. Though they all knew what I did, sometimes going through the motions of delivering information was better for us all. "It is important you understand that lives are at stake. Perhaps many lives. We need a plan, and quickly. Get to work."

Ivy finished distributing the sheets, ending next to me. She handed me the last group of papers.

"I already know the details," I said.

"Your sheet is different," Ivy said. "It's everything you know about I3's rival companies."

I glanced it over, and was surprised at how much information it contained. I'd spent the ride here pondering the things Yol had told me, and hadn't read his briefings beyond glancing at the names of the three companies he thought most likely to have stolen the corpse. Well, information about each company was apparently tucked in the back of my brain. I flipped through the pages, thoughtful. I hadn't done any research on biotech companies since Ignacio had . . . left us. I'd assumed that knowledge like this would have gone with him.

"Thanks," I said to Ivy.

"No problem."

My aspects spread through the White Room, each starting to work in his or her own way. Kalyani sat on the floor beside a wall and took out a bright red marker. Dylan paced. Lua sidled up to whomever was closest and started a conversation. Most wrote their ideas, using the walls like whiteboards. Some sketched as they wrote, others had a linear progression of ideas, others kept writing things and crossing them out.

I read through Ivy's pages to refresh my memory, then dug into the material Yol had given me. This included the coroner's report, with pictures of the dead man, who did indeed look very dead. Liza herself had filled out the report. Might need to visit her, unfortunately.

Once done reading, I strolled through the room looking over each aspect's work, Tobias at my side. Some aspects focused on whether or not Yol was playing us.

Others—like Ivy—extrapolated from what we knew about Panos, trying to decide where they thought he'd be most likely to hide the data key. Still others worked on the problem of the virus.

After one circuit through the room, I leaned back against the wall and picked up the larger stack of papers Yol had given me—the one that contained the record of Panos's web and email interactions over the last few months. It was thick, but this time I didn't worry about paying conscious attention to what I was reading. I just wanted to do a quick speed read to dump it into my brain so the aspects could play with it.

That still took over an hour. By the time I stood up, stretching, much of the white space in the room was filled with theories, ideas, and—in Marinda's case—large floral patterns and an impressively detailed sketch of a dragon. I clasped my hands behind my back and did another circuit of the room, encouraging those who had gotten bored, asking questions about what they'd written, breaking up a few arguments.

In the midst of it I passed Audrey, who was writing her comments in the middle of the air before her, using her finger instead of a pen.

I stopped and raised an eyebrow at her. "Taking liberties, I see."

Audrey shrugged. Self-described as "curvaceous," she had long dark hair and a pretty face. For an expert in handwriting analysis, her penmanship was awful.

"There wasn't space left on the wall," Audrey said.

"I'm sure," I said, looking at her hovering text. A second later a pane of glass appeared in the room where she had been writing, making it seem like she'd been writing on glass all along. I felt a headache coming on.

"Oh, that's no fun," she said, folding her arms.

"It is what must be, Audrey," I said. "There are rules."

"Rules you made up."

"Rules we all live by," I said, "for our own good." I frowned, reading what she'd written. "Biochemistry equations? Since when have you been interested in that?"

She shrugged. "I figured that somebody ought to do a little studying on the topic, and I had the time, since you pointedly refuse to imagine me a pet."

I rested my fingers on the pane of glass, looking over her cramped notes. She was trying to figure out the method Panos had used to create the virus. There were large gaps in her diagrams, however—breaks that looked as if they'd been ripped free of the writing. What was left went barely beyond basic chemistry.

"It's not going to work, Audrey," I said. "This just isn't something we can do anymore."

"Shouldn't it still be in there, somewhere?"

"No. It's gone."

"But—"

"Gone," I said firmly.

"You are one messed-up person."

"I'm the sanest one in this room."

"Technically," she said, "you're also the most insane."

I ignored the comment, squatting down beside the pane of glass, inspecting some other notations she'd made on other topics. "Searching for patterns in the things Panos wrote online?"

"I thought there might be hidden messages in his forum posts," Audrey explained.

I nodded. When I'd studied handwriting analysis—and in doing so, created Audrey—I'd done a little tangential research into cryptography. The two disciplines moved in the same circles, and some of the books I'd read had described decoding messages by noticing intentional changes in handwriting, such as a writer crossing some of their *T*s at a different slant to convey hidden information.

That meant Audrey had some small cryptography expertise. More than any of the rest of us did. "This could be useful," I said, tapping the pane of glass.

"Might be more useful," she noted, "if I—you—had any *real* understanding of cryptography. Do you have time to download some more books, perhaps?"

"You just want to go on more missions," I said, standing.

"Are you kidding? You get *shot at* on those missions."

"Only once in a while."

"Often enough. I'm not so comfortable with being imaginary that I want to see you dead on the ground. You're literally my whole world, Steve-O." She paused. "Though, to be honest, I've always been curious what would happen if you took LSD."

"I'll see what I can do about the cryptography," I said. "Continue with the analysis of his forum posts. Stop with the chemistry sham."

She sighed, but reached out and started to erase the equations with her sleeve. I walked away, pulling out my phone and bringing up some books on cryptography. If I studied further, would I create another aspect? Or would Audrey really acquire the ability, as she implied? I wanted to say the first was more likely, but Audrey—as the most self-aware of all my aspects—got away with things I wouldn't have expected.

Tobias joined me as I sorted through the volumes available electronically.

"Report?" I asked him.

"General consensus is that this technology is viable," Tobias said, "and the threat is real, though Mi

Won wants to think more about the effects of dumping rampant DNA strains into the body's muscles. J.C. says we'll want to confirm independently that I3 is in lockdown and that the feds are really involved. That will tell us a great deal about how honest Mr. Chay is being with us."

"Good idea. What's that contact we have at Homeland Security?"

"Elsie," Tobias said. "You found her cat."

Yes, her cat. Not all of my missions involve terrorists or the fate of the world. Some are far more simple and mundane. Like locating a teleporting cat.

"Give her a call," I said absently. "See if she'll confirm for us what Yol said about contacting the authorities."

Tobias stopped beside me. "Call her?"

I looked up from my screen, then blushed. "Right. Sorry. I've been talking to Audrey." She tended to throw me off balance.

"Ah, dearest Audrey," Tobias said. "I sincerely think she must be some kind of compensating factor in your psychology, a way to blow off a little steam, so to speak. Genius is often accompanied by quirks of the mind. Why, Nikola Tesla had an arbitrary, and baffling, aversion to *pearls* of all things. He'd send people away who came to him wearing them, and it is said . . ."

He continued on. I relaxed to the sound of his voice, choosing a book on advanced cryptography. Tobias eventually wound back around to his report on what the aspects had determined. "This brings us to our next course of action," he said. "Owen's suggestion is perhaps the most relevant, and Ivy won't be able to complete her psychological analysis unless we know more about the subject. Beginning by visiting Panos's family is advised. From there, Ngozi needs more information from the coroner. We may want to go there next."

"Reverse those," I said. "It's . . . what, three in the morning?"

"Six."

"Already?" I said, surprised. I didn't feel that tired. The engagement of a new mission, a puzzle to solve, kept me alert. "Well, still. I feel more comfortable about visiting a coroner office this early than I do about waking Panos's family. Liza gets to work at . . . what, seven?"

"Eight."

So I had time to kill. "What leads do we have on the corporations who might be behind this?"

"J.C. has some thoughts. He wants to talk to you."

I found him leaning against the wall near where Ivy was working; he was chattering away and generally distracting her. I grabbed him by the shoulder and pulled him aside. "Tobias said you have something for me."

"Our assassin," he said. "Zen Rigby."

"Yes, and?" J.C. couldn't have any new information on her—he only knew what I knew, and we'd dredged that well already.

"I've been thinking, Skinny," J.C. said. "Why did she show up when you were on your date?"

"Because her employers knew Yol was likely to go to me."

"Yeah, but why start surveillance on you that early? Look, they have the body, right?"

"So we assume."

"Therefore, the reason to watch you is to tail you and see if you find the data key. There was no reason to watch you *before* Yol arrived. It tipped their hand, you see? They should have waited until you were called in to I3."

I chewed on that for a minute. We liked to make fun of J.C., but the truth was, he was one of my most practical aspects. A lot of them spent their days dreaming and thinking. J.C. kept me alive.

"It does seem odd," I agreed. "But what does it mean?"

"It means we don't have all the facts," J.C. said. "Zen might have been trying to bug us, for instance, hoping we'd go to I3 and reveal information."

I looked at him sharply. "Wardrobe change?"

"Good place to start," he said. "But there are a host of other reasons she could have been there so early. Perhaps she's employed by a *third* company that knows something is up with I3, but doesn't quite know what. Or maybe she's not involved in this case at all."

"You don't believe that."

"I don't," he agreed. "But let's tread lightly, eh? Zen is dangerous. I ran across her a couple of times in black ops missions. She left corpses, sometimes operatives— sometimes just innocent bystanders."

I nodded.

"You'll want to carry a sidearm," J.C. said. "You realize that if it comes to a confrontation, I won't be able to shoot her."

"Because of past familiarity?" I said, giving him an out. I didn't like to push him to confront what he was—instead offering reasons why, despite being my bodyguard, he could never actually interact with anyone we met.

Except that one time when he had done just that.

"Nah," J.C. said. "I can't shoot her because I'm not really here."

I started. Had he just . . . ? "J.C.," I said. "This is a big step for you."

"Nah, I've got this figured out. That Arnaud guy, he's pretty smart."

"Arnaud?" I looked across the room toward the slender, balding Frenchman who was our newest addition.

"Yeah," J.C. said, hand on my shoulder. "He has this theory, see. That we're not figments, or whosits, or whatever crazy term you feel like using at the moment. He said . . . well, it's a lot of nerd talk, but it means I'm a real boy for sure. I'm just not here."

"Is that so?" I wasn't certain what to think of this.

"Yup," J.C. said. "You should hear what he has to say. Hey, chrome-dome!"

Arnaud pointed at himself, then hustled over as J.C. waved. J.C. put his hand around the diminutive Frenchman, as if they were best friends—the gesture seemed to make Arnaud distinctly uncomfortable. It was a little like the cat buddying up to the mouse.

"Let him have it," J.C. said.

"It? What it are you speaking of?" Arnaud spoke with a smooth French accent, like butter melting over a browned game hen.

"You know," J.C said. "The things you said about us?"

Arnaud adjusted his spectacles. "Well, um, you see, in quantum physics we talk about possibilities. One interpretation says that dimensions are infinite, and everything that can happen, has happened. It seems to follow if this is true, then each of us aspects somewhere has existed in some dimension or realm of possibility as a real person. A curious thought, would you not agree, Étienne?"

"Curious indeed," I said. "It—"

"So I'm real," J.C. interjected. "The smart guy just said it."

"No, no," Arnaud said. "I merely indicated that it is likely that somewhere, in another place and time, there really is a person who matches—"

J.C. shoved him aside and wrapped his arm around my shoulders, turning me away from Arnaud. "I've got it figured out, Skinny. We're all from this other place, see. And when you need some help, you reach out and *snatch* us. You're some kind of physics wizard."

"A . . . physics wizard?"

"Yup. And I'm no Navy SEAL. I've just got to accept that." He paused. "I'm an Interdimensional Time Ranger."

I looked at him, grinning.

But he was dead serious.

"J.C.," I said. "That's as ridiculous as Owen's ghost theory."

"No it's not," J.C. said, stubborn. "Look, back in that Jerusalem mission. What happened there at the end?"

I hesitated. I had been surrounded, hands shaking, holding a gun I barely knew how to use. In that moment, J.C. had *taken hold* of my arm and directed it, causing me to fire my gun in the precise pattern needed to bring down every enemy.

"I learn quickly," I said. "Physics, math, languages . . . I just need to spend a short time studying, and I can become an expert—via an aspect. Maybe gunplay isn't different. I studied it, fired a few times at the range, and became an expert. But this skill is different—you can't help me by talking—so I couldn't use you properly until I imagined you guiding me. It's not so different from what Kalyani does in guiding me through a conversation in another language."

"You're stretching," J.C. said. "Why hasn't this worked for any other skill you've tried?"

I didn't know.

"I'm a Time Ranger," J.C. said stubbornly.

"If that were true—which it's *not*—wouldn't you be angry at me for grabbing you from your other life and trapping your quantum ghost here?"

"Nah," J.C. said. "It's what I signed up for. The creed of the Time Ranger. We have to protect the universe, and for now that means protecting you as best I can."

"Oh, for the love of—"

"Hey," J.C. interrupted. "Aren't we tight for time? You should be moving."

"We can't do much until morning arrives," I said, but allowed myself to be moved on from the topic. I waved Tobias over. "Keep everyone working. I'm going to go take a shower and do some reading. After that, we're hitting the field."

"Will do," Tobias said. "And the field team is?"

"Standard," I said. "You, Ivy, J.C., and . . ." I looked through the room. "And we'll see who else."

Tobias gave me a curious look.

"Have the team meet me in the garage, ready to go, at seven thirty."

NINE

I turned the cryptography book to text-to-voice, cranked the volume, and set it to 5× speed. The following shower was long and refreshing. I didn't think about the problem—I just learned.

When I stepped into my bedroom in my bathrobe, I found that Wilson had set out breakfast for me, along with a tall glass of lemonade. I sent him a text, asking him to have the driver prep the SUV—much less conspicuous than taking the limo—for a seven-thirty departure.

I finished the book while eating, then made a call to Elsie, my contact in Homeland Security. I woke her up, unfortunately, but she was still willing to check on the matter for me. I put in a call to the coroner's office—got the voicemail, but left a message for Liza—and as I was finishing, got a text back from Elsie. I3 was indeed under lockdown, with the CDC investigating and the FBI involved.

I strode into the garage a short time later, dressed and

somewhat refreshed, right on time for our departure.
There I found Wilson himself—square faced, bifocaled,
and greying on top—flicking a speck of something off a
chauffeur's cap, which he proceeded to put on his head.

"Wait," I said. "Isn't Thomas supposed to be in this
morning?"

"Unfortunately," Wilson said, "he is not coming to
work today. Or ever, apparently, as per his message
this morning."

"Oh, no," I said. "What happened?"

"You do not recall explaining to him that you were
a Satanist, Master Leeds?"

"Two percent Satanist," I said. "And Xavier is very
progressive for a devil worshiper. He's never made me
sacrifice anything other than imaginary chickens."

"Yes, well . . ."

I sighed. Another servant lost. "We can call in a
driver for the day. We had a long night last night. You
don't need to do work this early."

"I don't mind," Wilson said. "Somebody needs to
look out for you, Master Leeds. Did you sleep at all?"

"Uh . . ."

"I see. And did you happen to eat anything at dinner
last night before you ended up in the tabloids?"

"The story is out already, is it?"

"Written up in the *Mag* and posted on Squawker
this morning—along with an exposé by Miss Bianca
herself. You skipped dinner, and you skipped lunch
yesterday as well, insisting that you didn't want to
spoil your appetite for the date."

More like didn't want to throw up from nervous-
ness. "No wonder that breakfast tasted so good." I
reached for the door handle to the SUV.

Wilson rested his hand on my arm. "Do not become
so preoccupied with saving the world, Master Leeds,

that you forget to take care of yourself." He patted my arm, then climbed into the driver's seat.

My team waited inside, all but Audrey, who burst into the garage wearing a sweater and a scarf. No other aspect had appeared upon my reading the book; Audrey had gained the knowledge, as she'd expected. I was glad—each new aspect put a strain on me, and I'd rather have old ones learn new things. Though, having Audrey along on the mission could be its own special brand of difficult.

"Audrey," I said as I opened the door for her, "it's almost June. A scarf?"

"Well," she said with a grin, "what good is being imaginary if you can't ignore the weather?" She threw her scarf dramatically over one shoulder, then piled into the car, elbowing J.C. on her way past.

"If I shoot you, woman," he growled at her, "it will hurt. My bullets can affect interdimensional matter."

"Mine can go around corners," she said. "And make flowers grow." She settled in between Ivy and Tobias, and didn't put on her seat belt.

This was going to be an interesting mission.

We pulled out onto the roadway. Morning was upon us, the day bright, and rush hour well under way. I watched out the window, lost in thought for a time, until I noticed J.C. fishing in Ivy's purse.

"Uh . . ." I said.

"Don't turn," J.C. said, batting away Ivy's hand as she tried to snatch the purse back. He came out with her compact makeup mirror and held it up to glance over his shoulder out the back window, not wanting to present his profile.

"Yeah," he said, "someone's probably following us."

"Probably?" Ivy asked.

"Hard to say for certain," J.C. said, shifting the mirror. "The car doesn't have a front license plate."

"You think it's her?" I asked. "The assassin?"

"Again," J.C. said, "no way to tell for certain."

"Maybe there is a way," Audrey said, tapping her head and the new knowledge inside of it. "Wanna try some hacking, Steve-O?"

"Hacking?" Ivy said. "As in computer hacking?"

"No, as in coughing," Audrey said, rolling her eyes. "Here, I'm going to write some instructions for you."

I watched with curiosity as she scribbled down a list of instructions, then handed them to me. It was imaginary paper—not that I could tell. I took it and read the instructions, then glanced at Audrey.

"Trust me," Audrey said.

"I only read you one book."

"It was enough."

I studied her, then shrugged and got out my phone. Worth a try. Following her instructions, I called up F.I.G., the restaurant where I'd eaten—or, well, ordered food—last night. It rang, and fortunately the breakfast staff was already in. An unfamiliar voice answered, asking, "Hello?"

I followed Audrey's instructions. "Yeah, hey," I said. "My wife ate there last night—but we had a family emergency, and she had to run before finishing her food. In fact, she was in such a hurry, she used the business credit card to pay instead of our home one. I was wondering if I could swap the cards."

"Okay," the woman on the phone said. "What's the name?"

"Carol Westminster," I said, using the alias Zen had used for her reservation.

A few minutes passed. Hopefully the receipts from

last night were still handy. Indeed, after shuffling about a moment, the woman came back on the phone. "Okay, what's the new card name?"

"Which one did she use?"

"It's a KeyTrust card," the woman said, starting to sound suspicious. "Ends in 3409."

"Oh!" I replied. "Well, that's the right one after all. Thanks anyway."

"Great, thanks." The woman sounded annoyed as she hung up the phone. I wrote the number down in my pocket notebook.

"You call that hacking?" J.C. said. "What was the point?"

"Wait and see," Audrey said.

I was already dialing the bank's credit card fraud prevention number. We continued in the car, taking an exit onto the southbound highway as I listened to holding music. Beside me, J.C. kept an eye on our supposed tail with Ivy's mirror. He nodded at me. They'd followed us onto the highway.

When I finally got through the menus, holding patterns, and warnings my call might be recorded, I ended up with a nice-sounding man with a Southern accent on the other side of the line. "How can I help you?" he asked.

"I need to report a stolen credit card," I said. "My wife's purse got taken from our house last night."

"All right. Name on the card?"

"Carol Westminster."

"And the card number?"

"I don't have it," I said, trying to sound exasperated. "Did you miss the part about the card being lost?"

"Sir, you just need to look online—"

"I tried! All I can see are the last four digits."

"You need to—"

"Someone could be spending my money *right now*," I cut in. "Do we have time for this?"

"Sir, you have fraud protection."

"I'm sorry, I'm sorry. I'm just worried. It's not your fault. I just don't know what to do. Please, you can help, right?"

The man on the other line breathed out, as if my tone change indicated he'd just dodged a potentially frustrating incident. "Just tell me the last four digits then," he said, sounding more relaxed.

"The computer says 3409."

"Okay, let's see . . . Do you know your PIN number, Mr. Westminster?"

"Uh . . ."

"Social Security number attached to the card?"

"805-31-3719," I said with confidence.

There was a pause. "That doesn't match our records, sir."

"But it *is* my Social Security number."

"The number I have is probably your wife's, sir."

"Why does that matter?"

"I can't let you make changes until I authenticate, sir," the man said in the neutral, patient voice of one accustomed to talking on the phone all day to people who deserved to be strangled.

"Are you *sure*?" I asked.

"Yes, sir. I'm sorry."

"Well, I suppose you could call her," I said. "She's off to work, and I don't have her social handy."

"I can do that," the man said. "Is the number we have on file all right?"

"Which one is that?" I asked. "Her cell was in her purse."

"555-626-9013."

"Drat," I said, writing down quickly. "That's the

stolen phone's number. I'll just have to call her when she gets to work and have her call you."

"Very well. Is there anything else, sir?"

"No. Thank you."

I hung up, then rotated the pad to display the number to the others. "The assassin's phone number."

"Great," J.C. said. "Now you can ask her out."

I turned the pad around and looked at the number. "You know, it was shocking how easy that was, all things considered."

"Rule number one of decryption," Audrey said. "If you don't have to break the code, don't. People are usually far less secure than the encryption strategies they employ."

"So what do we do with this?" I asked.

"Well, first there's a little app I need you to download onto your phone," Audrey said. "J.C., which of the three competitors do you think is most likely to have hired the woman?"

"Exeltec," J.C. said without missing a heartbeat. "Of the three, they're the most desperate. Years of funding with no discernible progress, investors breathing down their necks, and a history of moral ambiguity and espionage. Subject of three investigations, but no conclusive findings."

"That packet has their CEO's phone numbers," Audrey said.

I smiled and started working on the phone. In short time, I had my mobile set up to send fake information to Zen's caller ID, indicating I was Nathan Haight, owner of Exeltec.

"Have Wilson ready to honk," Audrey said.

I told him to be ready, then dialed.

It rang once. Twice.

Then picked up.

"Here," a curt, female voice said. "What is it? I'm busy."

I gestured to Wilson. He honked loudly.

I heard it over the phone as well. Zen was most certainly tailing us. I hit the button on my phone's app that imitated static on the line, then said something, which I knew would be distorted beyond recognition.

Zen cursed, then she said, "I don't care how nervous the other partners are. Bothering me repeatedly isn't going to make this go faster. I'll call in with a report when I know something. Until then, leave me alone."

She hung up.

"That," J.C. said, "was the strangest hacking I've ever seen."

"That's because you don't know what hacking really is," Audrey said, sounding smug. "You imagine geeks in front of a computer. But in reality, most people 'hacking' today—at least as far as the media calls it— just spend their time on the phone trying to pry out information."

"So we know she's following us," Ivy said, "*and* we know the name of our rival company. Which tells us who has the corpse."

"Not for certain," I said. "But it looks good." I tapped my phone, thoughtful, as Wilson pulled off the highway and started driving through downtown. "Advice?"

"We need to avoid getting in over our heads," Ivy said. "If that's humanly possible for us."

"I agree," Tobias said. "Stephen, if we can find proof that Exeltec stole the body, the CDC might be willing to raid their offices."

"We could just raid their offices ourselves," J.C. said. "Cut out the middleman."

"I'd rather not do anything specifically illegal," Tobias replied.

"Don't worry," J.C. said. "As an Interdimensional Time Ranger, I have code 876 special authorization to ignore local legal statutes in times of emergency. Look, Skinny, we're going to end up compromising Exeltec eventually. I can feel it. Even if they aren't storing the body in their local offices, there will be a trail to it in there somewhere."

"For what it's worth," Audrey added. "I'm with J.C. Breaking in sounds like fun."

I sat back, thinking. "We'll go to the coroner," I finally said, getting a nod from Tobias and Ivy. "I'd rather find proof incriminating Exeltec, and then set up an official raid." A plan was beginning to form in my head. "Besides," I added, "breaking in isn't the *only* way to find out what Exeltec knows. . . ."

T E N

The car rolled down a waking urban street, lamps
flickering off now that the sun was fully up, like ser-
vants lowering their heads before their king. The city
morgue was near the hospital, situated in a spread-
out office complex that could have easily held three
or four exciting internet start-ups. We passed carefully
trimmed hedges and trees with last year's Christmas
lights still wrapped around them, dormant until the
season started up again.

"All right," J.C. said to me. "You ready for this?"

"Ready?" I said.

"We're being tailed by an assassin, Skinny," he said.
"That feeling between your shoulder blades, that's the
knowledge that someone has you in their sights. She
could squeeze the trigger at any moment."

"Don't be silly," Ivy said. "She's not going to hurt us
as long as she thinks we're leading her to important
information."

"Are you sure?" J.C. said. "Because I'm not. At any

moment, her higher-ups could decide that you working for Yol is a very, very bad thing. They could decide to remove the competition and take their chances at finding the key on their own."

The way he said it, cold and straightforward, made me squirm.

"You just don't like being followed," Ivy said.

"Damn right."

"Language."

"Look," J.C. said, "Zen has information we'd really like to know. If we capture her, that alone might give us the proof we need. We know where she is, and we have a momentary advantage. How well do you think you could pull off a quiet evacuation?"

"Not well," I said.

"Let's try it anyway," J.C. said, pointing. "See that turn right ahead, as we move into the parking lot? The hedge there will hide us from the view of the car following us. You need to bail from the vehicle there— don't worry, I'll help you—and have Jeeves park in front of the building right beside the hedges. We can get the drop on Zen and turn this chase on its head."

"Reckless," Ivy said.

It was, but as the turn approached, I made a decision. "Let's do it," I said. "Wilson, I'm slipping out of the car at the next turn. Drive as if nothing has happened; don't slow more than normal. Park right in front of the morgue, then wait."

He adjusted the rearview mirror so he could meet my eyes. He didn't say anything, but I could see that he was concerned.

The turning of the mirror gave me a good glimpse of the dark sedan behind us. I felt under my jacket for the sidearm J.C. had insisted I bring. This was *not* how I liked missions to go. I'd rather spend ten hours in a room trying to figure out a puzzle or a safe with no lock. Why, lately, did guns always seem to get involved?

I moved to the side door, then crouched down, grabbing the handle. J.C. moved over behind me, hand on my shoulder.

"Five, four, three . . ." he counted.

I took a deep breath.

"Two . . . *One!*"

I cracked the door right as Wilson turned the car around the hedge. J.C. *heaved* against my back, somehow pushing me in just the right way so that when I left the car, I hit in a curling roll. It still hurt. The momentum of the car's turn clicked the door shut and I rolled up into a crouch beside the hedge, where I waited until I heard the car behind us start to turn.

I slipped through the hedge to the other side right as the car turned around it, following Wilson. This meant that I was separated from Zen by the squat wall of densely packed foliage. It ran all the way along the parking lot here.

I scurried along the hedge, head down, keeping pace with Zen's car. It passed Wilson as he parked, then continued on in a presumably nonsuspicious way toward another section of the parking lot. I caught brief glimpses of black car through holes in the hedge—a shadowed driver, but nobody else visible. The car pulled into a parking stall a short distance from where the hedge ended.

Ahead, the leaves rustled, and J.C. slipped through, handgun out, joining me. "Nice work," he whispered. "We'll make a Ranger out of you yet."

"It was your push," I said. "Sent me tumbling exactly the right way."

"I said I'd help."

I said nothing, too nervous to continue the conversation. I was manifesting something new, an extension of my previous . . . framework. What else could I learn to do by having one of my aspects guide my fingers or steps?

I peeked through the hedge, then took out my handgun. J.C. motioned furiously for me to hide it in front of myself, so cars passing along the street to my right wouldn't see. Then J.C. nodded toward an opening in the hedge.

I took a deep breath before scrambling through and crossing the short distance to Zen's car. J.C. tailed me. I came up beside the car in a crouch.

"Ready?" J.C. asked.

I nodded.

"Finger on the trigger, Skinny. This is for real."

I nodded again. The passenger's side window, just above me, was open. Palms sweating, I threw myself to my feet and leveled my gun through the open window at the driver.

It wasn't the assassin.

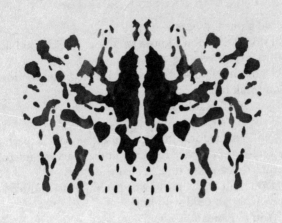

ELEVEN

The driver was a dark-haired kid, maybe eighteen, wearing a hoodie. He cried out, dropping the pair of binoculars he'd been using to look toward my SUV, his face going white as snow as he stared down my handgun.

That was most certainly *not* Zen Rigby.

"In the car, Skinny," J.C. said, looking around the parking lot. "Back seat, so he can't grapple you. Tell him to keep quiet. Don't look suspicious."

"Hands where I can see them," I told the kid, hoping he didn't see that my gun was shaking. "Don't say a word." I pulled open the back door and slipped in, but kept the gun on him.

The kid remained quiet save for a whine in the back of his throat. He was either terrified, or a very good actor.

"Where's Zen?" I said to him, lifting the gun up beside the youth's head.

"Who?" he said.

"No games. *Where is she?*"

"I don't . . . I don't know anything . . ." The kid actually started weeping.

"Damn it," J.C. said, standing by the front window. "You think he's acting?"

"No idea," I said back.

"I should fetch Ivy."

"No," I said, not wanting to be left alone. I inspected the kid's weeping face reflected in the rearview mirror. Mediterranean skin tone . . . Same nose . . .

"Don't kill me," the kid whispered. "I just wanted to know what you did with him."

"You're Panos's brother," I guessed.

The kid nodded, still sobbing.

"Oh hell," J.C. said. "No wonder it was so easy to spot the tail. *Two* people were following us: an amateur and a professional. I'm an idiot."

I felt cold. I'd heard Wilson's honk through the line when on the phone with Zen, so she had been nearby, yet we hadn't spotted her. Zen had been invisible to us all along.

Bad.

"What's your name?" I asked the youth.

"Dion."

"Well, Dion, I'm putting the gun away. If you are who you say, then you don't need to be afraid. I'm going to need you to come with me, and if you start to run, or cry out, or anything like that . . . well, I'll have to make sure you stop."

The youth nodded.

I climbed from the car, gun holstered, and pulled the kid out by his shoulder. A quick frisk determined he wasn't armed, though he considered himself quite the spy. Flashlight, ski mask, binoculars, a mobile phone which I took and turned off. I marched him across the parking lot, fully aware that this whole exchange would have looked *very* suspicious to anyone watching. With J.C.'s coaching, though, I maintained the air of someone who knew what he was doing—arm on the youth's shoulder, walking confidently. We were in the government complex; hopefully, anyone who spotted us would think I was a cop.

If they didn't, well, it wouldn't be the first time the police had been called to deal with me. I think they kept a department pool going on the frequency of it.

I shoved Dion into my SUV, then climbed inside, feeling a little more secure with the tinted windows and more of my aspects in attendance. Dion moved to the back seat and slumped there, forcing Audrey to climb onto Tobias's lap—an event so unexpected, the aging aspect almost seemed to choke.

"Wilson, please give me warning if anyone approaches," I said. "All right, Dion. Spill it. Why are you following me?"

"They stole Panos's body," Dion said.

"And by 'they' you mean . . ."

"I3."

"And why on earth would they do such a thing?"

"The information," Dion said. "He had it stored in his cells, you know? All of their secrets. All the terrible things they were going to do."

I shared a look with J.C., who then facepalmed. Panos had been talking to his family about his research. Wonderful. J.C. removed his hand and mouthed to me, *Security nightmare.*

"And what kind of terrible things," I said, "do you assume I3 was going to do?"

"I . . ." Dion looked to the side. "You know. *Corporate* things."

"Like take away casual Fridays," Audrey guessed.

So Panos hadn't completely confided in his brother. I tapped my fingers on the armrest. The family assumed that Yol and his people had taken the body to keep their information hidden—and, to be honest, that wasn't far from the truth. They'd been planning to see it burned, after all. Someone had merely gotten to Panos first.

"And you're following me," I said to the kid. "Why?"

"You were all over the internet this morning," Dion said. "Getting into a car with that weird Asian guy who owns I3. I figured out that you were supposed to crack the code on Panos's body. Seems obvious. I mean, you're some kind of superspy hacker or something, right?"

"That's *exactly* what we are," Audrey said. "Steve-O, tell him that's what we are." When I said nothing, she elbowed Tobias, in whose lap she was still sitting. "Tell him, grandpa."

"Stephen," Tobias said, somewhat uncomfortable, "this youth sounds earnest."

"He's being honest," Ivy said, inspecting him, "so far as I can tell."

"You should reassure him," Tobias said. "Look at the poor lad. He looks like he still thinks you're going to shoot him."

Indeed, Dion had his hands clasped, eyes down, but he was trembling.

I softened my tone. "I wasn't hired to crack the body's code," I told him. "I3 has plenty of backups on all their information. I'm here to find the corpse."

Dion looked up.

"No," I said, "I3 didn't take it. They would have been perfectly content to let it be cremated."

"I don't think he believes you, Steve," Ivy said.

"Look," I said to Dion, "I don't care what happens

with I3. I just want to make sure the information in that corpse is accounted for, all right? And for now, I need you to wait here."

"Why—"

"Because I don't know what to do with you." I glanced at Wilson, who nodded. He'd keep an eye on the kid. "Go climb in the front seat," I told Dion. "When I get back, we can have a long conversation about all of this. For now, I have to go deal with a very surly coroner."

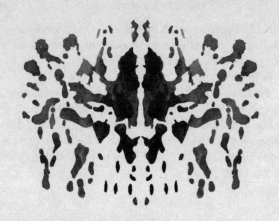

TWELVE

The city coroner was housed in a sterile-smelling little office beside the city morgue, which was only one set of rooms in a larger medical complex. Technically, Liza liked to be called a "medical examiner," and she was always surprisingly busy for a person who seemed to spend all of her time playing internet games.

At the stroke of eight, I strode through the medical complex lobby—suffering the glare of a security guard who was far too large for the little cubby they'd given him—and knocked politely on the coroner office door. Liza's secretary—I forgot his name—opened the door with an obviously reluctant expression.

"She's waiting for you," the young man said. "I wouldn't call her excited though."

"Great. Thanks . . ."

"John," Tobias filled in.

". . . John."

The secretary nodded, walking back to his desk and shuffling papers. I strolled down a short hallway to a nice office, hung with official-looking diplomas and the like. I managed to get a glimpse of Facebook reflected in one of them as Liza turned off her tablet and looked up at me.

"I'm busy, Leeds," she said.

Dressed in a white lab coat over jeans and a pink buttoned blouse, Liza was in her late fifties, and was tall enough that she was very tired of answering whether or not she'd played basketball in school. It was fortunate her clients were, for the most part, dead—as that was the only type of person who didn't seem to bother her.

"Well, this shouldn't take long," I said, leaning against the door frame and folding my arms, partially to block Tobias's adoring stare. What he saw in the woman, I'd never know.

"I don't have to do anything for you," Liza said, making a good show of turning toward her computer screen, as if she had tons and tons of work to do. "You're not involved in any kind of official case. Last I heard, the department had decided not to engage you anymore."

She said that last part a touch too triumphantly. Ivy and J.C. shared a look. The authorities weren't . . . particularly fond of us these days.

"One of your bodies went missing," I said to her. "Isn't anyone worried about that?"

"Not my problem," Liza said. "My part was done. Death pronounced, identity confirmed, no autopsy required. The morgue had a lapse. Well, you can talk to them about it."

Not a chance. They wouldn't let me in—they didn't have the authority. But Liza could; this *was* her department, no matter what she said.

"And the police aren't concerned about the breach?" I asked. "Sergeant Graves hasn't been poking around, wondering how such a terrible security snafu happened?"

Liza hesitated.

"Ah," Ivy said. "Good guess, Steve. Push more there."

"This is your division," I said to Liza. "Don't you even want to know how it happened? I can help."

"Every time you 'help,' Leeds, some kind of catastrophe follows."

"Seems like a catastrophe already happened."

"Hit her where it hurts," Ivy said. "Mention the hassle."

"Think of the paperwork, Liza," I said. "A body missing. Investigations, questions, people poking around, *meetings you'll have to attend.*"

Liza couldn't completely cover her sour grimace. Beside me, Ivy grinned in satisfaction.

"All this," Liza said, leaning back, "for a body that should never have been here."

"What do you mean?" I asked.

"There was no *reason* for us to keep the corpse. Kin had identified him; no foul play was suspected. I should have released the body to the family's chosen mortician for embalming. But no. Not allowed. This corpse had to stay here, and nobody would tell me why. The commissioner himself insisted." She narrowed her eyes at me. "Now you. What was special about that guy, Leeds?"

The commissioner? Yol had done some work to keep this body in custody. Made sense. If he'd had the corpse released, then given it some kind of crazy security, that would have advertised to the world that there was something special about it. A quick call to ensure Panos stayed in the city morgue, locked up tight, was far less suspicious.

It just hadn't worked.

"We're going to have to give something up, Steve," Ivy told me. "She's digging her heels in. Time for the big guns."

I sighed. "You sure?" I asked under my breath.

"Yes, unfortunately."

"One interview," I said, meeting Liza's eyes. "One hour."

She leaned forward in her chair. "Buying me off?"

"Yes, and?"

She tapped the top of her table with an idle finger. "I'm a medical examiner. I'm not interested in publishing."

"I didn't say the interview had to be with you," I said. "Anyone you like—anyone in the medical community you need something from. *You* get *me* as barter."

Liza smiled. "Anyone?"

"Yes. One hour."

"No. As long as they want."

"That's too open-ended, Liza."

"So is the list of ways you're annoying. Take it or leave it, Leeds. I don't owe you anything."

"We're going to regret this, aren't we?" Tobias asked.

I nodded, thinking of the hours spent being prodded by some psychologist who was looking to make a name for themselves. Another paper in another journal, treating me like a strange species of sea cucumber to be dissected and displayed.

Time was ticking though, and it was either this or tell Liza why the body was so important.

"Deal," I said.

She didn't smile. Smiling was far too human an expression for Liza. She did seem satisfied, as she grabbed her keys off the table and led me down the hallway, my aspects trailing.

The air grew appreciably colder as we approached

the morgue. A key card unlocked the door, which was of heavy, thick metal. Inside the room, one could see why Liza had chosen to work here—not only was it frigid, all this chrome probably reminded her of the spaceship that had dropped her off on our planet.

The door swung closed behind us, thumping into place. Liza settled in beside the wall, arms folded, watching to prevent any shenanigans. "Fifteen minutes, Leeds. Get to it."

I surveyed the room, which had three metal tables on wheels, a counter with various medical paraphernalia, and a wall full of large corpse drawers.

"All right," I said to the four aspects, "I want to know how they got the body out."

"We need proof too," J.C. said, poking through the room. "Something to tie Exeltec to the crime."

"That would be wonderful," I said to him, "but honestly, we don't want to be too leading. Maybe they don't have it. Focus on what we know. Find me clues on how the thieves stored or moved the body, and that might lead us right to it."

The others nodded. I turned around slowly, taking the whole room in, absorbing it into my subconscious. Then I closed my eyes.

My delusions started talking.

"No windows," J.C. said. "Only one exit."

"Unless those ceiling tiles are removable," Ivy noted.

"Nah," J.C. replied. "I've seen the security specs for this building. Remember the Coppervein case? No crawl space. No air ducts. Nothing funny about the architecture."

"This equipment *has* been used lately," Tobias said. "I know little of its purpose though. Stephen, you really *should* recruit a coroner of our own eventually."

"We *do* have Ngozi," Audrey said. "Forensic investigation. Why didn't we bring her?"

Because of you, Audrey, I thought. *My subconscious gave you an important skill and inserted you into my team.* Why? I missed the days when I'd had someone to ask about things like this. When Sandra had been with me, everything had made sense for the first time in my life.

"This place is secure," Ivy said, sounding dissatisfied. "Inside job, perhaps? One of the morgue workers?"

"Could one of the workers here have been bribed?" I asked, opening my eyes and looking toward Liza.

"I thought of that," she said, arms still folded. "But I was the last one in the office that night. I came in, checked everything, and turned off the lights. Security says nobody came in overnight."

"I'll want to talk to security then," I said. "Who else was here that day?"

Liza shrugged. "Family. A priest. Always accompanied. This room doesn't open for anyone other than me and two of our technicians. Even the security guard can't get in without calling one of us. But that's all irrelevant—the body was still here when I left for the night."

"You're sure?"

"Yeah, I had to write down some numbers for paperwork. I checked on it specifically."

"We'll want to fingerprint the place," J.C. said. "Like it or not, we might have to go through the precinct."

I nodded. "I assume the police have already done forensics."

"Why would you assume that?" Liza asked.

We all looked at her. "Uh . . . you know. Because there was a *crime*?"

"A corpse was stolen," Liza said dryly. "Nobody was hurt, we have no actual signs of a break-in, and there is no money involved. The official word is that they are 'working on' the case, but let me tell you—finding this body is low on their list of priorities. They're more worried about the break-in itself; they'll want someone's hide for that."

She refolded her arms, then repositioned and folded them again. She was trying to play it cool, but she *was* obviously worried. Ivy nodded at me, clearly pleased that I could read Liza so well. Well, it wasn't hard. I picked up things from my aspects now and then.

"Security cameras?" J.C. asked as he inspected the corners of the room. I repeated the question so Liza could hear it.

"Just out in the hallways," she said.

"Isn't that a little sparse?" I asked.

"The whole place is wired with alarms. If someone tries to break in, the security guard's desk will light up like Christmas." She grimaced. "We used to turn it on only at night, but they've had it on for two days straight now. Have to get permission to open a damn window these days . . ."

I looked at the team.

"Stephen," Tobias said, "we're going to need Ngozi."

I sighed. Well, it wasn't *too* long a drive to go back and pick her up.

"Here," J.C. said, pulling out his phone. "Let me give her a call."

"I don't think . . ." I said, but he was already dialing.

"Yeah, Achmed, we need your help," he said. "What? Of course I have your number. No, I have *not* been stalking you. Look, can you find Ngozi? How should I know where she is? Probably washing her hands a hundred times or something. No, I have *not* been stalking her either." He lowered the phone, giving the rest of us a suffering look. He raised it back up, and a short time later, continued. "Great. Let's video-conference."

Tobias and I looked over J.C.'s shoulders as Kalyani's face appeared on the screen, perky and excited. She waved, then turned the phone toward Ngozi, who sat reading on her bed.

What to say about Ngozi? She was from Nigeria, with deep brown skin, and had been educated at Oxford. She was also deathly afraid of germs—so much so that when Kalyani held the phone toward her, Ngozi shied away visibly. She shook her head, and Kalyani was obliged to stand there, holding the phone.

"What's up?" Ngozi asked with a clipped accent.

"Crime scene investigation," I said.

"You're going to come get me?"

"Well, I guess we kind of thought . . ." I hesitated, then looked to J.C. "I don't know if this is going to work, J.C. We've never done anything like this before."

"Worth a try though, right?"

I looked toward Ivy, who seemed skeptical, but Tobias shrugged. "What harm can it do, Stephen? Getting Ngozi out of the house is difficult sometimes."

"I heard that," Ngozi said. "It's not *difficult*. I just require proper preparation."

"Yeah," J.C. said, "like a hazmat suit."

"Please," Ngozi said, rolling her eyes. "Just because I like things clean."

"Clean?" I asked her.

"Very clean. Do you know the kinds of poisons that are pumped into the air every day by all those cars and factories? Where do you think that all goes? Do you ever wonder what that crusty blackness is on your skin after you hold a handrail on your way down the steps into the subway? And think of the *people*. Coughing into their hands, wiping their snotty nostrils, touching everything and everyone, and—"

"We get it, Ngozi," I said. I looked at Tobias, who nodded encouragingly. J.C. was right; phones among my aspects could be a valuable resource. I took the phone from J.C. Nearby, Liza watched me with what seemed like the first genuine emotion she'd displayed all morning: fascination. She might not be a psychologist, but physicians of all varieties tend to find my . . . quirks captivating.

Good for her. As long as it kept her from thinking about how much—or little—time I had remaining of her original "fifteen minute" restriction.

"We're going to try this over the phone," I said to Ngozi. "We're at the icebox. By all accounts, the body was here at night, but gone the next morning. Nothing suspicious on the hallway security cameras." Liza nodded when I checked with her on this one. "There isn't a camera in this room specifically, but the building does have an intense security system. So how did they get the body out?"

Ngozi leaned forward, still not taking the camera from Kalyani, but inspecting me with curiosity. "Show me the room."

I walked around it, scanning the place, fully aware that to Liza's perspective, I was holding nothing. Ngozi hummed to herself as I walked. Some show tune; I wasn't certain which one.

"So," she said after I'd spent a few minutes scanning the place, "you're sure the body is gone?"

"Of course it's gone," I said, pointing the camera toward the still-open corpse drawer.

"Well," Ngozi said, "it's going to be hard to do any traditional forensics here. But the question we should ask first is, 'Do we need to?' You'd be surprised at how often something is reported stolen, only to be found lost—or stashed—someplace very close to where the theft happened. If getting the body out of the room would be so hard, maybe it never did leave the room."

I looked at the other drawers. Then, with a sigh, I put the phone aside and began pulling them open one at a time. After a few minutes, Liza walked over and helped me. "We did this," she mentioned, but didn't stop me from double-checking. Only three of the other drawers had corpses, and we checked each one carefully. None were Panos.

From there, I looked in the room's cabinets, closets, and even drawers that were too small for a corpse. It was a long process, and one that I was actually pleased to find unfruitful. Discovering several bags full of elbows or whatnot wouldn't have been particularly appealing.

I dusted off my hands and looked toward the phone and Ngozi's image. Kalyani had joined her on the bed, and the two had been chatting about how I really *did* need to stop working so much and settle down with someone nice. And preferably someone sane.

"What next?" I said to the phone.

"Locard's principle," Ngozi said.

"Which is?"

"Basically," she said, "the principle states that whenever there is contact, or an exchange, evidence is left behind. We have very little to go on, as the victim was already dead when abducted, and presumably still zipped up tight. But the perpetrator will have left behind signs they were here. I don't suppose we can get a DNA sweep of the room. . . ."

I looked hopefully at Liza and asked, to which I got a sniff of amusement. The case wasn't nearly important enough for that. "We can try for fingerprints on our own," I said to Ngozi. "But the police aren't going to help."

"Let's do obvious contact points first," Ngozi said. "Close up on the drawer handle please."

I brought the phone over and put it very close to the handle of the corpse drawer. "Great," Ngozi said after a minute. "Now the door into the room."

I did so, passing Liza, who was checking her watch.

"Time might be running out, Ngozi," I said softly.

"My art isn't exactly something that can be rushed," she noted back at me. "Particularly long-distance."

I showed her the door handle, not really certain what she was looking for. Ngozi had me pull the door open to look at the other side. The door *was* heavy, made to swing shut after anyone who left. Once I was outside, I couldn't open it again. Liza had to unlock it with a key card.

"All right, Leeds," Liza said as I turned the camera to show the strike plate on the inside of the door frame. "You—"

"Bingo," Ngozi said.

I froze in place, then looked back at the door frame. Ignoring the rest of what Liza said, I knelt down, trying to see what Ngozi had.

"See those dust marks?" Ngozi asked.

"Um . . . no?"

"Look closely. Someone put tape here, then pulled it off, leaving behind enough gum to attract dust."

Liza stooped down beside me. "Did you hear me?"

"Tape," I asked. "Do you have some tape?"

"Why—"

"Yo," J.C. said from inside the room, holding up a roll of the translucent industrial tape that lay on the counter.

I brushed past Liza and fetched the tape—J.C. had to set down his imaginary copy before I could see the real one—then rushed back. I placed a strip of it over the strike plate, stepped out of the room, and let the door slide closed.

It thumped into place. That thump covered the lack of a click. When I pushed on the door, it opened without needing help from the inside.

"We know how they got into the room," I said.

"So?" Liza asked. "We knew they'd gotten in somehow. How does this help?"

"It tells us it was likely someone who visited the day before the body went missing," I said. "The last visitor, perhaps? They would be in a position to tape the door with the least chance of discovery during the day."

"I'm pretty sure I'd have noticed if the door were taped," Liza said.

"Would you have? With the key card unlocking, you never have to turn or twist anything. It's natural for you to push the door and have it just swing open."

She thought about it for a moment. "Plausible," she admitted. "But who did it?"

"Who was last into this room that day?"

"The priest. I had to let him in. The others had gone home for the evening, but I stayed late."

"Had a FreeCell game that you just *had* to finish?" I asked.

"Shut up."

I smiled. "Did you recognize the priest?"

She shook her head. "But he was on the list and his ID was valid."

"Creating a fake ID wouldn't be much," Ivy said to me, "considering what was at stake."

"That's probably our man," I said to Liza. "Come on, I want to talk to your security officer."

As Liza pulled the tape off the door, I thanked Ngozi for her help, turned off the camera, and tossed the phone back to J.C.

"Nice work," Ivy noted to him, smiling.

"Thanks," he said, slipping the phone into a pocket of his cargo pants. "Of course, it's not *actually* a phone. It's a hyperdimensional time—"

"J.C.," Ivy interrupted.

"Yeah?"

"Don't ruin this moment."

"Oh. Yeah, okay."

THIRTEEN

I hit the restroom in the hallway before going to the security station. I didn't really need to go to the bathroom, but Tobias did.

The room was clean, which I appreciated. The soap dispensers were full, the mirror spotless, and it even had a little chart on the door listing the last cleaning, where the staff had to sign to prove they'd done their job. I washed my hands, looking at myself in the mirror while Tobias finished his pit stop.

My own mundane face looked back at me. I'm never what people expect. Some picture me as some sort of eccentric scientist, others imagine an action star. Instead, they get a rather bland man in his thirties, perfectly normal.

In some ways, I often feel like my White Room. A blank slate. The aspects have all the character. I try very hard to not stand out. Because I am *not crazy*.

I dried my hands and waited for Tobias to wash

up, then we rejoined the others outside and walked toward the security station. It consisted of a circular desk with an open center, the type you'd find at a mall beneath a sign proclaiming INFORMATION. I walked up and the security guard looked me over—like I was a piece of pizza and he was trying to decide how long I'd been sitting in the fridge. He didn't ask what I wanted. Liza had called to tell him to prepare camera footage for me.

The desk really was too small for this hulk of a man. When he leaned forward, the inside front of the desk pressed into his gut; I was left with the impression of a grape being squeezed from the bottom.

"You," the guard said with a deep baritone voice, "are the crazy one, aren't you?"

"Well, that's not actually true," I said. "You see, the standard definition of insanity is—"

He leaned forward farther, and I pitied the poor desk. "You're armed."

"Uh . . ."

"So am I," the guard said softly. "Don't try anything."

"Okaaay," Ivy said from beside me. "Creepy guy manning the security station."

"I like him," J.C. said.

"Of course you do."

The guard slowly lifted a flash drive. "Footage is on here."

I took it. "You're certain the security system was on that night?"

The man nodded. His hand made a fist, as if me even *asking* something so stupid was an offense worthy of a pounding.

"Uh," I said, watching that fist, "Liza says you leave it on during the day now too?"

"I'm going to catch him," the guard said. "Nobody breaks into *my* building."

"Twice," I said.

The guard eyed me.

"Nobody breaks into your building twice," I said. "Since they did it once already. Actually . . . they might have done it twice already, since the first time they placed the tape on the door—but you might call that more of an infiltration than a break-in."

"Don't give me lip," the man said, pointing at me, "and don't make trouble. Otherwise I'll thump you so hard, it'll knock some of your personalities into the next state."

"Ouch," Audrey said, flipping through a magazine she'd found on his desk. "Ask him why, if he's so amazingly observant, he hasn't noticed that his fly is down."

I smiled, then made a quick exit. Liza watched me go from the doorway of her office.

Outside, I held up the flash drive, then began moving along the side of the building. I waved to Wilson, who was still in the car. Panos's brother sat sullenly in the front passenger seat, drinking a glass of lemonade.

I rounded the building, aspects trailing, so we could get a good look at the exterior. It had small windows, maybe large enough to fit through. No fire escape. I approached a back door; it was locked tight. I gave it a good shake anyway.

"Someone impersonated a priest," I said to the aspects, "and slipped in to inspect the body and place the tape. Then they came back at night to extract the corpse. So why didn't they just take a sample of the body's cells when they were first there, in the room with it?"

I looked toward the others, who all seemed baffled.

"I guess they didn't know where on the body the

modified cells were to be found," Tobias finally said. "There are many, many cells in the body. How were they to know which place held the information they wanted?"

"Perhaps." I folded my arms, dissatisfied. *We're missing something,* I thought. *A very important piece of all this. It—*

The back door burst open. The security guard stood there, puffing, hand on his sidearm. He glared at me.

"I just wanted to check," I said, inspecting the now-open doorway. Tape wouldn't work here; the door had a deadbolt. "Nice response time, by the way."

He poked a finger at me. "Don't push me."

He slammed the door. I continued on my way, rounding the corner into a little alleyway between this building and the next, looking for other entrances. I was about halfway down it when I heard the soft click behind me.

I spun, as did my aspects. There stood Zen Rigby beside a large trash bin, holding a paper bag with one hand inside of it, her posture innocent.

"SIG Sauer P239," J.C. said softly, looking at the bag, which undoubtedly held a gun.

"You can tell the type of gun by the way it sounds to *cock*?" Ivy asked.

"Well yeah," J.C. said. "Duh." He looked embarrassed as he said it though, and gave me a glance. He felt he should have spotted Zen sneaking up on us. But he could only hear or see what I did.

"Mr. Leeds," the woman said. Like last night, she wore a pantsuit and white blouse. She was dark and short with straight black hair. No jewelry.

I inclined my head toward her.

"I will need you to divest yourself of your sidearm,"

Zen said. "With attention and care, please, lest an unfortunate incident result."

I glanced at J.C.

"Do it," he said, though he sounded reluctant. "She probably won't try to kill us here."

"Probably?" Audrey asked, looking pale.

I slowly slid my gun out, then leaned down and set it on the ground before kicking it away. Zen smiled, sack still carried in a way that would make it easy to raise and shoot me.

"You called me earlier," she said. "A ploy which I must commend. I assume the purpose was to determine if I was following you or not?"

I nodded, hands at my sides, breathing quickly. I found myself in situations like this far too often. I wasn't a soldier or a cop; I wasn't cool under fire. I did *not* like having a gun pointed at me.

"Control the situation, Skinny," J.C. said from beside me. "The people who end up dead are the ones who lose control. Don't let your nerves determine how this plays out."

"Now," Zen said, "I'll need that flash drive."

I blinked. The flash drive . . .

She thought the flash drive contained the code to unlock Panos's data. How must it look to her? I got hired by Yol, then spent the night working. I headed to the coroner as soon as possible in the morning, then walked out with a flash drive.

She'd guessed that I'd recovered something important. Ivy laughed, though J.C. looked concerned. I glanced at him.

"If she thinks she has what she needs," he said softly, "we are in serious danger. If you give her the flash drive, don't go anywhere with her."

I backed away from Zen, hands still to the sides, until I was against the wall to the building. She studied me. Her gun was probably suppressed, but it would still make a sound. Relatively exposed as we were, she had to be worried about firing.

My heart beat frantically. Control the situation. Get her talking, perhaps? "Who did you get to impersonate the priest for you?"

She frowned. Then she raised her bag and the gun inside. "I asked you politely for something, Mr. Leeds."

"And I'm not going to give it to you," I said. "Until I at least know how you pulled off the heist. It's a quirk of mine. I'm certain you're aware that I'm prone to those."

She hesitated. Then she glanced to the sides.

Looking for my aspects, I thought. People did that, unconsciously, when they were around me.

"Good," Ivy said. "Playing the insanity card does tend to throw people off their game."

Think, think, think. I knocked my head back.

It hit the window behind me. I paused, then began slamming my head back repeatedly, rattling the glass.

Zen was beside me an instant later, grabbing me roughly by the shoulder and towing me away from the building. She glanced in the window—apparently saw nobody there—then threw me to the ground.

"I am not a patient woman, Mr. Leeds," she said softly.

I was tempted to give her the drive right then. But I held back, suppressing my worry and my fear.

Stall. Just a little bit more. "You realize this is all pointless," I lied to her. "Panos already gave the information away. On the internet. Free, for everyone."

She sniffed. "We know that I3 contained his attempts to do that."

He did? And . . . they did?

She pressed the gun down into my gut. Behind her, the window slammed open.

"Leeds!" the security guard shouted. "You crazy man! Do you *want* to die? Because I'm going to strangle you . . . Hey! What's up?"

Zen met my eyes, then threw herself off me and dashed away around the corner. I leaned back as the security guard cursed, stretching out the window. "Was that a gun she was carrying? Damn it, Leeds! What are you doing?"

"Surviving," I said, tired, looking at my aspects. "Move?"

"Now," J.C. said.

We left the shouting guard and made for my car. I scooped up my gun as I passed, and once out in the open, I didn't spot any sign of Zen. I climbed in the back of the vehicle and told Wilson to go.

I didn't feel much safer when we were on the road.

"I can't believe she tried that," Ivy said. "Practically in the open, without much proof that we even had what she wanted."

"She was likely told to bring us in," J.C. said. "She's a professional; she wouldn't have moved this recklessly without external pressure. She reported to her superiors we might have something, then was told to recover it."

I nodded, breathing in and out in deep, desperate breaths.

"Tobias," Ivy said, taking over for me. "What do we know about Exeltec?"

"Yol's report included some basic facts," Tobias said. "Biotech company much like I3, but far more . . . energetic, you might say. Founded five years ago, they soon released their key product—a pharmaceutical to help regulate the symptoms of Parkinson's disease.

"Unfortunately for them, a year later a rival company produced a much better alternative. Exeltec's product tanked. The company is owned by ten investors, with the largest stakeholder—the one Stephen imitated on the phone—acting as CEO and president of the board. Together they stand to lose a great deal of money on this company. Their last three products have flopped, and they are under investigation for cutting corners in overseas manufacturing. So, in a word, they're desperate."

I nodded, calmed by Tobias's voice. I plugged the flash drive into my laptop, then started the footage at 10× speed and set the machine on the floor so I could watch it with half an eye. Tobias, often the most observant of my aspects, leaned down to watch in detail.

In the front seat, Wilson and Dion began chatting about the youth's home life. I felt the tremors from being held at gunpoint finally fade, and took stock. Wilson pulled onto the freeway; he wasn't going anywhere in particular, but knew me well enough to realize I needed time to put myself together before giving him any specific directions.

Dion glanced in the rearview mirror to get a look at me. He caught me looking back at him and blushed, then slumped down into his seat, answering Wilson's questions about school. Dion had just finished high school, and was prepping for college in the fall. He readily answered Wilson's questions; it was difficult to resist the affable butler. Wilson could handle me, after all. Compared to that, normal people were easy.

"That must have been some event," Wilson said to the young man, in response to an explanation of a recent race. "Now, if you'll forgive the interruption, I should ask Master Leeds where it was he wanted to be going."

"You don't know already?" Dion asked, looking confused. "But where have we been driving?"

"Around," I said. "I needed time to think. Dion, your brother lived with you and your mother, right?"

"Yeah. You know Greek families. . . ."

I frowned. "Not sure I do."

"We're a tight lot," Dion said with a shrug. "Moving out on your own . . . well, that's just not done. Hell, I assume Panos would have stayed nearby even after he'd married. There's no resisting the pull of a Greek family."

The key to Panos's corpse might very well be at the family home. At the very least, going there would indicate to Zen that we were still looking for something, which might encourage her to postpone another confrontation.

"Let's head there, Wilson," I said. "I want to talk to the family."

"I *am* the family!" Dion said.

"The rest of the family," I said, getting out my phone and dialing. "Hold on a minute." The phone rang a few times before being picked up.

"Yo, dawg," Yol said.

"I don't think that's a cool phrase any longer, Yol."

"I'm bringing it back, dawg."

"I don't . . . You know what, never mind. I'm pretty sure our bad guys are Exeltec."

"Hmmm. That's unfortunate. I was hoping it was one of the other two. Let me step out so we can talk."

"I wasn't certain they'd even let you answer while on lockdown."

"It's a pain," he said, and I heard the sound of a door closing, "but I've managed a little freedom, since I'm not technically under arrest, I'm just quarantined. The feds let me set up a mobile office here, but nobody can get in or out until we convince them this thing wasn't contagious."

"At least you can talk."

"To an extent. It's a pain, dawg. How am I going to do press interviews for the new album?"

"Seclusion will just add to your celebrity mystique," I said. "Can you tell me anything more about Exeltec."

"It's all in the documents I sent," he explained. "They're . . . well, they're bad news. I had a hunch it would be them. We've caught them trying to slip in spies in the form of engineers seeking employment."

"Yol, they've got a hit woman working for them."

"That one you mentioned before?"

"Yeah. Ambushed me in an alley. Held me at gun-point."

"*Damn.*"

"I'm not going to sit around and let something like that happen again," I said. "I'm going to email you a list of instructions."

"Instructions?" Yol asked. "For what?"

"For keeping me from being killed," I said, taking my laptop from Tobias. "Yol, I have to ask you. What is it you're not telling me about this case?"

The line was silent.

"Yol . . ."

"We didn't kill him," Yol said. "I promise you that."

"But you *were* having him watched," I said. "You had his computer monitored. There's no other way you'd just naturally have a record of all of the things he'd been doing in the last few months, ready to print out when I arrived."

"Yeah," Yol admitted.

"And he was trying to give your information away," I said. "Post everything about the project online."

In the front seat, Dion had turned around and was watching me.

"Some of the engineers didn't like me getting involved," Yol said. "They saw it as selling out. Panos . . . that guy didn't believe in consequences. He'd have posted our research for everyone, so that every terrorist out there knew about it. I don't get such people, with their wikileaks and their open sources."

"You're making it very hard for me to believe," I said, "that you didn't just remove him."

Dion paled.

"I don't do things like that," Yol snapped. "Do you know how much a murder investigation can cost a company?"

I really wished I could trust him. To an extent, I *needed* to. Otherwise, I could very easily end this mission as a corpse myself. "Just follow the instructions in my email," I told him, then hung up.

I ignored Dion and began typing an email while the feed from the security camera continued to play on the other side of my laptop screen. Audrey stood up behind my seat and looked over my shoulder, watching me type.

"You shouldn't be out of your seat belt," Ivy said.

"If we wreck, I'm sure Steve-O will imagine some delightfully gruesome scars for me," Audrey said, then pointed at what I was typing. "Rumors to be spread? About Exeltec? This will make them even *more* desperate."

"I'm counting on it," I said.

"Which will put an even bigger target on our heads!" Audrey said. "What in the world are you planning?"

I didn't answer her, instead finishing up the instructions and shooting off the email to Yol. "Dion," I said, still half watching the video on the laptop. "Is your family religious?"

"My mom is," he said from the front seat. "I'm an atheist." He said it stubbornly, as if this were something he'd had to defend in the past.

"Panos?"

"Atheist," Dion said. "Mom refused to accept it, of course."

"Who's your family's priest?"

"Father Frangos," he said. "Why?"

"Because I think someone impersonated him last night when visiting your brother's remains. Either that, or Father Frangos is involved in the theft of the corpse."

Dion snorted. "He's, like, ninety years old. He's so pious, when my mother told him I was taking after my brother, he fasted for thirty-six hours to pray for me. *Thirty-six* hours. I think the idea of intentionally breaking one of the commandments would kill him on the spot."

The kid seemed to have gotten over his fear of me. Good.

"Ask him what he thought of his brother," Ivy said from the back seat.

"Seems he liked the guy," J.C. said with a grunt.

"Really?" Ivy said to him. "You deduced that all on your own, did you? Steve, I'd like to hear an opinion of Panos that didn't come through Yol's channels. Get the kid talking, if you please."

"Your brother," I said to Dion. "You seem to really dislike the company he was working for."

"It used to be all right," Dion said. "Before it went and got all corporate. That's when the lies started, the extortion. It became about money."

"Unlike other jobs," Audrey said, "which are never, ever about money."

"Your brother continued working there," I said to Dion, ignoring Audrey's commentary. "So he couldn't have been too torn up about the changes at I3. I expect he wanted in on a little of that cash."

Dion twisted around in his seat and fixed me with a glare that could have fried an egg. "Panos cared *nothing* for the money. He only stayed at that place because of their resources."

"So . . . he needed I3's equipment," I said. "And, by extension, their money."

"Yeah, well, it wasn't *about* the money. My brother was going to do great things. Cure diseases. He did things that even the others, traitors though they were, didn't know about. He—" Dion cut off, then turned around immediately in his seat, and refused to respond to further prying.

I looked at Ivy.

"Serious hero worship going on there," she said. "I suspect that if you prodded, you'd find Dion was planning to study biology and follow in his brother's footsteps. The philosophy, the mannerisms . . . We can learn a lot about Panos by watching his brother."

"So," J.C. said, "you're telling me Panos was an annoying little sh—"

"Anyway," Ivy interrupted, "if it's true that Panos was working on projects even Garvas and the others didn't know about, that could be the true secret Yol is trying to recover."

I nodded.

"Stephen," Tobias said, pointing at the laptop screen. "You'll want to watch this."

I leaned over, then rewound the footage. Tobias, Audrey, and J.C. huddled around, all ignoring Ivy's pointed complaints that none of us were bothering with seat belts. On the small screen, now playing at normal speed, I watched someone leave the bathroom in the medical complex.

The cleaning lady. She pulled a large trash can on wheels, and approached the doorway into the coroner's offices, then opened the door and went in.

"Does *nobody* in this world care about security anymore?" J.C. said, pointing at the screen. "Look at the security guard! He didn't even *glance* at her."

I froze the frame. The camera was positioned in such a way that we couldn't get a good look at the figure, even when I rewound and froze it again.

"Somewhat small in stature," Tobias said. "Dark haired, female. I can't pick out anything else. The rest of you?"

J.C. and Audrey shook their heads. I froze the frame on the security guard. It was a different man from the one we'd met, a smaller fellow, who was sitting in the station and reading a paperback novel. I rewound to try to find where the cleaning lady entered the building, but she must have come in the back. I did catch the security guard pushing a button, perhaps to open the back door for someone who had buzzed for the lock to open.

Fast-forwarding, we watched the cleaning lady leave the coroner's offices and go into each room along the hall. Whoever it was, she knew not to break pattern. She cleaned the other offices quickly, then disappeared down the hallway, towing her large trash can.

"That trash can could most certainly hide a body," J.C. said. "I thought the guard said nobody went into those rooms!"

"Cleaning staff is usually considered 'nobody,' " Tobias observed. "And the door into the morgue itself would be locked. Liza said even the security guard wouldn't be able to get in, so presumably the cleaning staff doesn't go into that room, at least not without supervision."

"Does that drive have footage from other nights?" Audrey asked.

"Good idea," I said, searching and finding the two previous nights' footage as well. We watched, and found that at around the same time each night, a cleaning person entered and engaged in a similar activity. But the trash can she brought was smaller, and it was obviously a different person. Female, yes, and with a similar build—but with lighter hair.

"So," Audrey said, "they replaced first the priest and then the cleaning lady."

"This should have been impossible," J.C. said. "Protocol should have made it so."

"And what protocol is that?" Audrey said. "This isn't a high-security facility, J.C. You spend year after year without any kind of incident, and of course you're going to grow lax. Besides, the people who pulled this off were capable. Fake ID, knowledge of the times the cleaning lady entered and left. The uniform is the same, and they even cleaned the entire set of offices so nobody would be suspicious."

I replayed the footage of the thief, wondering if it was Zen herself. The build was right. What was it Audrey had said before? People are usually far less secure than the encryption strategies—or in this case, security devices—they employ. This could have all been stopped if the guard had glanced at the cleaning lady. But he didn't, and why would he have? What was there *really* in these offices that someone would want to steal?

Just a corpse carrying a doomsday weapon.

I stifled a yawn as we eventually pulled into a residential area. Blast. I'd been hoping to find a chance to squeeze in a nap while we were driving. Even thirty minutes would do me some good. No chance for that now. Instead, I replied to Yol's return email, telling him that yes, I did want to make Exeltec more frantic and yes, I did know what I was doing. My next set of instructions seemed to placate him.

We pulled up to a quaint white suburban house, rambler style, with a neatly mowed lawn and vines growing up the walls. A careful air of cultivation helped offset the fact that this house—with its siding, its small windows, and its lack of an enclosed garage—was probably a decade or four past its prime.

"You're not going to hurt my family, are you?" Dion asked from the front seat.

"No," I said, "but I might embarrass you a little."

Dion grunted.

"Come introduce me," I said, shoving open the door. "We're on the same side. I promise that when I recover your brother's body, I won't let I3 do anything nefarious with it. In fact, I'll let you watch the cremation—with I3 getting no chance to lay hands on the body—if you want."

Dion sighed, but joined me in climbing from the car and walking toward the house.

F O U R T E E N

"Keep watch," I said to J.C. as we approached the house. "I haven't forgotten that Zen is out there."

"We might want to call in some backup," J.C. said.

"More Rescue Rangers?" Ivy asked.

"*Time* Rangers," J.C. snapped. "And no, we don't have temporal substance here. I was talking about real bodyguards. If Skinny hired a few of those, I'd feel a whole lot safer."

I shook my head. "No time, unfortunately."

"Perhaps you should have explained the truth to Zen," Tobias said, jogging up. "Was it wise to let her think we have the information she wants?"

Behind us, Wilson pulled the SUV away—I'd given him instructions to keep driving until I called him for a pickup. I didn't want Zen deciding to apply a little interrogation to my servant. Unfortunately, if she was determined, simply driving away wouldn't be enough to protect him. Perhaps I *should* have told Zen we didn't have her information. Yet my instincts said that the less she knew about what I'd discovered, the better off I'd be. I just needed to have a plan in place to deal with her.

Dion led us up to the house, glanced over his shoulder at me, then sighed and pushed open the door. I grabbed it and held it for my aspects, then slipped in last.

The house smelled old. Of furniture that had been polished over and over, of stale potpourri, and of burned wood from an old hearth. The careful clutter offered a new oddity on each wall and surface—a line of photos in novelty frames down one hallway, a collection of ceramic cats in a shadow box near the door, a sequence of colorful candles on the mantel with a religious tone to them. The house didn't look lived in, it looked decorated. This was a museum for a family's life, and they'd done a lot of living.

Dion hung his coat beside the door. The only coat there; the rest were stored neatly inside an open coat closet. He walked down the hallway, calling for his mother.

I lingered, stepping into the living room, with a rug on top of its carpet and an easy chair with worn armrests. My aspects fanned out. I stepped up beside the hearth, inspecting a beautiful wall cross made from glass.

"Catholic?" I asked, noticing Ivy's reverence.

"Close," she said. "Greek Orthodox. There's a depiction of Emperor Constantine."

"Very religious," I said, noting the candles, the paintings, the cross.

"Or just very fond of decoration," she said. "What are we looking for?"

"The decryption code," I said, turning. "Audrey? Any idea what it might look like."

"It's digital," she said. "For a one-time pad, the key

is going to be as long as the data being stored. That's why Zen was after the flash drive."

I looked around the room. With all of this stuff, a flash drive could be hidden practically anywhere. Tobias, Audrey, and J.C. started looking. Ivy remained beside me.

"Needle in a haystack?" I asked her softly.

"Possibly," she said, folding her arms, tapping one finger against the opposite forearm. "Let's go look at pictures of the family. Maybe we can determine something from them."

I nodded, walking over to the hallway that led to the kitchen, where I'd spotted pictures of the family. Four in a row were formal photos of each member of the family. The picture of the father was old, from the seventies; he'd died when the boys were children. The mother's picture and Dion's picture had what appeared to be pictures of saints hanging beneath them.

No saint beneath Panos. "A symbol that he'd given up on his faith?" I asked, pointing to the empty spot.

"Nothing so dramatic," Ivy said. "When a member of the Greek Orthodox Church is buried, a picture of Christ or their patron saint is buried with them. That picture would have been taken down in preparation for his funeral."

I walked on a little farther, searching for pictures of the family interacting. I paused beside one that showed a smiling Panos from not too long ago. He was holding up a fish while his mother—in sunglasses—hugged him from the side.

"Open and friendly, by all accounts," Ivy said. "An idealist who joined with friends from college to start their own company. 'If this works,' he wrote on a forum a few months back, 'then any person in any country could have access to powerful computing. Their own body supplies the energy, the storage, even the processing.' Others on the forum warned about the dangers of wetware. Panos argued with them. He saw all of this as some kind of information revolution, a step forward for humankind."

"Is there anything about those posts of his that doesn't add up?"

"Ask Audrey about that," Ivy said. "I'm focused on Panos the man. Who was he? How would he act?"

"He was working on something," I said. "Curing diseases, is that what Dion said? I'll bet he was really annoyed when the others pulled him off his virus research because of the cancer scare."

"Yol knows that Panos got further in his research than he let on. It's clear to me. Yol was spying on Panos and is really, really worried about all of this. That implies he's worried about a danger even more catastrophic than their little cancer scare. That's why Yol brought you in, and why he's so desperate for you to destroy the body."

I nodded slowly. "So what about Panos? What can you guess about him and the key?"

"If he even used one," Ivy said, "I suspect he'd give it to a family member."

"Agreed," I said as Dion finally headed out the back doors, calling for his mother in the back yard.

I felt a moment of concern. Had Zen been here before us? But no. Stepping into the kitchen, I was able to see the mother outside pruning a tree. Dion walked over to her.

I delayed a moment, walking up to Audrey and J.C.

"So," Audrey was saying, "in the future, do we have flying cars?"

"I'm not from *your* future," J.C. said. "I'm from a parallel dimension, and you're from another one."

"And does yours have flying cars?"

"That's classified," J.C. said. "So far as I can tell you, my dimension is basically like this one—only, I exist there."

"In other words, that one is way, *way* worse."

"I should shoot you, woman."

"Try it."

I stepped between them, but J.C. just grunted. "Don't tempt me," he growled at Audrey.

"No, really," Audrey said. "Shoot me. Go ahead. Then, when it doesn't do anything because we're both *imaginary*, you'll have to admit the truth: That you're crazy, even for a figment of a deranged man's psyche. That he imagined you as a repository for information. That in truth, you're just a flash drive yourself, J.C."

He glared at her, then stalked away, head down.

"And," Audrey shouted after him, "you—"

I took her by the arm. "Enough."

"It's good for someone to bring him down a notch or two, Steve-O," she said. "Can't have pieces of your brain getting too uppity, can we?"

"What about you?"

"I'm different," she said.

"Oh? And you'd be fine if I just stopped imagining you?"

"You don't know how to do that," she said, uncomfortably.

"I'm pretty sure that if J.C. *did* shoot you, my mind would follow through accordingly. You'd die, Audrey. So be careful what you ask for."

She glanced to the side, then shuffled from one foot to the other. "So . . . uh . . . what did you want?"

"You're the closest thing I've got to a data analyst right now," I said. "The information that Yol gave us. Think about the emails, forum posts, and personal information from Panos's computer. I need to know what he isn't saying."

"What he *isn't* saying?"

"What's hidden, Audrey. Inconsistencies. Clues. I need to know what he was really working on—his secret projects. There's a good chance he hinted at this online somewhere."

"Okay . . . I'll think about it." She'd gone from a niche expertise—handwriting analysis—to something broader. Hopefully this was the start of a trend. I was running out of space for aspects; it was getting harder and harder to contain them, manage them, imagine them all at once. I suspected that was why Audrey had insisted on coming on this mission—deep down, part of me knew that I needed my aspects to begin doubling up on skills.

She looked at me, eyes focusing. "Actually, as I consider it, I might have something for you right now. Viruses."

"What about them?

"Panos spent a *lot* of time on immunology forums, talking about disease, getting into very technical discussions with people who study bacteria and viruses. None of what he said is revelatory, but when you look at the whole . . ."

"His history was in microbial gene splicing," I said. "Makes sense for him to be there."

"But Garvas said they'd abandoned viruses as a method of data delivery," Audrey said. "However, Panos's forum posts on these subjects *increased* once I3 abandoned that part of the project." She looked at me, then grinned. "I figured that out!"

"Nice."

"Well, I mean, I guess *you* figured that out." She

folded her arms. "Being an imaginary person makes it difficult to feel any real sense of accomplishment."

"Just imagine your sense of accomplishment," I said. "You're imaginary, so imaginary accomplishment should work for you."

"But if I'm imaginary, and I imagine something, it's *doubly* unreal. Like using a copy machine to copy something that's just been copied."

"Actually," Tobias said, strolling up, "theoretically the imaginary sense of accomplishment would *have* to be imagined by the primary imaginer, so it wouldn't be an iteration as you suggest."

"It doesn't work that way," Audrey said. "Trust me, I'm the expert on being imaginary."

"But . . . if we are all aspects . . ."

"Yeah, but I'm *more* imaginary than you," she said. "Or, well, less. Since I know all about it." She grinned at him, triumphant as he rubbed his chin, trying to sort through that.

"You're crazy," I said softly, looking at Audrey.

"Huh?"

It had just struck me. Audrey was insane.

Each of my aspects was. I barely noticed Tobias's schizophrenia anymore, let alone Ivy's trypophobia. But the madness was there, lurking. Each aspect had one such condition, whether it be fear of germs, technophobia, or megalomania. I'd never realized what Audrey's was until now.

"You think you're imaginary," I told her.

"Duh."

"But it's not because you're actually imaginary. It's because you have a psychosis that makes you think you're imaginary. You'd think this even if you happened to be real."

It was hard to see. Many of the aspects accepted their lot, but few confronted it. Even Ivy did that with difficulty. But Audrey flaunted it; she reveled in it. That was because, in her brain, she was a real person who was crazy and therefore thought she wasn't real. I'd assumed she was self-aware, but that wasn't it at all. She was as crazy as the others. Her insanity just happened to align with reality.

She glanced at me, then shrugged, and immediately tried to deflect the conversation by asking Tobias about the weather. He, of course, referenced his delusion who lived in the satellite far above. I shook my head, then turned.

And found Dion standing in the doorway, a distinctly uncomfortable look on his face. How much had he watched? He gave me a look like one might give an unfamiliar dog that had just been barking frantically but now seemed calm. Through that whole exchange, I'd been a crazy man, stalking around and talking to himself.

No. I'm not crazy. I have it under control.

Maybe that was my only real madness. Thinking I could handle all of this.

"You found your mother?" I asked.

"In the back yard," Dion said, thumbing over his shoulder.

"Let's go talk to her," I said, brushing past him.

FIFTEEN

I found Ivy and J.C. outside, sitting on the steps. She was rubbing his back as he sat with hands hanging before him, gun in one of them, staring at a beetle crossing the ground. Ivy gave me a glance and shook her head. Not a good time to talk to him.

I headed across the well-tended lawn with Audrey and Tobias in tow. Mrs. Maheras had finished pruning and was now inspecting her tomato plants, picking off bugs, pulling weeds.

She didn't look up as I approached. "Stephen Leeds," she said. Her voice bore a distinct Greek accent. "You're famous, I hear."

"Only among people who like gossip," I said, kneeling down. "The tomatoes look nice. Growing well."

"I started them inside," she said, lifting one of the plump green fruits. "Tomatoes do better after the late frosts are past, but I can't help wanting to get an early start."

I waited for Ivy to give me a prompt on what to say,

but she was still on the steps. *Idiot,* I thought at my-self. "So . . . you like to garden a lot?"

Mrs. Maheras looked up and met my eyes. "I ap-preciate people who make decisions and act on them, Mr. Leeds. Not people who try to make small talk about things in which they obviously have no interest."

"Several pieces of me are very interested in garden-ing," I said. "I just didn't bring them along."

She regarded me, waiting.

I sighed. "Mrs. Maheras, what do you know of your son's research?"

"Almost nothing," she said. "Ghastly business."

I frowned.

"She thinks it took him away from the church," Dion said behind me, kicking at a clump of dirt. "All of that science and questioning. Heaven help us if a man spends his time *thinking.*"

"Dion," she said, "don't speak stupidity."

He folded his arms and met her gaze, defiant.

"You work for the people who employed my son," Mrs. Maheras said, looking at me.

"I just want to find his body," I said. "Before any-thing dangerous happens. What can you tell me of your priest?"

"Father Frangos?" she asked. "Why ever would you want to know about him?"

"He was the last person to see the body," I said. "He visited the coroner on the night before your son's corpse vanished."

"Don't be silly," Mrs. Maheras said. "He did noth-ing of the sort—he was here. I requested a house bless-ing, and he visited."

To the side, Tobias and Audrey shared a glance. So we had a witness that Father Frangos had *not* gone in to see the body. Proof an impostor was involved. But what good did that knowledge do us?

"Did Panos give you anything, before he passed away?" I asked her.

"No."

"It might have been something trivial," I said. "Are you sure? There's nothing you can think of?"

She turned back to her plants. "No."

"Did he spend time with anyone in particular during the last few months?"

"Just the men from that ghastly laboratory."

I knelt beside her. "Mrs. Maheras," I said softly. "Lives are at stake because of your son's research. Many lives. If you are hiding something, you could well cause a national disaster. You don't need to give it to me. The police—or better, the FBI—would work just fine. Just don't gamble with this. Please."

She glanced at me, lips pursed. Then her expression hardened. "I have nothing for you."

I sighed and rose. "Thank you." I walked away from her, back toward the steps, where J.C. had perked up a little at Ivy's prodding.

"Well?" he asked me.

"Stonewalled," I said. "If he did give the key to her, she wouldn't tell me."

"Coming here was a mistake," J.C. said. "A distraction from what we need to do."

I glanced at the mother, who continued to regard me, trowel in her hand.

"Admit it, Skinny," J.C. continued. "If we don't do something soon, the world is going to get cancer." He hesitated. "Smet, it sounds stupid when I say it like that."

". . . 'Smet'?" I asked.

"Future curse."

"Why does it sound so much like—"

"Future curses *always* sound like our curses," J.C. said, rolling his eyes. "But they're not, so it's okay to say them when prudes are around." He thumbed at Ivy, still sitting beside him.

"Wait," Ivy said. "I thought you were from another dimension, not from the future."

"Nonsense. I've always been from the future."

"Since when?"

"Since two days from now," J.C. said. "Look, Skinny, do I need to repeat myself? You know what our next move is."

I sighed, then nodded. "Yes. It's time to break into Exeltec."

PART THREE

PART THREE

SIXTEEN

"Are you sure about this?" Ivy said, rushing along beside me as I strode out of the front of the house.

"It's our best lead, Ivy," J.C. said. "We don't have time to investigate new threads. Exeltec has the body. We need to find out where it is and steal it back from them."

I nodded. "Panos's key could be almost anywhere, but if we destroy the corpse, then the key doesn't matter." I raised my phone, noticing that I'd missed a call from Yol. I nodded for J.C. to watch the perimeter as I texted Wilson for a pickup, then dialed Yol back.

Yol picked up the line.

"Hey," I said. "I—"

"I don't have much time," Yol interrupted, voice muffled. "This is bad, Legion. *Seriously* bad."

I grew cold. "What happened?"

"Panos," Yol said, talking quickly, his accent growing thicker in his haste. "He let something out. Damn it. It's—" He cut off.

"Yol?" I said, tensing as Ivy and Tobias crowded in, trying to hear what was being said. "Yol!"

I heard voices on the other end of the line, followed by rasping. "I'm being arrested," Yol said a moment later. "No more information in or out. They're going to take my phone."

"What did Panos let out, Yol?" I asked.

"We don't know. The feds tripped a hidden file on his computer. It erased the damn thing and popped up a screen that taunted us, saying he'd already released his infection. They're freaking out. I don't know anything else."

"And the things I asked you to do?"

"Did some. Set others in motion. Don't know if I'll be able to finish."

"Yol, my life could depend on whether or not—"

"*All* of our lives are in danger," Yol snapped. "Didn't you hear me? This is a disaster. Hell! They're here. Find that body. Find out *what that man did*!"

The phone rustled again, and the line went dead. I had the distinct impression that Yol hadn't hung up— someone had taken the phone from him. The feds now likely knew I was involved.

I lowered the phone and looked at my aspects as Wilson pulled up. Behind us, Dion trailed out of the house, hands in his pockets. He looked troubled.

"We need to get moving," J.C. said, rushing back from watching the perimeter. "Zen could show up here at any moment."

"If she does," I said, "Mrs. Maheras is in danger. I'm surprised Zen hasn't been here already—if not her, then another Exeltec flunky." I frowned. "I feel like we're a step behind. I do *not* like that sensation."

I ignored the car waiting for us, and I barely noticed

Dion as he walked up. Instead, I closed my eyes. "Tobias," I whispered.

"Have you noticed the beauty of the landscaping here?" Tobias said. "Those are tuberous begonia, challenging flowers to raise, particularly in this region. They require lots of light, but it can't be direct, and are very sensitive to frost. Ah, I remember a story about them . . ."

He talked on. The other aspects fell silent as we thought, collectively. I would not proceed, feeling I'd missed something. Something that one of us should have spotted. What was it?

"Zen," J.C. interrupted suddenly. "Her ambush."

"People are far less secure," I whispered, opening my eyes, "than their security measures." I reached up to my shoulder, where Zen had grabbed me in the alleyway to pull me away from the building, then I moved up to touch under my shirt collar.

My fingers brushed metal.

"Oh, *holy hell!*" J.C. said.

Zen had bugged me. *That* was what the attack in the alleyway had been about. It hadn't been nearly as reckless as she'd made it seem. My mind raced as J.C. explained to the other aspects what had happened. What had I said out loud? What did Zen know?

She'd heard that I intended to break into Exeltec. But what about the instructions I'd sent Yol? Did she know about those?

Sweating, I traced back through my memory. No. I'd only written that information down in the email. But she did know what I'd said to Mrs. Maheras. She knew that I was at a dead end.

"I'm an idiot," J.C. said. "We thought to have you scrub down after the restaurant, but not after actual *physical contact* with the assassin?"

"She hid her intentions well," Audrey replied. "Masked it as a frantic attempt to get the flash drive."

"At least now we probably don't have to worry about her coming to hurt Mrs. Maheras."

Probably. I stared at my phone. How had we missed this?

"Calm, Stephen," Tobias said, resting a hand on my shoulder. "Everyone makes mistakes, even you. We can use this one—the assassin is listening to us, but she doesn't know you've figured that out. We can manipulate her."

I nodded, taking a deep breath. Zen knew about the plan to infiltrate Exeltec, which meant I couldn't go through with that. I needed something new, something better.

That meant relying on the things I'd set in motion with Yol. Making Exeltec's owners frantic, then playing upon that. Why did missions always go this way, lately? I looked up at my aspects, then made the decision, punching a number on my phone.

Someone picked up. "Oh, honey," a sultry voice said on the other end of the line, "I was *hoping* you'd call me today."

"Bianca," I said.

Tobias groaned. "Not *her*."

I ignored him. "I need information," I said to the woman on the line.

"Sure thing, sugar," she said. How *did* she purr like that? I was half convinced she used some kind of sound effect machine. "What about? Your . . . date the other night? I can tell you the names of the people who set you up."

"It's not about that," I said. "There's something going on with a company called I3 and their rival, Exeltec. I think they might have released a deadly virus into the wild. Do you know anything about it?"

"Mmm . . . I can look," Bianca said. "Might take some time."

"Anything you can get me on Exeltec would be heartily appreciated," I said.

"Sure," she said. "And honey, next time you need a date, why not give me a call? I'm *so offended* that I wasn't even considered!"

"Like you'd show," I said. Three years, and I'd never seen Bianca face-to-face.

"I'd at least contemplate it," she said. "Now, you've got to give me *something* for the newspapers. About your date?"

"Get me information on Exeltec," I said, "and we'll trade." I hung up, looking over my shoulder as Dion stepped up to me on the sidewalk, looking confused.

"What are you hoping to find out?" the kid asked.

"Nothing," I replied, fully aware that Zen was listening to all this. "Bianca is a *terrible* informant. I've never gotten a drop of useful information out of her, and after I call her, most of what I say ends up on the internet within minutes."

"But—"

I dialed another informant and initiated a similar, but more circumspect, line of inquiry. Then a third. Within a few minutes I'd ensured that very, very soon everyone who cared about Exeltec would be reading about how they'd been involved in a major public safety breach. With I3 being investigated and me being involved, the kernel of truth to the rumors I'd started would set off a media frenzy.

"You're pushing them up against the wall, Steve,"

Ivy said as Wilson finally pulled up. "Zen's employers were desperate before; they'll be *rabid* once this hits."

"Hoping to make them ignore you and focus on damage control with the media?" J.C. asked. "Not smart. Whipping the tiger won't distract it; the thing will just get angrier."

I couldn't explain, not with Zen listening. Instead, I got out my notepad and scribbled a few instructions to Wilson, assuming the aspects would see and catch on.

Surprisingly, Audrey seemed to get it first. She grinned. "Oooh . . ."

"Dangerous," Ivy said, folding her arms. "*Very* dangerous."

Wilson rolled down the passenger window. "Master Leeds?"

I finished writing and leaned in through the window, handing him the message. "Some instructions," I said. "I need you to stay here, Wilson, and watch Mrs. Maheras. I'm worried the assassin might try to get to her. In fact, you should probably get her to the nearest police station."

"But who will drive you?"

"I can drive," I said.

Wilson looked skeptical.

"Funny," Audrey remarked, "how a man can trust you to save the world, but not to feed or drive yourself."

I smiled reassuringly at Wilson as he looked down at the instructions in his hand, then back at me with a worried expression.

"Please," I said to him.

Wilson sighed and nodded, climbing out of the car.

"You coming?" I said to Dion as I opened the side door of the SUV for my aspects and let them pile in.

"You said that people could be in danger," Dion said.

"They are," I replied, closing the door behind Audrey. "What your brother let out could cost the lives of millions."

"He said it wasn't dangerous," Dion said stubbornly.

Damn. The kid was holding out on me. Did *he* have the key? Unfortunately, I didn't want him to talk and let Zen hear. Well, in any case, I needed him with me. I might need an extra pair of nonimaginary hands, now that I'd sent Wilson away.

I settled into the driver's seat, and Dion climbed into the front passenger seat. "Panos didn't do anything wrong."

"And what *did* he do?" I asked, resigned. If I didn't prod, it would look suspicious to Zen.

"Something," Dion said.

"How pleasantly descriptive."

"He wouldn't tell me. I don't think he even actually finished it. But it wasn't dangerous."

"I . . ." I trailed off, looking back as J.C.'s mobile phone went off. The ringtone was "America the Beautiful." I shook my head, starting the car and pulling away—leaving an overwhelmed-looking Wilson on the curb—as J.C. answered his phone.

"Yo, Achmed," he said. "Yeah, I've got him here. Video? I can do that. Hey, you gonna fix that Chinese stuff for us again?"

"It was *Indian* food," Kalyani said, now on speaker. "Why would you assume it's Chinese?"

"Had rice, didn't it?" J.C. said, kneeling beside the armrest between driver's seat and passenger, then holding the phone out for me.

"Coconut rice, and curry, and . . . Never mind. Mr. Steve?"

"Yeah?" I said, glancing at the phone. Kalyani waved happily, wearing a simple T-shirt and jeans. Her bindi was black today and shaped like a little arrow between her eyebrows, rather than being the traditional red dot. I'd have to ask her about the significance.

"We've been talking," Kalyani said. "And Arnaud wants to tell you something." She turned the phone to the punctilious little Frenchman. He leaned forward, blinking at the screen. I kept my time divided between him and the road.

"Monsieur," Arnaud said, "I have spoken with Clive and Mi Won. The three of us, you see, had some upper-level chemistry and biology courses as part of our schooling. We cannot dig too deeply, because . . . Well, you know."

"I do." Ignacio. His death had ripped away most of my knowledge of chemistry.

"Regardless," Arnaud said, "we have been poring over the information given to us. Mi Won is insistent, and we have come to agree with her. It is our admittedly amateur opinion that I3 and the man named Yol are lying to you."

"About what specifically?"

"About giving up on a viral delivery method into the body," Arnaud said. "Monsieur, Panos had too many resources—was progressing too well—on his supposedly 'secret' project to have been cut off. They were investigating that line, no matter what they told you. In addition, we are not convinced that this cancer threat is as viable as it first seemed. Oh, that is *theoretically* where this research could lead, but from what we've gathered from the notes, I3 had not reached such a point yet."

"So they didn't want to tell me what the real crisis was," I said. "The rogue bacteria or virus that Panos spliced, whatever it is."

"That is for you to consider," Arnaud said. "We are

scientists. All we are saying is that there are layers here beyond what we are being told."

"Thank you," I said. "I suspected, but this confirmation is helpful. Is that everything?"

"One more item," Kalyani said, taking back the phone and turning it around toward her smiling face. "I wanted to introduce to you my husband, Rahul." An Indian man with a round, mustached face stepped into view beside her, then waved at me.

I felt a chill.

"I told you that he is a good photographer," Kalyani said, "but you do not need to use him that way. He is a *very* clever man. He can do all sorts of things! He knows computers well."

"I can see him," I said. "Why can I see him?"

"He's joined us!" Kalyani said, excited. "Isn't it wonderful!"

"Very pleased to meet you, Mr. Stephen," Rahul said with a melodic Indian accent. "I will be very helpful, I can promise you."

"I . . ." I swallowed. "How . . . did you . . ."

"This is bad," Ivy said from the back seat. "Have you ever manifested an aspect unintentionally?"

"Not since the early days," I whispered. "And never without researching a new topic first."

"Man," Audrey said. "Kalyani gets a husband and I can't even have a gerbil? Totally unfair."

I pulled over immediately, not caring about the car that honked beside me as I swerved. As we lurched to a stop I yanked the phone from J.C.'s hand and stared at the new aspect. This was the first time any family member of one of my delusions had appeared to me. It seemed a very dangerous precedent. Another sign that I was losing control.

I hung up, making their smiling faces wink out, then

tossed the phone over my shoulder to J.C. Sweating, I pulled the car forward, earning a honk from another car. I took the first off-ramp I saw, veering down into the city.

"You okay?" Dion asked.

"Fine," I snapped.

I needed a place to go, a place to think. A place that would look natural, but where I could stall and wait for my plan to proceed without Zen getting suspicious. I pulled into a Denny's. "Just need some food," I lied. This would work, right? Even a man trying to save the world had to eat.

Dion glanced at me. "You sure you're—"

"Yes. I just need an omelet."

SEVENTEEN

I held the restaurant door for my aspects, then walked in after them. The place smelled of coffee, and was occupied by the late-morning breakfast crowd, which was perfect. Zen was less likely to try something with so many witnesses. It took some work to get the waitress to give us a table for six; I had to lie and say we were expecting more people. Eventually, we settled down, Dion opposite me and two aspects on either side.

I held up a menu, fingers sticking to syrup on one side, but didn't read. Instead, I tried to calm my breathing. Sandra hadn't prepared me for this. The family members of aspects appearing suddenly, without research being done?

"You're crazy," a voice whispered across from me. "Like . . . *actually* crazy."

I lowered my menu, which—I only now realized—I'd been holding upside down. The kid hadn't touched his.

"No I'm not," I said. "I'll give you, I might be a touch insane. But I'm *not* crazy."

"They're the same thing."

"From your perspective, perhaps," I said. "I see it differently—but even if we admit that the word applies to me, it applies to you too. The longer I've lived, the more I've realized everyone is neurotic in their own individual way. *I* have control of my psychoses. How about you?"

Beside me, Ivy sniffed at my use of the word "control."

Dion chewed on this, leaning back in his chair. "What do they say my brother did?"

"He claims to have released something. A virus or bacteria of some sort."

"He wouldn't have done that," Dion said immediately. "He wanted to help people. It was the others that were dangerous. They wanted to make weapons."

"He told you this?"

"Well, no," Dion admitted. "But, I mean, why else would they try to force him to give up his projects? Why would they watch him so closely? You should be investigating *them*, not my brother. Their secrets are the dangerous ones."

"Typical pseudo-intellectual teen liberal prattle," J.C. said from my right, looking over his menu. "I'll have the steak and eggs. Rare and runny."

I nodded absently as the others spoke up. At the very least, the server wouldn't have reason to complain about us taking up so many seats—seeing as how I'd be ordering five meals. Part of me wished I could have them give the meals to others after I was done imagining my aspects cleaning their plates.

I turned my attention to the menu, and found I wasn't that hungry. I ordered an omelet anyway, talking to the waitress as the kid dug in his pocket, obviously determined not to let me pay for him. He came out with a few wadded-up bills and ordered a breakfast burrito.

I kept waiting for a beep from my phone, telling me that Wilson had followed my instructions. Nothing came, and I felt myself growing increasingly anxious; I wiped the sweat from my temples with my napkin. My aspects tried to relax me, Tobias chatting about the origin of the pancake as a food, Ivy engaging him and acting very interested.

"What's that?" I asked, nodding at Dion, who was staring at a little slip of paper he'd found among the wadded-up bills.

He blushed immediately, moving to tuck it away.

I snatched his hand, moving with reflexes I didn't know I had. Beside me, J.C. nodded appreciatively.

"It's nothing," Dion snapped, opening his hand. "Fine. Take it. Idiot."

I suddenly felt foolish. Panos's data key wouldn't be a slip of paper; it would have to be on a flash drive or some other electronic storage medium. I pulled my hand back, reading the piece of paper. *1 Esd 4:41*, it read.

"Mom slips them into my pockets when she's folding laundry," Dion explained. "Reminders to give up my heathen ways."

I showed it to the others, frowning. "I don't recognize that scripture."

"First Esdras," Ivy said. "From the Orthodox Bible—it's a book of Apocrypha that most other sects don't use. I don't know that particular verse offhand."

I looked it up on my phone. "Great is truth," I read, "and strongest of all."

Dion shrugged. "I suppose I can agree with that. Even if Mom won't accept what the truth really is . . ."

I tapped my finger on the table. I felt as if I was close to something. An answer? Or maybe just the right questions to be asking? "Your brother had a data key," I said, "which would unlock the information stored in his body. Would he have given it to your mother, do you think?"

Ivy watched Dion carefully to see if he reacted to mention of the key. He didn't have any reaction I could see, and Ivy shook her head. If he was surprised we knew about the key, he was hiding it very well.

"A data key?" Dion asked. "Like what?"

"A thumb drive or something similar."

"I doubt he'd give anything like that to Mom," Dion said as our food arrived. "She hates technology and everything to do with it, particularly if she thinks it came from I3. If he'd handed her something like that, she'd have just destroyed it."

"She gave me quite the cold reception."

"Well, what did you expect? You're employed by the company that turned her son away from God." Dion shook his head. "Mom's a good person—solid, salt-of-the-earth, Old World stock. But she doesn't trust technology. To her, work is something you do with your hands. Not this idle staring at computer screens." He looked away. "I think Panos did what he did to prove something to her, you know?"

"Turning people into mass storage devices?" I asked.

Dion blushed. "That's just the setup, the work he had to do in *order* to do the work he wanted."

"Which was?"

"I . . ."

"Yeah," Ivy said. "He knows something here. Man, this kid is not good at lying. Take a dominant position, Steve. Push him."

"Might as well tell me," I said. "Someone needs to

know, Dion. You don't know that you can trust me, but you have to tell someone. What *was* your brother trying to do?"

"Disease," Dion said, looking at his burrito. "He wanted to cure it."

"Which one?"

"All of it."

"Lofty goal."

"Yeah, Panos admitted as much to me. The actual curing wasn't his job; he saw the delivery method as his part."

"Delivery method?" I asked, frowning. "Of the disease."

"No. Of the cure."

"Ahhh . . ." Tobias said, nodding as he sipped his coffee.

"Think about it," Dion said, gesturing to the sides, animated. "Infectious disease is pretty awesome. Imagine if we could design a fast-spreading virus which, in turn, *immunized* people from another disease? You catch the common cold, and suddenly you can never get smallpox, AIDS, polio . . . Why spend billions immunizing, trying to reach people? Nature itself could do all the work for us, if we cracked the method."

"That sounds . . . incredible," I said.

"Incredibly *terrifying*," J.C. said, pointing at the kid with his knife. "Sounds a little like using a smarkwat to fight a viqxuixs."

"A what?" Ivy asked, sighing.

"Classified," J.C. said. "Smet, this steak is good." He dug back into the food.

"Yeah, well," Dion said. "I was going to help him, you know? Go to school, eventually start a new biotech company with him. I guess that dream is dead too." He stabbed at his food. "But you know, each day he'd come home and Mom would ask, 'Did you do any good today?' And he'd smile. He knew he was doing something important, even if she couldn't see it."

"I suspect," I said, "that your mother was prouder of him than she let on."

"Yeah, probably. She's not as bad as she seems sometimes. When we were younger, she worked long hours in menial jobs, supporting us after Dad died. I shouldn't complain. It's just . . . you know, she thinks she knows *everything*."

"Unlike your average teenager," Audrey said, smiling toward Dion.

I nodded, toying with my food, watching Dion. "Did he give you the key, Dion?" I asked him directly.

The kid shook his head.

"He doesn't have it," Ivy said. "He's too bad a liar to hide this from us, in my professional estimation."

"What you should be doing," Dion said, digging back into his burrito, "is looking for some crazy device or something."

"Device?"

"Sure," Dion said. "He'd have built something to hide it, you know? All that maker stuff, you know? He was always gluing LED lights to things and making his own name badges and things. I'll bet he hid it like that. You pick up a potato, and it knocks over a penny, and a hundred geese fly into the air, and the key drops on your head. Something like that."

I looked at my aspects. They seemed skeptical, but maybe there was something to this. Not a device like Dion described, but a process. What if Panos had set up some sort of fail-safe that would reveal the truth if he died—but it hadn't been tripped for some reason.

I forced myself to eat a bit of omelet, just to be able to tell Wilson I'd done so when he inevitably asked.

Unfortunately, my phone still hadn't beeped by the time we finished. I stalled as best I could, but eventually felt it would look suspicious to Zen if we stayed any longer.

I led the way back out to the SUV, and held open the side door for my aspects before rounding to the driver's seat. I'd just settled in, planning my next move, when I felt the cold metal of a gun barrel press against the back of my neck.

EIGHTEEN

Dion climbed into the passenger seat, oblivious. He looked at me, then froze, going all white. I glanced at the rearview mirror and caught a glimpse of Zen squatting behind my seat, gun pressed against my head.

Damn. So she hadn't been as willing to wait as I'd hoped. My phone hung in my pocket like a dead weight. What was taking Wilson so long?

"Join me in the back, if you would please, Mr. Leeds," Zen said softly. "Young Maheras, remain in place. I assume that I needn't warn you how willing I am to resort to violence?"

Sweating, I noticed J.C. in the rearview mirror, his face red. He'd been sitting in the seat that Zen now squatted before, but hadn't seen her until now. Twice she'd gotten the drop on us, and J.C. hadn't been able to do a thing. Her skill at this was far better than my own.

J.C. took out his gun, for all the good it would do,

and nodded for me to obey Zen. Getting into the back would put me into a better position to engage her.

She moved to the far back seat—scrunching Ivy and Audrey to the sides—as I moved, her gun on me at all times.

"Your weapon," she said.

I removed it, just as I had in the alley, and placed it before me on the floor. Why was I even carrying the blasted thing?

"Phone next."

I passed it over.

"Good job on finding the bug," she noted to me. "We will discuss the matter further, Mr. Leeds, as we go for a stroll together. Young Maheras, you are not involved in this. Move to the driver's seat of the car. Once we are out, you are to leave. I don't care what you do—go to the police, if you wish—but stay away. I don't like killing people I haven't been hired to hit. It's bad business to . . . give away too many freebies."

Dion was all too quick to move, scrambling into the driver's seat, where I'd left the keys.

"This is good," J.C. said softly. "She's letting the boy go and is moving us out into the open." He scrunched up his face. "I can't figure out why she'd do either one, but I think it indicates that her superiors have demanded she not actually kill anyone."

I nodded, sweat trickling down the back of my neck. Zen waved with her gun and I opened the side door, letting my aspects file out, J.C first, then Ivy, then To-bias. Audrey rested a hand on my arm encouragingly and I nodded, then moved to climb out before her.

Zen snapped forward, grabbing me by the shoulder and throwing me back. She snatched the door and slammed it closed.

"Maheras," she said, turning the gun on him. "Drive. *Now.*"

"But—"

"Go or you're a dead man!"

The kid floored it, running over a parking lot divider. I lay stunned against the side of the car, blinking, tracking what had happened. Zen . . .

My aspects!

I cried out, turning and pressing my face against the window. Ivy and Tobias stood in the parking lot, looking baffled. Zen instructed Dion to pull out of the parking lot onto the street, and then told him to continue at a normal speed—no trying to get picked up by cops, please.

I barely listened. She'd lured my aspects out, then isolated me from them. Only Audrey was left, and that was by a fluke. Another moment, and she'd have been gone too. I turned, stunned, to look at Zen, who had settled into the seat by the now-closed door, her gun held on me.

"I do my research," she said. "As a side note, the amount that has been written about you in psychological journals was *quite* useful, Mr. Leeds."

Audrey sank down onto the floor between us, wrapping her hands around her knees, whimpering. She was all I had for now, and—

Wait.

J.C. I hadn't seen J.C. out the window. I turned, searching, and there he was! Charging along the sidewalk at a full run, gun in one hand, look of determination on his face. He kept pace with us, barely.

Bless you, I thought toward him. He'd reacted when the other two were caught flat-footed. He dodged around some people on the sidewalk and leaped a bench in an almost superhuman move.

Audrey perked up, looking out the window. "Wow," she whispered. "How is he *doing* that?"

The car was moving at around forty miles an hour. Suddenly, I couldn't pretend any longer. J.C. ran out of breath, lurched to a stop on the sidewalk, his face flushed. He collapsed, exhausted from a run he shouldn't have been able to manage.

The illusion. I *had* to keep the illusion. Audrey looked at me, then seemed to shrink upon herself, realizing what she'd done. It wasn't her fault, though. I'd have eventually noticed how fast we were going.

"You," Zen said to me, "are a very dangerous man."

"I'm not the one holding the gun," I said, turning to face her. How was I going to do this without Ivy and Tobias to help me interact? Without J.C. to pull me out of a deadly situation?

"Yes, but I can only kill the occasional individual," Zen said. "You bring down companies, destroy hundreds of lives. My employers are . . . concerned about what you've done."

"And they think having you grab me is going to help?" I asked. "I won't find Panos's key for you at gunpoint, Zen."

"They're not worried about the body anymore," she said, and sounded faintly troubled. "You've toppled their fortunes and sent the government after them. They don't want to be associated with this hunt any longer. They just want . . . loose threads to be pulled out and disposed of."

Great. My plan was working.

Too well.

I tried to come up with something more to say, but Zen turned from me, giving Dion a series of driving instructions. I tried to get her talking again, but she refused, and I wasn't about to try anything physical. Not without J.C. to give advice.

Maybe . . . maybe the other aspects would find their way to wherever we were going. Given time, they probably would.

I wasn't sure how long that would take.

Audrey spent the ride seated in the middle of the floor between our two seats, arms wrapped around her legs. I wanted to talk to her, but didn't dare say anything with Zen watching. The assassin thought she'd isolated me without any aspects. If I let her know that one was still here, I would lose a big advantage.

Unfortunately, our drive took us to an area on the outskirts of the city. There were some new housing developments out here, as the city's creeping expansion slowly consumed the countryside, but there were also big patches of fields and trees waiting for condos and gas stations. Zen had us pull into one of these large wooded spots, and we drove on a dirt road up to a solitary house of the "my fathers farmed this land for generations" variety.

This was far enough from neighbors that shouts would not be heard and gunshots would be attributed to the removal of vermin. Not good. Zen marched Dion and me to a cellar door set in the ground and ordered us down the stairs. Inside, sacks slumped against the wall, spilling potatoes so old they'd probably witnessed the Civil War. A bare lightbulb glared where it hung from the center of the ceiling.

"I'm going to go report," Zen told us, taking Dion's phone from him. "Get comfortable. My expectation is that you're going to be living down here for a few weeks while things blow over for my employers."

She walked up the steps and locked the cellar door.

NINETEEN

Dion let out a deep breath and put his back to the cinder-block wall, then slumped down to a sitting position. "Weeks?" he asked. "Trapped in here with you?"

I paused a moment before speaking. "Yeah. That's going to suck, eh?"

Dion looked up at me, and I cursed myself for hesitating before giving my reply. The kid looked frazzled—he'd probably never been forced to drive at gunpoint before. First time is always the worst.

"You don't think we're going to be down here for weeks, do you?" Dion guessed.

"I . . . No."

"But she said—"

"They're trained to talk that way," I said, fishing out Zen's bug from under my collar, then smashing it just in case. I walked around the chamber, looking for exits. "Always tell your captives they have more time than they do; it makes them relax, sets them to planning, instead of trying to break out immediately. The last thing you want to do is make them desperate, since desperate people are unpredictable."

The kid groaned softly. I probably shouldn't have explained that. I was feeling the lack of Ivy's presence. Even when she didn't guide me directly, having her around made me better at interacting with people.

"Don't worry," I said, kneeling down to inspect a drain in the floor, "we probably won't be in real danger unless Zen decides to take us individually into the woods 'for questioning.' That will mean she's been told to execute us."

I prodded at the grate. Too small to crawl through, unfortunately, and it looked like it just ended in a small pit of rocks anyway. I moved on, expecting—despite myself—to hear commentary by my aspects analyzing our situation, telling me what to investigate, theorizing on how to get out.

Instead, all I heard was retching.

I spun on Dion, shocked to find him emptying his stomach onto the floor of the cellar. So much for the breakfast burrito he'd so stubbornly paid for. I waited until he was done, then walked over, taking an old towel off of a dusty table and draping it over the sickup to smother the smell. I knelt down, resting my hand on the young man's shoulder.

He looked awful. Red eyes, pale skin, sweat on his brow.

How to interact? What did one say? "I'm sorry." It sounded lame, but it was all I could think of.

"She's going to kill us," the youth whispered.

"She might try," I said. "But then again, she might not. Killing us is a big step, one her employers probably won't be willing to make."

Of course, I *had* made them very desperate. And desperate people were . . . well, unpredictable.

I stood up, leaving the kid to his misery, and walked to Audrey. "I need you to get us out of this," I whispered to her.

"Me?" Audrey said.

"You're all I have."

"Before this, I'd only been on a *single* mission!" she said. "I don't know about guns, or fighting, or escaping."

"You're an expert on cryptography."

"Expert? You read *one* book on cryptography. Besides, how is cryptography going to help? Here, let me interpret the scratches on the walls. They say we're *bloody doomed!*"

Frustrated, I left her trembling with worry and forced myself to continue my inspection of the room. No windows. Some sections of bare earth where the cinder-block wall had fallen in. I was able to dig at one, but heard the floor groaning above as I did. Not a good idea.

I tried the exit next, climbing the steps and shoving my shoulder at the doors to see how strong they were. They were tight, unfortunately, and there was no lock to pick—just a padlock on the outside that I couldn't reach. I might be able to find something to use as a ram and break us out, but that would certainly alert Zen. I could hear her through the floor above, talking. Sounded like a tense conversation over a cell phone, but I couldn't make out any specifics.

I went over the room again. Had I missed anything? I was sure I had, but what? Without my aspects, I didn't know what I knew. Being alone haunted me. As I passed Dion, I found the expressions on his face alien things, no more intelligible as emotions than lumps in mud. Did that expression mean happiness? Sorrow?

Stop, I told myself, sweating. *You're not that bad.*

I was without Ivy, but that didn't suddenly make me unable to relate to members of my own species. Did it?

Dion was upset. That was obvious. He stared down at a few small slips of paper in his hands. More scriptures he'd found in his pockets from his mother.

"She just left the verse numbers," he said, glancing at me, "so I don't even know what the scriptures say. As if they'd be a help anyway. Bah!" He closed his fist, then threw the papers, wadded up. They burst apart from each other and fluttered down like confetti.

I stood there, feeling almost as sick as Dion looked. I needed to say something, connect with him somehow. I didn't know *why* I felt that, but I was suddenly desperate for it.

"Are you so frightened of death, Dion?" I asked. Probably the wrong words, but speaking was better than remaining silent.

"Why wouldn't I be?" Dion said. "Death is the end. Nothing. All gone." He looked at me, as if in challenge. When I didn't respond immediately, he continued. "Not going to tell me everything will be all right? Mom always talks about how good people get rewarded, but Panos was as good a man as there was. He spent his life trying to cure disease! And look at him. Dead of a stupid *accident*."

"Why," I said, "do you assume death is the end?"

"Because it *is*. Look, I don't want to listen to any religious—"

"I'm not going to preach at you," I said. "I'm an atheist too."

The kid looked at me. "You are?"

"Sure," I said. "Almost fifteen percent—though admittedly, several of my pieces would argue that they are agnostic instead."

"Fifteen percent? That doesn't count."

"Oh? So you get to decide how my faith, or lack thereof, works? What 'counts' and what doesn't?"

"No, but even if it did work that way—if someone could be *fifteen percent* atheist—the majority of you still believes."

"Just like a minority of you probably still believes in God," I said.

He looked at me, then blushed. I settled down beside him, opposite the place where he'd had his little accident.

"I can see why people want to believe," Dion told me. "I'm not just a petulant kid like you think. I've wondered, I've asked. God doesn't make sense to me. But sometimes, looking at infinity and thinking of myself just . . . not being here anymore, I understand why people would choose to believe."

Ivy would want me to try to convert the boy, but she wasn't here. Instead, I asked a question. "Do you think time is infinite, Dion?"

He shrugged.

"Come on," I prodded. "Give me an answer. You want comfort? I might have a solution for you—or at least my aspect Arnaud might. But first, is time infinite?"

"I don't think we know for certain," Dion replied. "But yeah, I'd guess that it is. Even after our universe ends, something *else* will happen. If not here, then in other dimensions. Other places. Other big bangs. Matter, space, it'll continue on without end."

"So you're immortal."

"My atoms, maybe," he said. "But that's not *me*. Don't give me any metaphysical bull—"

"No metaphysics," I said, "just a theory. If time is infinite, then anything that *can* happen *will* happen—and *has* happened. That means you've happened before, Dion. We all have. Even if there is no God—even supposing that there are no answers, no divinity out there—we're immortal."

He frowned.

"Think about it," I said. "The universe rolled its cosmic dice and ended up with you—a semi-random collection of atoms, synapses, and chemicals. Together, those create your personality, memories, and very existence. But if time continues forever, eventually that random collection will happen again. It may take hundreds of trillions of years, but it *will* come again. You. With your memories, your personality. In the context of infinity, kid, we will keep living, over and over."

"I . . . don't know how comforting that is, honestly. Even if it is true."

"Really?" I asked. "Because I think it's pretty amazing to consider. Anything that is *possible* is actually *reality*, given infinity. So, not only will you return, but your every iteration of possibility will play out. Sometimes you'll be rich. Sometimes you'll be poor. In fact, it's plausible that because of a brain defect, sometime in the future you'll have the memories you have now, even if in *that* future time you never lived those memories. So you'll be you again, completely, and not because of some mystical nonsense—but because of simple mathematics. Even the smallest chance multiplied by infinity is, itself, infinite."

I stood back up, then squatted down, looking him in the eyes and resting my hand on his shoulder. "Every variation of possibility, Dion. At some point, you—the same you, with the same thought processes—will be born to a wealthy family. Your parents will be killed, and you will decide to fight against injustice. It has happened. It will happen. You asked for comfort, Dion? Well, when the fear of death seizes you—when the dark thoughts come—you stare the darkness right back, and you tell it, 'I will not listen to you, for I am *infinite Batmans*.'"

The kid blinked at me. "That ... is the weirdest thing anyone has ever told me."

I winked at him, then left him lost in thought and walked back to Audrey. I wasn't sure how much of that I actually believed, but it was what had come out. Honestly, I don't know that the universe could really handle everyone being infinite Batmans.

Perhaps the point of God was to prevent nonsense like that.

I took Audrey by the arm, speaking softly. "Audrey, focus on me."

She looked at me, blinking. She'd been crying.

"We're going to think, right now," I told her. "We're going to scrounge everything we know, and we're going to come up with a way out of this."

"I can't—"

"You *can*. You're part of me. You're part of all of this; you can access my subconscious. You can *fix this*."

She met my eyes, and some of my confidence seemed to transfer to her. She nodded sharply, and adopted a look of complete concentration. I smiled at her encouragingly.

The door to the building up above opened, then shut.

Come on, Audrey.

Zen's footsteps rounded the building, then she began working on the lock down into the cellar.

Come on ...

Audrey snapped her head up and looked at me. "I know where the body is."

"The body?" I said. "Audrey, we're supposed to be—"

"Zen's company doesn't have it," Audrey said. "I3

doesn't have it. The kid doesn't know anything. *I know where it is.*"

The door down into the cellar opened. Light flooded in, revealing Zen silhouetted above. "Mr. Leeds," she said. "I need you to come with me so I can question you alone. It will only take a short time."

I grew very cold.

TШЕПТУ

"Oh hell," Audrey said, backing away from me. "You need to do something! Don't let her kill you."

I turned to face Zen—a woman dressed in chic clothing, like she was the CFO of a Manhattan publishing company, not a paid assassin. She walked down the steps, feigning nonchalance. That attitude, mixed with the tension of the call above, told me all I needed to know.

She was going to eliminate me.

"They're really willing to do this?" I asked her. "It will leave questions. Problems."

"I don't know what you're talking about." She got out her gun.

"Do we have to play this game, Zen?" I replied, frantically searching for a way to stall. "We both know what you're up to. You'll really follow through with orders that are so incompetent? It leaves you in danger. People *will* wonder where I've gone."

"An equal number will be glad to have you out of

their hair, I assume," Zen said. She took out a suppressor, affixing it to her gun, all pretense gone now.

Audrey whimpered. To his credit, Dion stood up, unwilling to face death sitting down.

"You pushed them too hard, Mr. Crazy," Zen said. "They have it in their heads that you're trying specifically to destroy them, and so they have responded as any bully does when shoved. They hit as hard as they can and hope it will solve the situation." She raised the gun. "As for me, I can take care of myself. But thank you for your concern."

I stared down the barrel of that gun, sweating, panicking. No hope, no plan, no aspects . . .

But she didn't know that.

"They're around you," I whispered.

Zen hesitated.

"Some people theorize," I said, "that what I see are ghosts. If you've read about me, then you'll know. I do things I shouldn't be able to. Know things I shouldn't know. Because I have help."

"You're just a genius," she said, but her eye twitched to the side. Yes, she'd read about me. Deeply, if she knew how to drive off without my aspects.

And nobody could dig into my world without coming away a little bit . . . touched.

"They've caught up to us," I said. "They stand on the steps behind you. Can you feel them there, Zen? Watching you? Hands at your neck? What will you do with them if you remove me? Will you live with my spirits stalking you for the rest of your life?"

She set her jaw, and seemed as if she was trying very, very hard not to look over her shoulder. Was this actually working?

Zen took a deep breath. "They won't be the only

spirits that haunt me, Leeds," she whispered. "If there is a hell, I earned my place in it long ago."

"So you say," I replied. "Of course, what you really should be wondering is this: I'm a genius. I know things I shouldn't. So why have I placed us here, right now? Why is it that I *want* you right there?"

"I . . ." She held the gun on me. A cool breeze blew in down around her, rustling the lips of old potato sacks.

My cell phone chirped in her pocket.

Zen practically jumped to the ceiling. She cursed, sweating, and rested her hand on the pocket. She thrust the gun at me and fired. Wild. The support beam beside me popped with exploding bits of wood. Dion dove for cover.

Zen—eyes so wide, I could see the whites all around her pupils—held the gun in a trembling hand, focusing on me.

"Check the phone, Zen," I said.

She didn't move.

No! It couldn't go this way. So close! She had to—

Another phone rang. Hers this time, I assumed, buzzing in her other pocket. Zen wavered. I met her stare. In that moment, one of the two of us was mad, insane, on the edge.

And it wasn't the crazy guy.

Her phone stopped ringing. A text followed. We waited, facing one another in the cold cellar until, at long last, Zen reached down and took out her phone. She stared at it for a few moments. Then she laughed a barking laugh. She backed up, placing a call, and had a whispered conversation.

Letting out what had to be the biggest breath of my life, I walked to Dion and helped him to his feet. He looked up at Zen, who laughed again, this time louder.

"What's going on?" Dion asked.

"We're safe," I said. "Isn't that right, Zen?"

She giggled wildly. Then she hung up and looked right at me. "Whatever you say, sir."

". . . 'Sir'?" Dion asked.

"Exeltec was on unstable footing," I said. "I released rumors that it was involved in a federal investigation, and had Yol push all the right buttons economically."

"To make them desperate?" Dion asked.

"To crash the company," I said, walking back to Zen, passing a flummoxed Audrey. "So I could afford to buy it. Yol was supposed to do that part, but only got halfway done. I had to have Wilson do the rest, calling the various Exeltec investors and buying them out." I proffered my hand to Zen. She gave me my phone.

"So . . ." Dion said.

"So I now own a sixty percent stake in the company," I said, checking the text from Wilson. "And have voted myself president. That makes me Zen's boss."

"Sir," she said. She was doing a good job of regaining her composure, but I could see a wildness in the way her hands still trembled, the way she stood with her expression too stiff.

"Wait," Dion said. "You just defeated an assassin with a *hostile takeover*?"

"I use the cards dealt to me. Probably wasn't particularly hostile, though—I suspect that everyone involved was all too eager to jump ship."

"You realize, of course," Zen said smoothly, "that I was never actually going to shoot you. I was just supposed to make you worried so you'd share information."

"Of course." That would be the official line, to protect her and Exeltec from attempted murder charges.

My buyout agreement would include provisions to prevent me from taking action against them.

I pocketed my phone, took my gun back from Zen, and nodded to Audrey. "Let's go collect that body."

TШEПTУ - ΠE

We found Mrs. Maheras in the garden still. She knelt there, planting, nurturing, tending.

I walked up, and from the way she glanced at me, I suspected she realized that her secret was out. Still, I knelt down beside her, then handed over a carton of half-grown flowers when she motioned toward them.

Sirens sounded in the distance.

"Was that necessary?" she asked, not looking up.

"Sorry," I said. "But yes." I'd sent a text to Yol, knowing the feds would get it first. Behind me, Audrey, Tobias, Ivy, and a dispirited J.C. stepped up to us. To my eyes they cast shadows in the fading light, and blocked my view of Dion standing just behind. We'd found the other aspects walking along the road, miles from Zen's holding place, trying to reach me.

I was tired. Man, was I tired. Sometimes in the heat of it all, you can forget. But when the tension ends, it comes crashing down.

"I should have seen it," Ivy said again, arms folded.

"I *should* have. Most Orthodox branches are pointedly against cremation. They see it as desecration of the body, which is to await resurrection."

We had been so focused on the information in Panos's cells that we didn't stop to think there might be other reasons entirely that someone would want to take the corpse. Reasons so powerful that they would convince an otherwise law-abiding woman and her priest to pull a heist.

In a way, I was very impressed. "You were a cleaning lady when you were younger," I said. "I should have asked Dion more about your life, your job. He mentioned menial labor, a life spent supporting him and his brother. I didn't ask what you'd done."

She continued planting flowers upon her son's grave, hidden in the garden.

"You imitated the cleaning lady who worked at the morgue," I said. "You paid her off, I assume, and went in her place—after having the priest place tape on the door. It really was him, not an impostor. Together, you went to extremes to protect your son's corpse from cremation."

"What gave me away?" Mrs. Maheras asked as the sirens drew closer.

"You followed the real cleaning lady's patterns exactly," I said. "Too exactly. You cleaned the bathroom, then signed your name on the sheet hanging on the door, to prove it had been done."

"I practiced Lilia's signature exactly!" Mrs. Maheras said, looking at me for the first time.

"Yes," I said, holding up one of the slips of paper with scriptures on them that she put in her son's pockets. "But you wrote the cleaning time on that sheet as well, and you didn't practice imitating Lilia's *numbers*."

"You have a very distinctive zero," Audrey explained,

looking supremely smug. Cryptography hadn't cracked this case after all. It had just required some good old-fashioned handwriting analysis.

Mrs. Maheras sighed, then placed her spade into the dirt and bowed her head, offering a silent prayer. I bowed my head as well, as did Ivy and J.C., but Tobias refrained.

"So you'll take him again," Mrs. Maheras whispered, once she had finished. She looked at the ground before her, now planted with flowers and tomatoes.

"Yes," I said, climbing to my feet and dusting off my knees. "But at the very least, you're unlikely to be in too much trouble for what you did. The government doesn't recognize a body as property, so what you did wasn't actually theft."

"A cold comfort," she muttered. "They'll still take him, and they'll burn him."

"True," I said idly. "Of course, who knows what secrets your son had hidden in his body? He'd been splicing secret information into his DNA, and he might have hidden all kinds of things in there. The right implication at the right time might prod the government into a very, *very* long search."

She looked up at me.

"Scientists disagree on how many cells there are in the human body," I explained. "Somewhere in the trillions, easily. Perhaps many more than that. Could take decades upon decades to search them all, something I doubt the government will want to do. However, if they think there *might* be something important, they could likely put the body into cold storage just in case they need to do a thorough search at some point.

"It wouldn't be a proper burial, as you want—but it also wouldn't be cremation. I believe the church does make provisions for people donating organs to help others? Perhaps it's best to just consider it in that light."

Mrs. Maheras seemed thoughtful. I left her then, and Dion stepped forward to comfort her. My suggestions did seem to have made a difference, which baffled me. I'd have rather seen a family member cremated than spend forever being frozen. But as I reached the building and looked back, I found that Mrs. Maheras seemed to have perked up visibly.

"You were right," I told Ivy.

"Have I ever *not* been right?"

"I don't know about that," J.C. said. "But you *do* make some really bad relationship choices sometimes."

We all looked at him, and he blushed immediately.

"I was talking about her *dumping* me," he protested. "Not picking me in the first place!"

I smiled, leading the way into the kitchen. I was just glad to have them back. I walked down the little hallway lined with pictures, toward the front door. I'd want to meet the feds when they arrived.

Then I stopped. "There's a bare patch on the wall. It looks so odd. Every surface, desk, and wall in this place is covered with kitsch. Except here." I pointed at the four pictures of the family, then the two pictures of saints. Two spots empty save for little nails. Ivy had said that Mrs. Maheras had probably taken down the picture of Panos's patron saint in preparation for his funeral.

"Ivy," I said, "would you say it's safe to assume that Panos knew if he died, this picture would be removed and placed with his corpse?"

We looked at each other. Then I reached up and pulled on the nail below Panos's picture. It resisted in an odd fashion. I yanked harder, and the nail came out—but had a knob and string tied around the back end.

Behind the wall, something clicked.

I looked at the aspects, suddenly worried, until the wall's nearby light switch—plate behind it and all—rotated forward like a hidden cupholder in a car's dashboard. The portion that had been hidden inside the wall had LED lights blinking on the sides.

"Well I'll be damned," J.C. said. "The kid was right."

"Language," Ivy mumbled, looking closely at the contraption.

"What happened to the future curses?" Audrey said. "I kind of liked those."

"I realized something," J.C. said. "I can't be an Inter-dimensional Time Ranger. Because if I am, that means all of *you* are too. And that's just a little too silly for me to accept."

I reached into the holder that had come out and extracted a thumb drive. Written on it, with a label maker, were a few words.

"1 Kings 19:11–12," I read.

"And He said," Ivy quoted in a quiet voice, "Go forth, and stand upon the mount before the Lord. And behold, the Lord passed by, and a great and strong wind rent the mountains and broke in pieces the rocks before the Lord, but the Lord was not in the wind; and after the wind an earthquake, but the Lord was not in the earthquake. And after the earthquake a fire, but the Lord was not in the fire; and after the fire a still small voice."

I looked at my aspects as a fist pounded on the door. Then I pocketed the thumb drive and pushed the holder back into the wall before going to meet with the feds.

EPILOGUE

Four days later, I stood alone in the White Room. Tobias had covered over the hole in the ceiling, as he'd promised. The place was refreshingly blank.

Was this what I would be, without my aspects? Blank? I'd certainly felt that way while being held by Zen. I'd barely been able to do anything to save myself. No plans, no escaping. Just some stalling. Ivy had sometimes wondered if I was growing good enough on my own that I eventually wouldn't need her or the others any longer.

From what had happened to me when I'd lost them, I figured that day—if it ever came—was a long, long way off.

The door cracked open. Audrey slipped in, wearing a blue one-piece swimsuit. She trotted up to me and delivered a sheet of paper. "Have to go catch a pool party. But I did finish solving this. Wasn't too hard, once we had the key."

On the thumb drive, we'd found two things. The first was the anticipated key to unlocking the data on Panos's body. The body had been seized by the government, and I'd convinced them to put it on ice for the foreseeable future. After all, there might be very, very important data on it, and someday the key might turn up.

Yol had offered me an exorbitant amount to track down the key. I'd refused, though I had forced him to buy Exeltec from me for another exorbitant sum, so I came away from this in a good enough position.

The CDC failed to find evidence that Panos had released any kind of pathogen, and eventually determined that the note on Panos's computer had been an idle threat, meant to send I3 into a panic. Earlier that morning, Dion had sent me a thank-you note from him and his mother for stopping the government from burning the body. I hadn't yet told them I'd stolen this thumb drive.

It contained the key, and a . . . second file. A small text document, also encrypted. We'd stared at it for a time before realizing that the key had been printed on the outside of the thumb drive itself. Chapter nineteen of First Kings. Any string of letters or numbers, or mixture of the two, can be the passphrase for a private-key cryptogram—though using a known text, like Bible verses, wasn't a particularly secure option.

Audrey went out, but left the door cracked open. I could see Tobias outside, leaning against the wall, arms folded, wearing his characteristic loose business suit, no tie.

I raised the sheet of paper, reading the simple note Panos had left.

I guess I'm dead.

*I shouldn't be surprised, but I didn't think they'd
ever actually go through with it. My own friends, you
know?*

He'd gotten that wrong. So far as I or anyone else
could determine, his fall really had been an accident.

*Did you know every person is a walking jungle of
bacteria? We're each a little biome, all to ourselves.
I've made an alteration. It's called Staphylococcus epi-
dermidis. A strain of bacteria we all carry. It's harmless, for the most part.*

*My changes aren't big. Just an addition. Several megs
of data, spliced into the DNA. I3 was watching me, but
I learned to do my work, even when supervised. They
watched what I posted though, so I decided to use their
tools against them. I put the information into the bacteria of my own skin and shook hands with them all.
I'll bet you can find strains of my altered bacteria all
across the world by now.*

*It won't do anything harmful. But if you've found
this, you have the key to decoding what I've hidden.
You make the call, Dion. I leave it in your hands. Release the key on this thumb drive, and everyone will
know what I've studied. They'll have the answers to
what I3 is doing, and everyone will be on an even playing field.*

I studied the paper for a time, then quietly folded
it and slipped it into my back pocket. I walked to the
door.

"Are you going to do it?" Tobias asked as I passed
him. "Let it out?"

I pulled out the flash drive and held it up. "Didn't
Dion talk about starting a new company with his
brother? Curing disease? Doing good each day?"

"Something like that," Tobias said.

I tossed the drive up into the air, then caught it. "We'll set this aside, to be mailed to him on the day he graduates. Maybe that dream of his isn't as dead as he thinks. At the very least, we should honor his brother's wishes." I hesitated. "But we'll want to see if we can get the data ourselves first and check out how dangerous it might be."

As my aspects had guessed, my contacts among the feds said the cancer scare had been a fake on Yol's part, an attempt to make my task urgent. But we had no idea what Panos had really been working on. Somehow, he'd hidden that even from the people at I3.

"Technically," Tobias said, "that information is owned by Yol."

"Technically," I said, pocketing the flash drive again, "it's owned by *me* as well, since I'm part owner of the company. We'll just call this my part."

I passed him, heading to the stairs. "The funny thing is," I said, hand on the banister, "we spent this entire time searching for a corpse—but the information wasn't just there, it was on every person we met."

"There's no way we could have known," Tobias said.

"Of course there was," I said. "Panos warned us. That day we studied I3—it was proclaimed right there, on one of the slogans he'd printed and hung on his wall."

Tobias looked at me, quizzical.

"Information," I said, wiggling my fingers—and the bacteria that held Panos's data, "for every body."

I smiled, and left Tobias chuckling as I went searching for something to eat.

LIES OF
THE BEHOLDER

A STEPHEN LEEDS STORY

ONE

"So . . ." J.C. said, hands on hips as he regarded the building. "Anyone else worried that this doctor's office is in a slum?"

"It's *not* a slum," Ivy said, extending her hand to help me from the back of the limo.

"Sure," J.C. said. "And those *aren't* crack dealers on the corner over there."

"J.C., those kids are like *six*."

He narrowed his eyes. "Starting early, are they? Nefarious little entrepreneurs."

Ivy rolled her eyes, but Tobias—an African American man who was growing a little unsteady on his feet, now that he was getting on in years—just laughed a hearty, full-throated laugh. He climbed out of the limo with my help, then slapped J.C. on the back. They'd been joking the whole way here.

J.C. grinned, showing he was at least a little aware of his buffoonery.

I eyed the building. Though it was your typical,

generic suburban office structure, it *was* across the street from a pawnshop and next door to an auto mechanic. Not a slum, but hardly prime real estate either. So maybe J.C. had a point.

I rapped on the front passenger window of the limo, which rolled down, revealing a young woman with short blonde hair. Wilson's grandniece was shadowing him again. Right. I wished he'd left her behind today; I tend to be a little more . . . erratic when visiting with reporters.

I looked past her toward the tall, distinguished man in the driver's seat. "Why don't you wait here, Wilson," I said, "instead of going to the service station? In case we've got the wrong location or something."

"Very well, Master Leeds," Wilson said.

His grandniece nodded eagerly. As comfortable as Wilson looked in his traditional buttling gear, she seemed awkward wrapped in a coachman's coat and cap. Like she was playing dress-up. Had she been listening as I talked to my hallucinations in the back seat? I was used to Wilson, but it felt wrong to expose myself to someone from the outside. I mean, I was used to people seeing my . . . eccentricities when I was in public. But this felt different. An intrusion.

I turned and walked with my aspects into the office building, which had a familiar, sterile quality. Not quite like a hospital, but scrubbed often enough to give it the off-white scent of one. The first door to the right was number sixteen, where we were supposed to meet the interviewer.

J.C. glanced in through the side window. "No reception area," he said. "Just one large room. Feels like the sort of place where someone grabs you the moment you walk in. You black out, and then . . . *BAM* . . . three kidneys."

"*Three?*" Ivy asked.

"Sure," J.C. replied. "They need unwitting mules for their illegal organ trade."

"And exactly *how* unwitting are you going to be when you wake up with an incision in your abdomen? Wouldn't you immediately run to the doctor?"

His eyes narrowed. "Well, the doctor's obviously *in on it*, Ivy."

I looked to Tobias, who was still smiling. He nodded toward a painting on the hallway wall. "That's by Albert Bierstadt," he said. "*Among the Sierra Nevada Mountains*. The original hangs in the Smithsonian, as one of the most famous works of the Hudson River School." His calming tone was a relaxing contrast to J.C.'s jovial—but still deep-seated—paranoia. "I've always loved how the clouds part to illuminate the dark wilderness: a representation of the Creation through the lens of the American frontier. Our eyes are inexorably drawn toward that central light, as if we are being accepted into heaven."

"Or," Ivy observed, "perhaps the clouds are closing, and the landscape is dimming as God withdraws and leaves men in darkness."

Startled, I glanced sharply at Ivy. She was usually the religious one, sticking up for all things Christian and holy. She shrugged and looked away.

I knocked, and the door opened to reveal a tall, mature Asian woman with a square face and prominent smile lines. "Ah! Mr. Leeds. Excellent." She gestured for us to enter, and J.C.—of course—went first.

He ducked under her arm, deftly avoiding touching a real person, then looked around, hand on his weapon. Finally he nodded for the rest of us to enter.

The interviewer had set out a group of chairs for us, and she stood by the door a conspicuously long

time for all of us to enter. She'd done her homework. Though she waited too long—she couldn't see
the aspects—her effort did help with the illusion, for
which I was grateful.

Ivy and Tobias settled themselves while J.C. continued to inspect the room. Large windows to our right
looked out on the curb, where Wilson stood beside my
limo. The far left wall of the room was dominated by
a large saltwater fish tank. The rest of the décor was in
a "writing den" theme, with hardwood bookcases and
deep green carpeting.

I stepped up to the window and nodded toward Wilson, who waved back.

"Three today, then?" the interviewer asked.

I turned around, frowning.

"I followed your eyes," she said, pointing to the
chairs where Ivy and Tobias sat, then to where J.C.
had been standing—though he'd moved to search the
bookshelves for secret passages.

"Only three," I said.

"Ivy, Tobias, J.C.?"

"You *have* done your homework."

"I like to be prepared," the woman said, settling
down in her own seat. "I'm Jenny, by the way, in case
Liza didn't say."

This woman was Jenny Zhang, reporter and bestsell-
ing writer. She specialized in salacious pop-biographies
that rode the lines between information, entertainment, and voyeurism. She had won awards, but really,
she was just another hack who had fought her way
out of the clickbait trenches and earned a measure of
respectability.

I wished I'd never promised Liza the favor of doing
an interview with one of her friends, but I was stuck.

Hopefully Jenny wouldn't keep me too long, and her eventual book wouldn't be *too* painful.

She nodded toward the seats, but I remained beside the window. "Suit yourself," she said, getting out a notepad. She pointed at my aspects. "J.C., Tobias, Ivy. Id, ego, superego."

"Oh, *great*," Ivy said. "One of those. Tell her we've been over this. It doesn't fit."

"We're not fans," I said to Jenny, "of that psychological profile."

"Ivy's the one complaining?" Jenny asked. "She's a repository of your understanding of human nature—you've externalized in her your people skills and your understanding of relationships. She's reportedly very cynical. What does that say about you, I wonder?"

I shifted uncomfortably.

"Hey," J.C. said. "That's not bad."

"But you've also created a personification of peace and relaxation." Jenny pointed her pencil toward one of the seats. She had them reversed, but obviously she meant Tobias this time. "You say he's a historian, but how often does his knowledge of history prove relevant?"

"Frequently," I said.

"That's not what I hear," Jenny said. "You claim to have limited 'slots' in a given team of aspects. Imagining too many at once is difficult, so you bring only a few with you at a time. Yet you always take these three. J.C.—your sense of paranoia and self-preservation—is a logical inclusion. As is Ivy, who can help you cope with the social norms of the outside world. But why Tobias?"

"She knows too much," Ivy said. "Something's wrong with this interview."

"Do we really need to panic?" Tobias said. "So she's read the previous profiles people have done of Stephen. Surely, we should expect that. Wouldn't we be more suspicious if she hadn't come in with some theories about our nature?"

I idled by the window, but finally J.C. nodded and sat down. He was satisfied. I stepped away from the window, but didn't sit. Instead, I walked up to the fish tank. It was extravagant, with variegated corals and beautiful lighting. So much work to create what amounted to a prison.

Jenny was writing on her notepad. What *did* she find so fascinating? I'd barely said anything.

I watched the fish pick at the coral, eating at their own confines. "Don't you have any other questions for me?" I finally asked Jenny. "Everyone else wants to know how I distinguish reality from hallucination. Or they want to know what it feels like to assimilate knowledge—then manifest it as an aspect."

"What happened to Ignacio?" Jenny asked.

I spun on her. Tobias raised a hand to his lips, gasping softly.

"You mentioned Ignacio in past interviews," Jenny said, watching me with poised pencil. "One of your favorite aspects. A chemist? And yet, in your recent case with the motor-oil-eating bacteria, you didn't involve him at all. Curious."

Ignacio. He, like Justin, was . . . was no longer one of my aspects.

Tobias cleared his throat. "Did you see she has an Algernon Blackwood book on the shelf? Original Arkham House edition, which is my favorite. The feel of the paper—the scent . . . it is the scent of lore itself."

"You've frozen up," Jenny noted. "Can you *lose* aspects, Mr. Leeds?"

"Original Arkham House editions are ... are rare ... though that depends on who you want to read. I once had a copy of Bradbury's *Dark Carnival* from them, though the cover ..."

"What happened?" Jenny asked. "Did they simply move out?"

"The cover ... did not ... age ... well. ..."

"Ivy," I whispered.

"Right, right," she said, standing up. "Okay, so she's acting like this is an innocent question, but I don't buy it. She knew this would touch a nerve. Look how tightly she holds that pencil, hanging on your words."

"I'm sorry," Tobias said, dabbing at his brow with a handkerchief. "I am not helpful right now, am I?"

"She's goading us," J.C. said, standing up. He rested his hand on Ivy's shoulder. "What do we do?"

"She wants to push us off balance," Ivy decided. "Steve, you need to reassert control of the conversation."

"But *how much does she know*?" Tobias asked. "Did she really guess what happened to Ignacio? You don't speak of these things often." He cocked his head. "Stan says ... Stan says she must be working for *them*."

"Not helping, Tobias!" Ivy said, glaring at him.

"Quiet," I said to them. "Quiet, *all of you*."

They quieted. I locked eyes with Jenny, who now sat calmly twirling her pencil between two fingers. Feigned nonchalance.

I couldn't keep unraveling every time Ignacio or Justin came up. I had to control this.

I was *not* crazy.

"I'm not comfortable talking about this topic," I said, finally walking over and taking the seat she'd provided for me.

"Why not?"

"Different question, please."

"Have you lost any aspects besides Ignacio?"

"I can sit here all day, Jenny," I said. "Repeating the same words over and over. Is that how you want to waste your interview?"

The pencil stopped twirling. "Very well. Another question then." She shuffled through her papers. "You've maintained throughout all your interviews that you are not insane—that by your definition, 'insanity' is the line beyond which an individual's psychology impinges upon their ability to live a normal life. A line you've never crossed."

"Exactly," I said. "The media pretends that 'insanity' is this magical state that is simply on or off. Like it's a disease you can catch. They miss the nuance. The human brain's structure and chemistry are incredibly complex, and certain traits which—in the extreme—are deemed insane by society can be present in many so-called normal people, and contribute greatly to their success."

"So you deny that mental illness is, indeed, an illness?"

"I didn't say that." I glanced at my aspects. Ivy, who sat down, primly crossing her legs. Tobias, who stood and strolled over to the window, looking up to where he thought he could see Stan the astronaut up in his satellite. J.C., who had moved to lounge by the door, hand on his gun.

"I'm just saying," I continued, "that the definition of the word 'insanity' is a moving target, and depends greatly upon the person being discussed. If someone's means of thinking is different from your own, but those thought patterns don't disrupt their life, why try to 'fix' them? I don't need to be fixed. If I did, my life would be out of control."

"That's a false dichotomy," Jenny said. "You could be both in need of help *and* in control."

"I'm fine."

"And your aspects don't disrupt your life?"

"Depends on how annoying J.C. is being at the moment."

"Hey!" J.C. said. "I don't deserve that."

All three of us looked at him.

". . . today," he added. "I've been good."

Ivy cocked an eyebrow. "On the way here, you said—and I quote—'The police shouldn't be so racist to them towel-heads, because it isn't their fault they were born in China or wherever.'"

"See, being good." J.C. paused. "Should I have called them 'towel-headed Americans' or something . . . ?"

"Your id is speaking out?" Jenny looked from me to J.C. She was good at following my attention.

"He is *not* my id," I said. "Don't try to pretend he somehow articulates my secret desires."

"I'm not certain he can *articulate* anything," Ivy added. "As doing so would, by definition, require more than grunts."

J.C. rolled his eyes.

I stood up and walked over to the fish tank again. I always wondered . . . did the fish know they were in a cage? Could they comprehend what had happened to them, that their entire world was artificial?

"So," Jenny said. "Perhaps we could track your status, Mr. Leeds. Three years ago, during your last interview, you said you were feeling better than you ever had. Is that still the case? Have you gotten better, or worse, over the years?"

"It doesn't work that way," I said, watching a little black and red fish dart behind some fake yellow coral.

"I don't get 'better' or 'worse' because I'm not sick. I simply am who I am."

"And you never before considered your . . . state . . . to be an affliction?" Jenny asked. "Because very early reports paint a different picture. They describe a frightened man who claimed he was surrounded by demons, each whispering instructions to him."

"I . . ."

That had been a long time ago. *Find a purpose,* Sandra had taught me. *Do something with the voices. Make them serve you.*

"Hey," J.C. interrupted, "I'm gonna go grab some jerky or something at that gas station. Anyone want anything?"

"Wait!" I said, spinning away from the fish tank. "I might need you."

"What?" J.C. said, hand on the doorknob. "Need me to be the butt of more jokes? I'm sure you'll live."

He stepped out, then pulled the door closed. I stood, speechless. *He'd actually left.* Usually when J.C. disobeyed, it was because I tried to leave him behind—or because I didn't want him practicing with his guns. He disobeyed to protect me. He didn't just . . . just walk away.

Ivy ran to the door and peeked after him. "Want me to go after him?"

"No," I whispered.

"So," Jenny said. "We were talking about you getting worse?"

I . . . I . . .

"That's an Achilles tang," Tobias said, stepping up to me and nodding toward the little red and black fish. "It looks black, but it's actually dark brown, sometimes even a dark purple. A beautiful, but difficult fish to keep; that spot on the tail is the origin of its name—as it looks a little like a bleeding wound on the heel."

I took a deep breath. J.C. was just being J.C. We were talking too much about aspects—and he hated being reminded he wasn't real. That was why he'd left.

"I've had some rough patches lately, perhaps," I said to Jenny. "I need something to focus my aspects and my mind."

"A case?" Jenny said, pulling a few sheets out from behind her notepad. "I might be able to help with that." She set the sheets on the coffee table in front of her.

"Ah . . ." Ivy said, walking over to me. "That's her angle, Steve. This is all preamble. She wants to *hire* you."

"She was pushing you off balance," Tobias said with a nod. "Perhaps to get herself into a better bargaining position?"

This was familiar ground. I relaxed, then walked over and settled down in the seat across from Jenny. "All this to offer me a case? You people. You realize that you can just *ask*."

"You have a tendency to return letters unopened, Leeds," the reporter said, but she did have the decency to blush.

"What is this . . ." I said, skimming. "Machine that can use big data to predict a person's exact wants, updated minute by minute, incorporating brain chemistry with historic decisions, removing the need for most choices . . ."

"Kind of interesting," Ivy said, reading over my shoulder. "I guess it will depend on what she's willing to pay, and what exactly she wants us to do."

"What do you need from me?" I asked Jenny.

"I need you to steal a—"

My pocket buzzed. I absently glanced at the phone, expecting a text from J.C. He'd probably sent me a picture of himself trying to drink straight from the soda machine at the gas station, or some similar nonsense.

But the text wasn't from J.C. It was from Sandra. The woman who originally taught me to use my aspects; the woman who had brought me sanity. The woman who had vanished soon after.

The text read, simply, *HELP*.

TWO

I tore from the room, followed by Ivy and Tobias. Out
on the street, Wilson and his niece saw something was
up, and he alertly opened the car door for me. I waved
Ivy and Tobias in. J.C.? Where was J.C.?

No time. I climbed into the back seat of the limo.

"Wait!" Jenny shouted from the door of the building. "What about my interview! I was promised a full
session!"

"I'll start it up again another time!"

"But the case!" she said, holding up her papers. "I
need to see how your aspects respond to this situation.
Aren't you intrigued by—"

I slammed the door shut. On a normal day, perhaps
I *would* have been intrigued. Not today. I held up the
phone for Ivy and Tobias.

"You're sure it's from her?" Ivy asked.

"It's from the number she left on the table that
morning," I said. "I've kept it in my contacts list on

every phone I've had since." We'd tried tracing it in the past, but phone records always listed it as unassigned.

Wilson climbed into the passenger-side front door, and his grandniece pulled on her coachman's cap and took the driver's seat. The car rumbled to life. "Where to, sir?" she asked.

I looked from Tobias to Ivy.

"It could be someone else spoofing the number," Ivy said. "Be careful."

Is it really you? I typed to her.

Destiny Place, she typed back. It was her nickname for Cramrid Hotel, the place where we'd first met. Another text soon followed: a sequence of numbers and nonsense characters.

What? I typed to her.

No reply.

"Sir?" Wilson asked from the front. "We're leaving?"

"Take us home," I said to Wilson.

His niece pulled us out onto the street and made a U-turn, heading back the way we'd come.

"What are those numbers?" Ivy asked, looking toward Tobias. "Do you recognize them?"

He shook his head.

"Sandra is worried that I might not be the one who has the phone," I said. "It's a cipher. She often did this sort of thing."

The other two shared a look. Both of them had been around when I'd known Sandra—or at least they'd been among the many shadows and apparitions I'd seen back then. But they hadn't been *completely* themselves until Sandra taught me to create aspects. Focusing my attention, meditating, compartmentalizing my mind. They'd transformed naturally from shadows and whispered voices into distinct individuals.

"We should ignore it," Ivy said. "She's playing with you again, Steve. If that's really her."

"If he ignores it, Ivy," Tobias said softly, "it will haunt him for the rest of his life. You know he needs to pursue this."

Ivy sat back, folding her arms. With her blonde hair in a tight bun and her no-nonsense pantsuit, you might easily think her cold. But when she looked away out the window, there were tears in the corners of her eyes.

Tobias placed his hand on her shoulder.

Oddly, I felt out of place. I should have offered her comfort, reassured her I wasn't looking for a cure, or a way to be rid of her. I'd always promised Ivy that wasn't the point of finding Sandra.

I did none of this. Instead, I stared at the phone screen. *HELP.* Twelve years ago, Sandra had saved me from the nightmare my life had become. Dared I hope that I'd be able to be with her again? Dared I hope that she'd be able to do something about the way I was sliding, my aspects getting worse, my—

The image on my screen was obscured as a new text popped up.

Dude. DUDE! Tell me I didn't just see you drive off.

We're heading home, I wrote to J.C. *Grab an Uber or something.*

I got you a doughnut and everything. With sprinkles. And you haven't eaten it yet?

Sure I did, he wrote back. *But I knew I probably would, so I bought two. Can't promise the second will survive the trip home. These are dangerous times, Skinny, and it's a rough neighborhood for a tasty doughnut to be wandering about on its own.*

J.C., Sandra just texted me. She needs help.

I didn't get a response for a good minute and a half.

Stay at home until I get there, he wrote.

I'll try.

Skinny. I'm telling you, wait.

I tucked the phone into my pocket. Three more texts came from him, but I ignored them. I wanted J.C. to hurry, and nothing would make that happen more efficiently than letting him think I was going into danger without him.

Not that there was anything he'd be able to do. He was a hallucination, not a real bodyguard. Though . . . there *had* been that one time, when he'd moved my hand—as if he were controlling it. And that time he'd pushed me out of the car . . .

I texted Kalyani en route, so the aspects were waiting by the windows when I got back to the mansion. I pushed open the car door as soon as we were near the house. Wilson's niece yelped, then stopped the car.

I strode across the lawn.

"Want me to get the White Room ready?" Ivy asked, hurrying up.

"We don't have time for that," I said. "Get me Audrey, Ngozi, Armando, and Chin."

"Got it."

We reached the front doors, and I took a deep breath, bracing myself. All of my aspects would be here. That could—*would*—be taxing.

"Master Leeds?" Wilson asked, stepping up to my side. "Might I discuss something with you?"

"Can it wait?" I said, then pushed open the doors.

It hit me like a sudden weight—as if someone had slipped bars of lead in my pockets. Some fifty people, standing inside, all talking at once. Some were panicked. Others excited. A few haunted. The same name was on all their lips. Sandra.

Tobias joined me, and he seemed winded. From that

short walk from the car? He *was* getting old. What . . . what happened when one of my aspects died of old age?

"Can you quiet the crowd?" I asked him.

"Certainly," Tobias said. He stepped among them and began explaining. His calming voice worked for most of them, though as I walked up the stairs of the grand entry hall, one woman broke off from the others and chased after me.

"Hey," Audrey said. Plump with dark hair, she tended to be a little unusual even for an aspect. "Sandra's back, eh? Is she going to un-crazy you? I'd like forewarning if I'm going to vanish forever; I've got plans for to-night."

"Date?" I asked.

"Binge-watching *Gilmore Girls* and eating like seventeen bowls of imaginary popcorn. I can't *technically* gain weight, right, since I already weigh nothing?"

I smiled wanly as we reached the top steps.

"So . . ." she said. "You doing okay?"

"No," I said. "Take this, see if you can figure out what this sequence of numbers means." I tossed her the phone.

Which, of course, she fumbled and dropped. I winced. Audrey looked at me sheepishly, but it wasn't her fault. My mind had *forced* her to fumble it—because she wasn't actually real. I'd thrown my phone toward empty space. It had been a while since I'd made that kind of mistake.

I picked up the phone—its screen had cracked, but not badly—and showed Audrey what Sandra had sent. Audrey was the closest thing we had to a cryptographer. Actually, she was getting pretty good at it, now that I'd read a few more books on the subject.

"Thoughts?" I asked.

"Give me a few minutes," she said. "Those characters in the string are probably wildcards . . . but for what . . ." She scribbled the string on her hand with a pen. "You going to deal with that mess?" she asked, gesturing toward the aspects down below.

"No," I said.

"You going to at least count who didn't show up?"

I hesitated, then leaned against the banister and did a quick count, already feeling a headache coming on. No Armando, but that wasn't odd. He rarely left his room, or his "kingdom in exile" as he put it. Ngozi had come, which was good. She wore a face mask and gloves, but Kalyani had been working with her—and they'd been going out lately. Like, the actual outdoors.

Let's see . . . no Arnaud, he's probably sitting in his room, oblivious as always. No Leroy. Isn't he on a skiing vacation? No Lua. Maybe in the yard, working on his hearth? He'd been constructing his own "stone age" house in the back yard, using only technology he could build by himself.

I hastened through the second floor's hallways to Arnaud's room. The light above the door was on, indicating that he didn't want to be disturbed, so I knocked. Finally he answered, a diminutive balding man with a soft French accent.

"Oh!" he said. "Monsieur!"

"How's the device, Arnaud?" I asked.

"Come and see!" He opened the door, letting me into his laboratory. There were blackout curtains over the windows, since he was frequently developing film these days. Bits and pieces of machinery were neatly laid out on the workbench. A cigar in an ashtray indicated that Ivans had been helping him. He was the only aspect that still smoked.

Taped to the wall was a series of pictures. Winter scenes of the mansion.

"I've only been able to get it to go back about six months at most," Arnaud said, stepping over to a device sitting on the table: a big old-school camera, like the ones you'd see news photographers use in old movies. "Just as you surmised, the flash is the most important part. But I still haven't figured out exactly how it penetrates time."

I took the camera, feeling its weight in my hands. A camera that could take photos of the past. The device had been involved in one of my most dangerous cases.

"I've now fitted it with instant film," Arnaud said. "It should work. This dial here? That sets the time focus. It's most accurate at short range, just a few days. The farther back you go, the blurrier the pictures become. I do not know how the original inventor solved this, but so far, I am at a loss. It is perhaps related to moments blurring together the farther back we try to make the light penetrate."

"It'll do, Arnaud. It's fantastic." I glanced to the side and noticed a few prints on the ground, each cut in half. "What are those?"

"Oh." Arnaud shuffled, looking embarrassed. "I thought it would be good to have Armando look them over, as he is the expert in photography. I know physics, but not the taking of good shots. Armando agreed and destroyed several of my photos, as they were not 'significant' enough."

I sighed, then packed the camera in a bag that Arnaud pointed out. Part of me already knew that the device would be ready. I'd been spending evenings in this room, working with my hands as Arnaud instructed me on the repairs. But those sliced photos were new.

I was getting very, *very* tired of Armando's shtick. Each of my aspects could be challenging in their own way, but none were so outright disobedient.

I shouldered the camera. "You did well, Arnaud. Thank you."

"Thank you! I am pleased to hear it." He hesitated beside the door as I opened it. "Could I . . . return to France now? And my family."

I froze. "Return?"

"Yes, Étienne. I understand how important our work here was, and it was truly engaging. But my job, it is finished, correct? I could return now?"

"You want to . . . leave. Not be an aspect any longer?"

"If it would not be too much trouble."

"I . . ." I'd never had an aspect want to leave, other than for a brief vacation. "Let me get back to you. I mean, I won't keep you here against your will, but the camera isn't completely finished yet. Maybe . . . maybe we could work out . . . for your family to come here . . . or for you to live part-time back in Nice?"

"Thank you," he said.

I pulled the door shut, troubled. Wilson walked up, bearing a tray of much-needed lemonade. "Master Leeds," he said. "I *do* need to talk to you about a small matter. Insignificant, really, but I don't want you growing too distracted to . . ."

I took a long pull on a glass of lemonade, then slung the camera bag off my shoulder. "Would you pack this camera in the car for me, Wilson? I need to talk to Armando. I'll make time to chat with you then, all right?"

I just . . . Sandra. I had to keep focused on Sandra. Sandra had *texted* me.

I checked the phone again as I walked up toward Armando's attic room. Nothing more from Sandra, just a few texts from J.C., complaining that his Uber driver had a "Gun-Free Zone" sticker on his car window.

As if that means anything, J.C.'s text said. *You can't simply "sticker" your way out of the Constitution, buddy.*

It was followed by: *And yeah, I just ate your dough-nut.*

I shook my head, knocking at the attic door. No response from Armando. Was he imposing "royal auditory sanctions" on me again? I pushed the door open, preparing myself to be shouted at. Armando claimed to be the rightful emperor of Mexico, and . . .

His room had been destroyed.

And there was blood on the walls.

THREE

Gouges in the plaster, like the claw marks of a feral beast. The bedding had been shredded. Stylish night photographs from cities around the world—Armando's prize collection—lay in confetti on the floor.

And the blood. Sprays were flung across nearly every surface. Suddenly, I felt thoughts fading from my memory. Knowledge and expertise dispersed like smoke from a snuffed candle.

I'd first gained Armando about eight years ago, when working on a missing person case. A woman had vanished, but then continued to upload selfies with famous monuments—though the security footage showed she'd never been at any of them. I'd used Sandra's technique, binge-reading about photo manipulation and imagining the information as a reservoir within me. I hadn't consciously created Armando, no more than I'd consciously given any of the aspects personalities, but he'd been the result. In the early days, we'd joked about his claim to the throne of Mexico, just as I now joked with J.C.

I felt that reservoir leaking away like blood from my veins. I grew cold and stumbled backward, horrified by the scene of carnage inside his room. I couldn't . . . I had to . . .

It was gone.

He was gone. I fell to my knees and let out a low moan that became a cry of agony. A breeze through the room's open window blew scraps of torn photographs into the hallway around me.

Mi Won was the first to arrive. She gasped, but—ever the professional—went inside to assist anyone who might need her medical skills. The other aspects began arriving in a steady stream, gathering around me, though in that moment . . . in that moment they seemed to fade into the background. A group of shadows. Mere silhouettes.

"Master Leeds!" Wilson said, rushing up. He passed right through several of the aspects, then knelt beside me. "Stephen? Please. What is wrong?"

Slowly, I let my hands relax. I let out a long sigh, and felt a strange calm come over me. I had to keep control. That was . . . that was what Sandra taught me.

"Wilson," I said, surprised at how even my voice sounded, "what was it you wanted to talk to me about?"

"Oh, never mind that! Sir? What is wrong? Why did you cry out?" He peered into the room.

"What do you see?" I whispered.

"Sir? It looks like it always does. Empty guest room. The bed made with a yellow comforter, tucked in."

"Pictures on the floor?" I asked.

"No, sir. Would you . . . like me to pretend there are?"

I shook my head.

"Sir, if I may say, you've been *most* strange lately. More, I mean. More than usual." The elderly butler wrung his hands. Behind him, his niece stood in the mouth of the attic stairwell, looking at us uncertainly.

"Am I causing it?" Wilson asked.

"Causing it?" I asked, blinking.

"Because of . . . today, sir."

"Today?"

"My retirement, Master Leeds. We've discussed it. Remember? It was going to be last month, but you asked me to stay on. But sir, today, I'm *seventy* today."

"Nonsense. You can't be . . ."

Retirement? We'd discussed it?

I could vaguely remember . . .

Mi Won left Armando's room and shook her head. The other aspects brightened into full color again, and their worried chattering suddenly filled my ears. Ivy pushed through them, then stepped toward the room. Mi Won grabbed her arm.

"I'm sorry," Mi Won said. "He's gone."

"What kind of gone?" Ivy demanded, then turned toward me. "Justin and Ignacio didn't just *go*. They became something else, something terrible. It's happening again, isn't it, Steve?"

I hauled myself to my feet, using the wall for support. "I can't . . . I can't keep imagining you all right now. Go to your rooms. Everyone who isn't on the mission. Ngozi, Ivy, Tobias."

"Did you want me?" Chin—Chowyun Chin—asked. He was wearing sunglasses as always, no matter the time of day.

"Sandra was always fond of puzzles," I said to him, "and so I might need to crack some computer codes. I want you and Audrey to stay ready and near her phone. But I think . . . I think I can only manage a few of you with me today. Please."

"Sure," Chin said. "You've got those new programs installed?"

I wiggled my phone. We'd been making enhancements.

"You cracked the screen?"

"Sorry."

He sighed, but then—with the others—retreated. Fifty figures, each distinct, each a chunk of my mind. People with lives, pasts, families, passions. At times, it was just *so much* to track. Kalyani gave me a hug as she joined Rahul. Ivans gave me a fist bump. Oliver let me hold his stuffed corgi, which I did for an embarrassingly long time, before they finally left me.

I tried to imagine what this was like for them, discovering that for the first time in years, I was losing control. That Sandra had returned—a figure who to most of them was mere legend.

Wilson looked on, helpless, though his niece—Barb—was more visibly disturbed by it all. Ivy studied her, shaking her head.

He's been training her for months now, I thought, remembering. *Because he's retiring. Leaving me.*

"Wilson," I said. "I . . . I realize—"

I cut off as I spotted something. The withdrawal of most of the aspects left a conspicuous figure standing in the hallway, holding a notepad. She was tall, Asian, and wearing a relaxed pantsuit. Jenny Zhang. The reporter.

I lurched toward her, shoving past Wilson and grabbing her by the shoulders. "How did you get in here!" I shouted, feeling betrayed, embarrassed. How *dare* she see me at my most vulnerable!

"You broke our promise," she snapped. "I need to get this down. For the book."

"Steve?" Ivy said.

"What book?" I said to Jenny. "I didn't give you permission to write a book! You're trespassing!"

"Steve, I think she can *see us.*"

I froze, my eyes locked with Jenny's. Then she turned and looked right at Ivy.

"Wilson," I said, growing cold, "can you see the person I'm holding right now?"

"Master Leeds? Is it one of your aspects?"

"*Can you see her?*"

"No. Unless you wish for me to . . . to pretend?"

Oh hell.

"What did we do earlier today?" I said to Wilson. "Where did we go?"

"Sir? Barb and I drove you around a poorer section of town, and we stopped at an abandoned building. I must admit I was worried, though grateful you told me to stay close by. You stood in an empty room for a while, then came running out."

I let go of Jenny, who straightened her jacket with an unperturbed air.

I put my hand to my head. It wasn't possible. I wasn't supposed to be crazy. The aspects . . . shielded me from that. *They* were insane, and I kept them organized. I . . . I could tell what was real. . . .

"Was Sandra real?" I asked Wilson.

"Yes, sir," he said. "You've never questioned that before. . . . Master Leeds? This *is* caused by my leaving, isn't it? I'm sorry. But sir, I just can't keep doing this. Not after the case with that assassin, and then the fire last year. Barb, though, she's *excited* to help you. She'll be good at it, sir."

I stood there until the sound of footsteps announced Tobias's arrival. Ivy ran to him and whispered to him, and the old historian nodded, running a hand through his powder-white hair. Then he smiled.

"It's all right," he said. "He's bound to be a little upset. Why, we've finally found Sandra!"

Ivy whispered something else, and Tobias glanced at Armando's room, lips pursing grimly. Then he smiled again, walked over, and gripped me—gently but firmly—on the shoulder. "Strength, Stephen. Let's pull through this. You can do it. You've always been able to do it."

"Armando . . ." I whispered.

"It happened. We just have to make sure it doesn't happen again. *Focus*. Sandra has returned."

I looked to Ivy, who pointedly did not look at Armando's room. "I think . . . I think maybe I've been wrong. You're right, Steve. We need to find Sandra. Maybe she's back for a reason; maybe someone up above is watching out for us."

Nearby, Jenny was writing all of this down. How on Earth had I created her? And why?

"Wilson?" I asked, showing him my phone. "Yes, I know it's cracked. Not that. The text."

"Help," he read, tilting his glasses and squinting. "And a sequence of numbers and letters. From . . . Sandra?"

I sighed in relief. So the text was real. Unless . . . unless Wilson was a hallucination too.

I couldn't go down *that* particular rabbit hole. I had to believe I had at least that shred of sanity left.

"Where's Ngozi?" I asked Ivy.

"Didn't you see her back off? The sight of the blood . . . I think she's getting some air."

My forensic scientist was a germophobe who couldn't stand the sight of blood. My brain was a very strange place sometimes.

"See if you can find her," I said to Ivy. "I want her along. You, her, me, Tobias, J.C.—once he catches up."

Ivy nodded and ran off.

"And me," Jenny noted.

"*Not* you," I said, walking toward the stairwell. Tobias walked with me and kept his hand on my shoulder, as if I were the frail old man, not him. We passed Barb and I looked her up and down. Short blonde hair, perky grin. So young. "I haven't scared you off?" I asked.

"Honestly, this is really interesting," she said. "You are *so* crazy."

"Go start the car and wait for me."

She ran off, and I looked back at Wilson. "Can she at least make lemonade?"

"My own recipe, sir. And I must say, she's taken to it with acumen." He hesitated. "Perhaps I could add another day or two—"

"No. This had to happen eventually, Wilson. You've given more than enough. More than anyone probably should have given." I'd already made sure there was something nice in the bank for him—I'd done that years ago, and for some reason, he'd just kept on with me. Perhaps he was the crazy one.

I started down the steps with Tobias. From above us on the stairs, Wilson watched us go. "Sir," he called after me. "If, for some reason, you aren't fighting terrorists or finding teleporting cats tonight, I would love to have you at the party. My brother is hosting it."

"A party?" I said, looking over my shoulder. "With *real people*?"

"The best kind, sir."

"Yeah. I'll pass. But thanks anyway."

FOUR

I haven't always been this bad about real people. It was only . . . what, a year and a half ago that I'd been going out on dates? All had been unmitigated disasters, but at least I'd tried.

Ivy claimed I unintentionally sabotaged those interactions. She had all kinds of theories as to why, none of them particularly flattering.

I found Audrey, Chin, and a few of the others in the game room. It was a place they could be around each other for mutual support in facing what was coming. Stormy was making drinks. Entering the room, I braced myself and tried to keep my focus. Sandra. Sandra would know how to help me.

To be honest, I'd been sliding for months now. Maybe years. But I *could* turn it around.

Near the bar, Audrey had her feet up on an ottoman, chewing on some Sugar Babies candies while watching cat videos on her phone. Ever since J.C. had gotten a phone, the rest had wanted one—except Harrison, the technophobe.

"Check it out," Audrey said, showing me a cat meowing as its owner opened a can of food—then stopping abruptly every time the owner stopped. "I can't get enough of this stuff."

I just stood there, staring at her.

"What?" she asked.

"We're in the *middle* of a disaster," I whispered. "Aspects are being corrupted, Audrey."

"Yeah. Can't decide if I'll be the next to go, since I know too much, or if it would be more ironic for me to go last."

"You were supposed to be—"

"Relax," she said, showing me a piece of paper. "I cracked it. I needed a key to the cipher, which turned out to be the room number at the hotel where you two first met. With that plugged in, it didn't take long. These are GPS coordinates."

I took the paper with a relieved sigh. "Where is it?"

"City fairgrounds. There's an outdoor performance tonight. Starts in a half hour." Audrey checked her phone. "Right at sundown."

That sounded like Sandra. I tucked the paper in my pocket, then turned to go.

"Hey," Audrey said, "you think . . . maybe you can imagine me a shotgun or something?" She bit her lip. "In case, you know, this goes south? And . . . the nightmares come to . . ."

"That won't happen."

"And if it does?"

"Break into J.C.'s room."

"And set off the inevitable booby traps? You know he has them. Even if we haven't seen them, he has them."

She was right. He probably had a minefield installed under the floor or something.

Audrey chuckled as Stormy brought her a mimosa, and I left, a bitter taste in my mouth. If Audrey was worried, that was very bad.

The halls of the mansion were oddly quiet, contrasting with the disturbance earlier. I didn't pass a soul, human or imaginary, as I walked toward the door. The place felt so hollow, I almost worried that they'd all just . . . vanished on me. Then I heard Ivans shouting from the conservatory, where another group had gathered.

I tried calming myself with some deep breaths, and checked outside. I spotted Ivy and Ngozi near the far hedge. Ivy was very careful not to put her arm around Ngozi, but her posture was encouraging. Eventually, the two walked over.

Ngozi was still wearing a face mask and gloves, but she removed the mask as she stepped up to me. I always forgot how tall she was; she easily had five inches on me. She spoke with a lofty accent, Nigerian with a hint of her British education. "I'm sorry. I . . . panicked."

"Can you handle this?" I asked.

"Yes. If you're sure you need me."

I wasn't sure. I couldn't be sure *what* this case would require—but I had a hunch. Things were never simple when Sandra was involved. And if we couldn't find anything at the coordinates Sandra had sent, Ngozi was our best bet at investigating a possible crime scene.

"I am sure I need you," I said. "But there might be a crowd at the fairgrounds. Are you going to freak out, like last time?"

"Depends. Is someone going to try to give me leprosy this time?"

"*One* person sneezed on you, Ngozi."

"Did you *hear* that sneeze? Do you know how many germs the average uninterrupted sneeze can produce? Projected into the air, hanging like little mines, sticking to your face, your skin, infiltrating your system . . ." She shivered, then held up a gloved hand to interrupt my next complaint. "I can do it, Stephen Leeds. I *will* do it. This is . . . a special case."

Ivy and Ngozi walked to the limo, which was still parked by the curb. Barb was polishing the hood ornament, but she'd left the back door open, in case aspects needed to enter. Tobias sat inside already, reading a thick book to keep his mind off our troubles. That made three. I could handle three.

Four, I thought, checking my phone. There was no response from J.C., so I texted him. *Did you stop to catch a movie or something?*

A response came shortly after. *Stupid Uber stopped and picked someone else up, then drove the wrong direction. I finally managed to get out at Seventeenth and State.*

I sighed. J.C., *did you just climb in a random Uber?*

. . . Maybe.

What were you thinking!

I've got my stealth suit on. They can't see me. Figured I could head the right direction, then get out and take another.

It was as close as he ever came to admitting he wasn't real. Where another aspect would have been fine fudging things a little, catching an imaginary Uber, J.C. . . . well, J.C. didn't play by the same rules. He tried to be real.

Or my brain tried to make him real. Or . . . or I don't know. My head was pounding, and as I composed a reply, a large shadow fell over me. I glanced back and noticed Lua—a three-hundred-pound Pacific Islander—trying to read over my shoulder. Instead of his traditional survivalist gear, he was wearing his Cub Scout shirt. *That's right.* Tonight had been pack meeting. He'd entirely missed the chaos inside.

"Hey, boss," he said. He nudged his chin toward my phone. "You need me? I can do a J.C. impression. Grab a big knife. Glare at everyone."

"No," I said. "Thanks anyway."

"You sure? If we're tracking someone, I can track people."

"We won't be leaving the city—I'm hardly likely to get trapped in the wilderness or something."

"No problem, boss," he said. Then he clapped me on the shoulder. "Hey. Surviving isn't just about making shoes from vines and an oven from mud and stones, you know? Keep your eyes up, boss. Shoulders back."

"I . . . It's getting hard, Lua. Harder every day. My own brain fights against me."

"No. We're your brain, boss. We fight *with* you." Before stepping away, he clasped my arm and then gave me a hug.

And honestly, I felt a little better as I settled into the car. *Meet us at the fairgrounds on Thirtieth,* I told J.C. *That might be easier.*

I suppose, he texted back. *But can't you just wait?*

Just meet us there. Don't take someone else's Uber. Here, I'm sending a cab for you. I had a few drivers around town who were willing to accept large sums to drive to a spot, open the door, then close it and drive an empty car to another spot. I should have done that for J.C. in the first place. I would have, if I'd been thinking straight.

Fine, he sent back. *But be careful. Something feels wrong about all of this.*

I mumbled to Barb where I wanted to go, and she pulled out. But I continued staring at the phone.

"You have to tell J.C. what happened, Stephen," Tobias said from the seat beside me.

But I didn't. Not yet. At least one of us could go on pretending, for a little while, that we hadn't lost Armando. I locked the phone and tucked it into my jacket pocket.

F I V E

Dusk had fallen by the time we reached the fairgrounds, which—this time of year—was just a tramped-down field of dirt on the east side of the city. A large swell of people had gathered as if for a concert—they were common here—but were currently milling among vendors. The performance wasn't to start for another few minutes.

Barb dropped us off at the curb. I absently bought us all tickets—paying for my aspects without thinking—then led us among the evening throng. The crowd made it difficult to see, but announcements were being made from a stage set up on the dirt ahead.

I hated crowds. Always had. It's difficult for my aspects to maintain the illusion when people are milling around, mashed together, breathing the same stale air and conversing in a buzzing cacophony. . . .

So maybe Ngozi came by her germophobia honestly. She stuck closest to me, eyes forward, hand on my shoulder. I was proud of her, all things considered.

Ahead of us, the announcer quieted, and bright flares of light came from the stage.

"Are those *fireworks?*" Ivy asked from just behind us.

"No," Tobias said. He dodged to the side, narrowly avoiding a collision with a little girl who shot past holding an ice cream cone. "I've read about what this is." He gestured to an open spot up ahead.

We took refuge from the crowds under the eaves of a small toolshed for the fairgrounds staff, and I got my first good look at the performance. Men in protective clothing stood on the stage and threw *molten metal* up against a black fireproof backdrop.

The effect was dazzling, and for a moment the crowd seemed to vanish. Even my urgent worry about Sandra faded. The performers would dip a ladle into a bucket of the metal, then fling it up in a burning swirl. When the metal hit the wall, it splashed outward, exploding into thousands upon thousands of glittering sparks. These fell in waves, like molten rain.

It *was* like fireworks, but somehow more primal. No gunpowder or smoke. Just buckets, a steady hand, and perhaps an unhealthy disregard for one's own safety.

"It's called Da Shuhua," Tobias said. "I've always wanted to see the performance in person. The story goes that hundreds of years ago, blacksmiths in Nan-chuan, China, had no money for fireworks. So they came up with something else, using what they had on hand."

The performers threw with frantic energy, ladle after ladle—as if they were trying to stay ahead of gravity and get all the fire into the air at once. The explosions of sparks created streaky patterns in the air, like tiny sprites flaring to life for a mayfly existence—one brilliant moment of life and glory, before succumbing to the cold.

"That *can't* be safe," Ngozi said.

"Wonder and irresponsibility are often bedfellows, Ngozi," Tobias responded. I glanced at him, watching sparks reflect in his eyes. "The name Da Shuhua translates to something like 'tree flowers' and implies that you beat the tree and the flowers appear. You take something ordinary and make it *extraordinary*. All it takes is two thousand degrees."

We watched until the performance reached an intermission. The crowd in the immediate vicinity started to disperse, seeking out food vendors or nearby carnival rides. I checked my phone, showing it to the others. Sandra's coordinates indicated a spot ahead near the edge of the fairgrounds.

"We should be careful," Ngozi said. "What would J.C. say?"

"Probably something vaguely racist and/or threatening," Tobias noted.

"No, no, he'd say something like . . ." Ivy adopted a husky voice. "'Guys, stop. Look very carefully. Do you see it? Do you see that? Is that . . . *funnel cake*?'"

Ngozi chuckled. But she was right, we should be careful. Fortunately, I'd prepared for this. I rounded the dusty fairgrounds, eventually positioning us a close—but safe—distance away from the coordinates. Judging by my phone's map, our goal was a small path running near some trampled grass. *That bench,* I thought. I texted Barb, then settled down near some bushes where I could watch the bench without getting too close.

"Ngozi," I said, unpacking some binoculars she could use. "Give that spot a look. Tell me what you see. Pretend it's a crime scene."

"What good is that going to do?" Ivy said. "She can't just *pretend* there's blood around."

"Forensics isn't just used to study homicides," Ngozi said absently, reaching into my pack with her handkerchief, then taking out another pair of binoculars. "The various forensic disciplines are simply studies of the way that science interacts with the law, or applying science to the law." She scanned the area. "I usually start with a question. What about the scene is odd, out of place . . . ?"

I unpacked the camera, then tried to affix it to the tripod—and failed. Damn it.

"That's because you lost Armando?" Jenny asked. "You can't even work a *tripod* now that you no longer have your photo expert?"

I looked up sharply. Yes, there she was, the aspect with the notepad.

"How did you get here?" I demanded.

"Uber."

Sure, *she* could work it out and not get lost. I sighed, then gave up on the tripod. I probably didn't need it anyway.

"How are you going to use that?" Jenny asked, taking notes, narrowing her eyes. "Isn't it the flash that's the important part—the part that lets you take photos of the past? We've set up too far away for that to work."

She was right, but it was also true that I was likely to drop the stupid thing if I tried to take a picture. Losing an aspect left me bizarrely incompetent, particularly right after they left. Eventually, the others could compensate a little.

I'd still never be the same. But again, I'd allowed for that. As Ngozi continued her investigation, I stood up, looking past Jenny—trying to ignore her—toward Barb, who was approaching.

"Wow," she said, chauffeur's cap tucked under her

arm. "Did you see those spark things? That was *awesome*."

"I need you to do something that might be dangerous," I said.

"Sure!"

I tried not to let her naive enthusiasm put me off. I should be *glad* she wanted to help, not annoyed. It was just that she felt like the others. Regular people. Who treated what I did as some kind of carnival act.

"There's a bench over there near that hot dog cart. See it?" I handed her the camera. "Leave your cap and jacket here—they're too conspicuous. Go over there and pretend you're taking pictures of the stage and the crowds, but get the bench in every shot."

"Cool," she said.

"Here's the important part," I said, holding up the camera and showing her the dial on the flash that would change the time of day—in the past—that she was taking pictures of. "Rotate this one tick each picture, all right? It's *very important*."

She rolled her eyes, which didn't inspire confidence, then handed me her coachman's cap and jacket. She wandered off inspecting the camera, which was more user friendly than it looked. Arnaud simply liked a retro aesthetic. Theoretically, the . . . um . . . thing with the . . . er . . . other things . . . wouldn't need . . . to be twisted . . . or . . .

Well, I was reasonably certain it would take pictures just fine for someone who didn't know picture taking.

"Clever," Jenny said. "Using a real person to do what you cannot."

"I am a real person."

"You know what I mean," she said, scribbling some notes in her pad. "Why do you always insist on doing so much alone? If you had a team of real assistants, not just the occasional chauffeur forced to pitch in, how much further could you go?"

Tobias settled down on a boulder to wait, while Ivy demanded that I show her my phone to see where J.C. was—the app tracked the car I'd sent for him. It was at a stoplight nearby, though it appeared to have been caught in the traffic surrounding the festival.

Another round of tree flowers started as Barb was taking her photos. Well, that would just give her some extra cover. Ngozi watched carefully to see if anyone reacted to Barb, and so I took a turn with the real pair of binoculars. Naturally, Ngozi could only notice something if I saw it.

I watched the sparks. They seemed more . . . violent to me this time. Angry. The flashes from Barb's camera and its unique bulb seemed stark to me, flagrant.

I saw no sign of Sandra.

Barb strolled back and delivered the photos, which were starting to develop. "Great," I said, distracted as I looked through them. "Go wait in the car. Keep that camera safe."

"That's it?" she said. "That's all I get to do?"

"Other than wait in the car? Yes."

She took back her cap and coat, and left, muttering to herself. I looked up and found Jenny regarding me, then making another note.

"All right," Ngozi said as I sat down on the boulder by Tobias. "Let's see . . ."

Though it was getting dark, the pictures—all save the first—were during the day. Timestamps at the bottom indicated that each successive picture was a half hour farther back in the past. With eight total, we had four hours of data.

Hopefully Ngozi could make something of them,

treating the area as a crime scene. I flipped through the pictures one after another to give Ngozi a glimpse, then we'd spend time analyzing each one for—

That was Sandra.

I froze, holding the next-to-last picture. A narrow face, with almost ghostly features. Her hair was longer and straight, but it was her. Sitting on the bench, reaching toward the wastebasket beside her.

Ivy gasped. Jenny took notes. Ngozi lowered her face mask and pulled off a surgical glove, then rested her fingertips on the picture. Tobias put his hand on my shoulder and squeezed.

She'd been here. She'd actually been here, not four hours ago. But where had she gone?

"She texted you," Ngozi said, "then dropped something in the rubbish bin."

"Then let's go get it!" I said, suddenly heedless of any risk.

"Hold on a moment," Ngozi said, making me check the last photo. "I said *wait*. Tobias, restrain him." She shivered, putting her glove back on as Tobias held me still. His wasn't a strong grip, but there was something demanding about it.

"See here," Ngozi continued. "This man buying a hot dog from the vendor? He's back again in this other picture, and *again* in this picture."

I sat back and squinted at the photos. At a prompt from Ivy, I used my phone for light so we could see them better.

Behind us, the crowd oohed and aahed over another round of sparks in the air.

"So . . ." I said. "He likes hot dogs?"

Ngozi cocked an eyebrow at me.

"Either that," I said, "or both the patron and the vendor are involved."

"Look here," Ngozi said, pointing at another picture. "They're whispering together. They're definitely involved."

My heart sank, and I looked back. The same vendor as in the pictures—a younger black man—was selling hot dogs now. "They're surveying the drop site," I said. "Waiting to grab me, perhaps?"

"Well," Ngozi said, "you're not exactly hard to find. If they wanted to snatch you, they wouldn't do it here, in a crowded area. They'd come to your home, or ambush you on the street."

Ivy grunted. "So maybe they just want to see what you do?"

"Or maybe they're after Sandra," Ngozi said. "Or maybe they don't know who is going to respond to her texts. Or, most likely, they're connected to this in a way we can't guess—because we don't have the right information."

I turned back to the photo of Sandra. Then I stood up and started walking toward the bench.

My aspects scrambled to catch up. "Steve?" Ivy said. "What are you doing? Shouldn't we think about this?"

I didn't want to think about this. I'd had enough of thinking and worrying. Maybe I was making this harder than it needed to be. Or maybe I was doing something willfully stupid, and wanted to be done with it before J.C. got back to stop me.

Either way, I ignored the sputtering aspects as I strode right up to the wastebasket. I dug into it, ignoring the ends of half-eaten hot dog buns—and heard Ngozi retch at my side.

I pulled my arm out holding a small black bag, which turned out to contain a smartphone. It needed a PIN to open—and I tried the room number from Destiny Place, the one Audrey had used in the cipher. It worked, and the phone opened to the photo archive, showing selfies of Sandra sitting on the bench. She'd captioned the last of them.

It's really me. Here is your proof. More to come.

"The vendor at the hot dog cart is right over there," Ivy said from my side. "But I can't find the other man from the pictures. We need J.C. Where *is* he?"

I turned to face the hot dog cart, with its vendor.

"Here we go . . ." Ivy said with a sigh.

"Ngozi," I said softly, "see if you can pick out where this man came from or who he works for."

"It doesn't work that way!" she said. "I'm not Sherlock Holmes."

I ignored her complaint and—as flashes of light behind us lit the fairgrounds a shimmering red-orange—I strode right up to the man at the hot dog cart, placed Sandra's phone on the counter, and looked him right in the eyes.

"I'm tired," I told him. "And I feel old."

The man stood up straight, eyes going wide. He had his hair in a buzz cut, and was lean and muscular. J.C. could have told me whether he was packing, but even I noticed how poor a fit he was for his hot-dog-vendor role.

"Sir," he said, "I'm not certain if a hot dog can help."

Too formal. Military training, perhaps?

I sighed, wiping my hands on one of his napkins. Then I reached for my pocket. He immediately responded by reaching for his gun, flipping back his apron and revealing a holster.

I held my hand back up, splaying my fingers, showing I'd gotten nothing. I nodded toward his gun. "We can stop playing. I told you. I'm too old for this."

"Old?" the man finally said, lowering his hand. "You don't look that old, sir."

"And yet, parts of me are wearing out. Like a car with faulty brakes and a secondhand engine. Looks and runs fine until you put it under stress, and then . . . well, all hell starts to break loose." I spun the phone on the counter, then turned and scared away someone else who got into line wanting a hot dog.

"I think he must be the junior of the two," Ivy guessed, inspecting the hot dog vendor. "See how nervous he is? He was set here to watch and send word if you showed up. I'd guess he wasn't supposed to actually deal with you."

"So who sent you?" I asked him. "And why didn't you just take this phone yourself and run?"

The man shut right up, practically stood at attention, and didn't answer as I pressed further. Yes, military for sure.

"I guess I should go then?" I said, taking the phone.

The man put his hand on it—not pulling it away from me, but also preventing me from walking off with it.

"So you *do* want to talk?" I said. "Then—"

"You can stop bullying him, Mr. Legion," another voice said. I looked to the side as the other man from the photos approached: older, Caucasian, with flecks of grey in his beard. "He can't answer your questions."

"Then who can?" I asked.

The man pointed at the phone. Which started ringing.

I frowned, then answered and held it up to my ear. "Hello?"

"Hey," Sandra said on the other end. "It's good to hear your voice again."

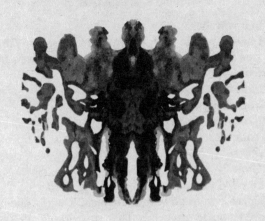

S I X

Sandra.

Sandra.

Her voice was full and husky, like the sound of a solitary cello. It reminded me of peace, of nightmares stilling. Of quiet talks at night, with a candle flickering between us, because modern lights weren't alive enough for Sandra.

"Why?" I said to her. "Why dump this phone here, and go through all of this? Why not just *call me*."

"We needed a secure line, Rhone."

My middle name. I closed my eyes, imagining lazy days near the end, after I'd silenced and embodied the voices. Days when I got to just lie there, Sandra beside me, speaking softly. She'd always said I wasn't a "Stephen." That was too common a name.

"My line *is* secure," I told her.

"Secure *from* you, I'm afraid."

"So you're working with these men?" I asked, glancing at the two beside the hot dog cart.

"In a way."

"I need to meet with you, Sandra," I said. "I'm . . . I'm not as strong as I was when you left. Things have started to fall apart."

"I know."

"You've been watching me?"

"No. It happened to me too."

"Your aspects. Jimmy, Orca, Mason . . . how are they?"

"Gone."

It felt like she'd punched me in the stomach.

"I need you to go with these men, Rhone," she said. "I need you to trust me. They're working on something that can help you. Has helped me."

The longer she spoke, the more *wrong* she sounded. Like she was drugged or something. I lifted the phone from my ear and pointed for the aspects to gather in closer and listen.

"Sandra?" I said. "What happened to your aspects? What's going on?"

"I gave them away," she said softly. "For sanity. Come see me, Rhone. It's . . . better this way."

I looked up to Ivy, who nodded curtly. I hit mute on the phone, looking toward the two men. The young one was a soldier, but the older one—now that I got a good look at him—didn't have the feel of a security officer. A little too pudgy, a little too relaxed in that sport coat, even if I did spot a gun peeking out from an underarm holster. J.C. would be proud of me.

"What have you done to her?" I demanded.

"Rather," the older man said, "you should ask what she's chosen to do to herself."

"Which is?"

"She's found peace," the man said. "We can offer it to you too. A simple business arrangement. Your brain—

safe within your skull, don't look at me like that—and our technology. We can make the world a better place, and your world a saner one, all through the power of our proprietary solution."

"He sounds like a businessman," Tobias said, "giving a pitch to the board of directors."

"He's intrigued by you," Ivy said, eyes narrowing. "Maybe even amused."

I lifted the phone to my ear, unmuting it. "Sandra? I want to talk to you in private. Just you and me. No phones. No listeners."

"And if I ask you for help?"

I felt a sudden need to give back to her. All those years ago, she'd saved my life, and I was desperate to repay our debt. To put us on even footing. Because, deep down, I suspected she'd left because I had been too needy and our relationship had been unbalanced.

She's playing me. She knows how I feel and she's playing me. Help. It was such a *difficult* word to ignore.

I turned away from the two men, speaking more softly into the phone. "Are they holding you? Have they drugged you?"

"If I say yes, will you come?"

"I . . ."

"I almost came back, you know," she said. "Two years ago, when it started going badly for me? I came to visit. But I left before speaking with you. Rhone . . . it's going to get worse for you. You're like me, only a few years behind. The brain, it just can't take the strain. You're going to start losing them again. Unless you submit."

"To what?"

"To a perfect world."

"Well," Ivy noted beside me, "*that's* not ominous."

"Sandra," I said. "It's not supposed to go this way. I've imagined . . . I mean, I pictured . . ."

"Rhone, Rhone . . . You should know by now. The two of us are too good at imagining. But when have the daydreams ever played out as we wanted them to? Go with Kyle."

"But—"

"I'll see you then. Come."

She hung up.

And I realized I was weeping. My arm went limp, and I nearly dropped the phone as I turned toward the two men.

"Mr. Legion," said the older man, who was probably Kyle, "the paradigm you live in *can* be expanded. Please, let me show you the nature of our work, and let it redefine your vision of what is possible."

"You're holding her."

"You'll find that we have done nothing outside the moral and ethical bounds of good business."

I sneered.

"Leeds," Ngozi said, taking me by the arm. Light flared behind us, and the crowd cheered.

"I don't know what you've done to her," I said to Kyle. "But I'm not going with you. I'm going to find Sandra. I'm going to *free* her."

"And if she doesn't want your freedom?"

I snarled. "You can't—"

"Stephen," Tobias said. "Perhaps you should calm down. Deep breaths, remember? Let me tell you a little more about these fire displays. Listen to my voice. The displays are so beautiful because . . ."

I breathed in and out, calming myself to the rhythm of Tobias's words. Kyle and the other man backed off, and I turned to look across the crowd toward the flashes of sparks against the wall. They were beautiful, as Tobias said. I listened to his voice until . . .

What was that chill?

I looked into the crowd. Most everyone was facing the display, but one nearby figure moved in my direction. I frowned as this person walked *right through* a couple—as if they weren't really there. The figure had . . . had sunken eye sockets and pale, milky eyes with no pupils.

His skin had gone ashen white, even faintly translucent, so you could see the shadows of the skull beneath. But I *recognized* that face anyway. Armando.

Armando—what was left of him—howled and leaped toward me, slashing with a large knife. I jumped back, but only then realized he wasn't aiming for me.

Instead, he cut down Tobias midsentence.

SEVEN

Tobias collapsed without a sound, leaving Armando's knife dripping with blood. Wraithlike, Armando lunged toward me, slashing the blade, reflecting the red-orange light of the performers' sparks.

I threw my hands up in a panic, stumbling backward and taking a gash in my arm from the attack. It *hurt*. It seemed to actually bleed.

I crashed into the hot dog cart, barely noticing as the younger of the two men pulled out his weapon. I didn't care, couldn't care. Armando had become a nightmare. And Tobias . . .

No. Please. Not Tobias.

Ivy cried out, kneeling and trying to help Tobias. Ngozi backed away, horrified.

I reeled.

NOT TOBIAS!

Armando came at me again, and I fled. I pushed off the hot dog cart and ran with my bleeding arm cradled against my chest. Warm liquid soaked through my shirt, wetting my skin. I shoved through the crowd, knocking people over in a wild attempt to stay ahead of Armando.

He flowed after me, more ghost than man or aspect. Obstructions didn't stop him; he passed right through a crowd of people unhindered. He didn't bother to pretend like the others. He didn't need to try to preserve my sanity.

I shoved past a family, scrambling, and somehow got to the front of the crowd, right up near the stage. I'd gotten turned around, confused in my flight.

Red sparks splashed against the wall, then flickered and died. I looked over my shoulder. Radiant, inconsistent, dying light illuminated Armando. His eyes were dead, the eyes of a drowned corpse. He followed, inexorable, brandishing the bloody knife.

"I will cut them out of you," he whispered, voice somehow audible over the sounds of people cheering the show or yelling at me. "I will cut them *all out*."

I collided with someone in the crowd, and they shoved me the other way. My arm protested as I hit another group, and these crushed the wind from me, smashing me between them. Armando flowed through them, his face appearing from someone's back like a stain seeping through a wall.

I screamed again, pushing people away from me, my arm flaring with pain. I squeezed through the stuffy, sweating, screeching, horrible mass. I squirmed and shouted and scrambled and finally . . . I burst from the back of the crowd into open air.

Armando slammed into me from behind, hitting me with his shoulder, throwing me to the ground. I hit the concrete sidewalk and gasped at the pain.

"Cut *them all out*."

I rolled over, and stared up at Armando—who was

backlit by an explosion of sparks in the night. He grinned.

Then a bullet took him in the forehead.

He stumbled, shaking his head. More shots followed, like fireworks. Each took him in the face, with almost no spread. He finally collapsed back to the dusty ground, dropping the knife.

I pulled myself away from the corpse, up onto the sidewalk, then twisted about. Never had I been so happy to see J.C. Still holding his sidearm out before him, he stepped over to me and squatted down. "Yup," he said, "a part of me knew I'd have to shoot that guy someday."

I looked back at Armando, lying in an expanding pool of his own blood. J.C. nodded for me to hold my arm out so he could inspect the wound, and I did so, feeling numb.

"So," J.C. said, pulling a bandage from his pocket, "you going to tell me why you were so eager to keep me away?"

"Wha . . . what?"

"Leaving me in a slum, running off from the mansion before I could get back to you. Even my car here got caught in traffic."

"That was real."

"Still feels like you're being reckless. On purpose."

No. I wasn't. I just . . . just wanted to get to Sandra. I tried to explain, but then I felt a *ripping* sensation. Nauseatingly familiar, as it had happened to me earlier today, with Armando. Loss. Information leaving me forever.

This one was much worse. A thunderbolt compared to a twig snapping.

I moaned, huddling into myself, as it left me forever:

all the random bits of knowledge that didn't fit into another aspect's expertise. The trivia that touched everything I did, everything I had learned, wrapped up in a single wonderful man.

Tobias . . .

Tobias was gone.

"What?" J.C. asked. "What is that look on your face, Skinny? What happened?"

"He got Tobias," I croaked.

"Where?" J.C. demanded.

I pointed the way back through the crowd.

J.C. took off running, and I lurched to my feet and followed, leaving Armando's corpse. I didn't *think* it could get up and come after us again . . . but there was no guarantee. Nightmares didn't follow the rules.

By now, the real people had opened a space around me, and backed away as I moved. One got used to this sort of thing in a big city, even if I didn't look like the usual homeless drunk. A few Good Samaritans asked if I needed help, but I managed to brush them off and make my way back toward the hot dog cart.

The two men from earlier had left. Ngozi knelt by Tobias's body, her arms covered in blood. She'd tried, bless her, to bandage him.

It hadn't been enough. J.C. was down on one knee beside Tobias, his handgun held limply. Ivy stood nearby, one arm wrapped around herself while she smoked a cigarette with the other hand. Damn. She'd given that up *years* ago. J.C. rose and walked over to her, and she leaned into him, crying softly on his shoulder.

I just . . .

I stared at the body.

Tobias had been the very first. A calming, optimistic voice pulled from the shadows and nightmares. I remembered sitting at night in a chair, lights off, surrounded by whispers—and then hearing him for the first time.

He had been my lifeline to sanity.

"What . . ." Ngozi said. "What do we do now?"

I didn't know.

"We have to keep moving," J.C. said, still holding Ivy. He needed the comfort as much as she did. "We've drawn attention. Look."

Though the spark show had ended—and someone was starting to spray down the stage with water—security was making its way past the dispersing crowd. A few people turned toward me, gesturing animatedly.

"We can't . . . just leave him," Ivy said.

"There's a way out," I whispered. "A way to fix this. Sandra. She knows." I stumbled over to the hot dog cart. On the counter was a note and the pouch with the cell phone in it. The note read simply, "We'll be in touch."

I grabbed both pouch and note, and—though it pained me to do so—I left Tobias's remains. It felt wrong. It felt awful. I'd come back for him though. I'd give him a proper burial.

He'll just lie there, I thought, *with people walking through him. Never knowing what they're treading on. The great man they could never see, could never know.*

Had to keep moving.

I limped away, still cradling my cut arm as the security guards called after me. They hurried to catch up, but then I approached my limo, which was still parked at the curb.

Barb opened the door, and the two guards backed off. I'd suddenly moved from "random homeless drunk" to "above my pay grade."

I climbed in, then used my foot to kick the door

back open as Barb tried to close it after me. Ivy, J.C., then Ngozi entered and slumped into seats.

Barb peeked in. "Um, all in?"

"No," I whispered. "But we can go anyway."

"Sure thing!" she said, chipper. "Anything I can get you? Some water, or—"

"You can shut up."

She closed the door, perhaps a little too firmly. I missed Wilson, and . . .

Oh, hell, *Tobias was dead.*

I lay down on the seat as J.C. knelt by me and worked on the bandage some more.

"Right," Ivy said, taking a deep breath. "Right. We need a plan. I can't believe how much this hurts . . . but we *need a plan.* Steve, this *can't happen again.*"

The car started. Barb flipped on the intercom. "Are we going anywhere specific?"

"No," I said. "Just drive. Please."

Anywhere but here.

EIGHT

I didn't know what type of phone this was.

I turned it over in my hands as the car pulled onto the freeway. Beside me, Ivy helped Ngozi clean the blood off her hands using the limo's sink and water bottles.

Why did it matter what kind of phone it was? Because Tobias had known everything about phones. Not just the devices themselves, but all about the companies that made them. The history of technology was just one of his many little quirks. I'd grown used to having that knowledge comfortably in the back of my brain, not really that important, but still . . . there.

I tried texting Sandra a few times, but she didn't respond. Finally, at a suggestion from J.C., I texted saying I'd turn the phone back on in an hour—then took out the battery, so I couldn't be traced using the phone, just in case.

"J.C.," Ivy said. "Call the mansion."

He did so, dialing Kalyani, then putting her on speaker.

"Is there news?" she asked immediately.

"We . . ." Ivy took a deep breath. "We lost Tobias."

Silence.

"You lost him," Kalyani finally said. "As in . . . he ran away?"

"He's dead," J.C. said. "Gone."

Kalyani gasped.

"We need to prevent something like this from happening again," Ivy said. "I want you to gather all the aspects and get them into the White Room. Let us know if *anyone* is unaccounted for."

"Yes. Yes, okay," Kalyani said. "But . . . Tobias. Are you *sure*?"

"Yes, unfortunately."

"How is Mr. Steve?"

Ivy looked at me. "Not well. Call us back when everyone is together." She hung up.

I stared straight ahead, numb, feeling only the motion of the car on the road.

Get to Sandra.

But would she be able to do anything? Her voice on the line, the way she'd spoken, hadn't sounded like someone who had the answers. Not the right ones, at least.

It was something to think about other than Tobias. Looking up, I was startled to find my aspects all frozen. Like statues, not moving, not breathing. As I realized it, they jerked into motion again, Ngozi drying her hands and telling J.C. about the two men from the hot dog cart.

I checked my phone, and saw that half an hour had passed while I'd sat there, zoned out, thinking about Sandra and Tobias.

The phone buzzed. It was Kalyani calling me.

"Hello," I said, switching it to speaker.

"Everyone is accounted for, Mr. Steve," Kalyani said. "Nobody has vanished. We're all here. Even Leroy, who just got back."

That meant no more nightmares. For now.

"What do you want us to do?" Kalyani asked.

I looked at Sandra's phone. Did we just wait for her, or that Kyle fellow, to "be in touch"? Or did I do something more?

"Options?" I said, looking at my team.

"The older man," Ivy said, "Kyle, he sounded like he was a business type. Not security. So . . ."

"So maybe there's a record of him, and where he works," I said, nodding. "But we'll need a way to search him out. Ngozi. How's your mental image of him?"

"Excellent," she said.

"Great. Kalyani, you still there?"

"Yup."

"Grab Turquoise."

Turquoise was one of my older aspects. He came on, speaking with a weird mix of a Texas accent and a stoner drawl. "Hey, man. This has been crazy, huh?"

"Don't use that word lightly around me, Turquoise," I said. "Ngozi is going to describe someone to you. Can you draw him?"

"Sure. Like one of those guys. From those shows."

"Exactly."

"Cool."

I nodded to Ngozi, who started describing Kyle. Round face, thinning hair, big forearms—like he worked out—but not really an athletic build. Big nose.

Kalyani turned the phone to video mode and showed what Turquoise was drawing. Ngozi coached him to make tweaks, with some input from Ivy, and he did a remarkable job. My brain could memorize complex details quickly. We just needed a way to get the information out.

"Cool," Turquoise said when we were done. "Kind of looks like a potato who is pretending to be a man, and is worried someone will call his bluff."

"You're a weird dude, Turquoise," I said.

"Yeah. Thanks."

"Hey, Chin?" I asked. "You listening?"

"Here," my computer expert said, leaning down and waving into the camera.

"Can you run that sketch through some kind of facial recognition software?" I asked.

"No, but I can tell you who he is anyway."

"What? Really?"

"Sure," Chin said. "I read an article on him recently— that's Kyle Walters, a local entrepreneur. He's made a few waves in local tech circles."

I frowned, Googling the name. "Kyle Walters. President of Walters and Ostman Detention Enterprises."

". . . Detention Enterprises?" Ngozi asked. "Like, prisons?"

"For-profit prisons," Chin said, reading. "He made news by purchasing a game company. It was a moderately big deal in some circles."

I nodded slowly. Whatever Chin knew came from me. I must have read about Kyle during one of my many information binges, where I tried to absorb as many news stories and articles as possible, for future reference.

"Video games and prisons?" Ivy said. "That's an odd pairing."

"Yeah." I scrolled up on the article. "President of the company. Why did he bother coming to meet me himself?"

"Meeting you is quite the experience," Chin said. "He's said to be a hands-on type. Guess he just wanted to see you for himself."

I frowned, studying the article.

"What?" Ivy asked.

"Nothing," I said. "I just . . . I think I used to know something about that structure he's standing in front of." I glanced at the caption below the picture. "'Eiffel Tower'? Looks like some kind of art installation."

"Yeah. A big one." Ivy shook her head. "Strange."

"That's 'art'?" J.C. said. "Looks like someone forgot to finish the thing."

I sat there, waiting for Tobias to explain it to us, then felt again like I'd been punched. He was gone. I took a deep breath and did some further searching into our Kyle Walters fellow. I found some clips of him talking at tech conferences, giving speeches full of buzzwords.

But he owned *prisons*. What was he doing at these conferences? They weren't even security conferences. *Applied Virtual Reality Summit*, I read. Huh.

"He's based locally?" I asked. "Where?"

"Here," Ivy said, showing me her phone, with an address listed. "He owns an entire building in a suburban office park." It appearing on her phone meant I had that address tucked in the back of my brain somewhere, from when I'd memorized local business lists. So I hadn't lost everything with Tobias.

"You seem to be coping remarkably well," Jenny said, "now that the initial shock has worn off. Can you explain how your aspects are helping you to recover?"

Startled, I looked up. There she was, sitting across from me in the limo. J.C., with wonderful presence of mind, pulled his gun and leveled it right at her head.

"Is that necessary?" she asked.

"We just had an aspect go crazy and kill one of my

best friends," J.C. said. "I *will* blow the back of your head across that seat if I think it will save anyone else."

"You're not following the rules," I said to her. "Appearing and vanishing? That's dangerous. Nightmares don't follow the rules."

She pursed her lips, and for the first time seemed to *get* that idea. She nodded, and J.C. looked at me.

"You can put it away," I said to him. "She's obviously not a nightmare. Not yet."

He obeyed, holstering it with deliberation as he leaned back in his seat, still watching her. We made fun of J.C., but I'll admit he can be casually intimidating when he really wants to be. Ivy settled in next to him, legs crossed, staring daggers at Jenny. Ngozi had missed the entire exchange, because she was suddenly fixated on how dirty the inside of the cupholder was.

"It seems to me," Jenny said, "that you all are very quick to point a gun—but very slow to ask the difficult questions."

"Such as?" I asked.

"Such as *why* is this happening?" Jenny asked. "*Why* are you losing aspects? What is causing your hallucinations to behave in this way?"

"My brain is overworked. Too many aspects, too much going on with them. Either that or I'm emotionally incapable of handling change in my life."

"False dichotomy," Jenny said. "It could be a third option."

"Such as?"

"You tell me. I'm just here to listen."

"You realize," I said to her, "that I *already* have a psychologist aspect." I nodded toward Ivy. "She gives me lip, but she's good at her job, so I don't need another."

"I'm not a psychologist," Jenny said. "I'm a biographer." She wrote some things in her notepad, as if to prove the point.

I looked out the window, watching streetlights pass on the side of the road. We'd pulled off the freeway, and were heading down a dim neighborhood street. The patches between the lights were dark—almost like nothing existed, except where those streetlights created the world.

I pushed the intercom button. "Barb, GPS an office building called Walters and Ostman Detention Enterprises. Should be on 206th. Take us there."

"Roger, boss," she said.

"Tell me, Mr. Leeds," Jenny said. "Do you want to be cured?"

I didn't answer.

"Say you'd lose us all," Jenny said. "No more aspects. No more knowledge. No more being special. But if you could be normal, would you take that trade?"

When I didn't answer immediately, Ivy shot me a betrayed look. But what could I say? To be well.

To be *normal*.

I did everything I could to remain sane, to shove my psychoses off onto the aspects. I was the most boring of the lot, by design. That way I could pretend. But did that mean . . . mean that I'd welcome losing the aspects?

Could I really live without them?

"I miss Tobias already," J.C. said softly. "He'd have broken this silence. Said something to make me smile."

"Tell me about him," Jenny said. "I barely got to meet him."

It felt like she was trying to worm her way in, dig information from my brain.

"He was wonderful," Ivy said. "Calm with everyone. Interested in everyone."

"He loved a mystery," Ngozi added. "He loved *questions*. He was the part of us that kept wanting to learn."

"I swear," I noted, "half the aspects exist because he was interested enough to get me digging into some strange topic."

"He hated charging people for our work," J.C. said. "Always wanted to give everyone a pro bono deal. Terrible businessman. Good *man* though."

"He was crazy in his own wonderful way," Ivy said. "Remember how people would get when they found out that one of your hallucinations had *his own* hallucination?"

I smiled. Maybe . . . maybe I could imagine Stan, Tobias's astronaut friend. I didn't usually have that much control.

The others continued to reminisce, telling stories about Tobias. Jenny sat back, writing it all down. And it did feel better to talk about it. To remember. Maybe for once she'd actually helped.

Eventually we pulled up to a small business building—maybe four stories high. I didn't know if Sandra was inside, but hopefully they'd at least have information on where she was being held.

I just had to break in and steal it.

NINE

"Same car," Ngozi said, peering through the binoculars out the window of our limo. "Big silver SUV that was parked on the street near the hot dog cart. I can barely make out the license plate by the streetlights." She hesitated. "Anyone heard of a 'Lexus' make of cars?"

The aspects shook their heads. How many more aspects could I lose before I was just . . . gone? A drooling vegetable?

J.C. waved for the binoculars, and Ngozi wiped them down with a disinfecting wipe, then passed them over. He looked over the building. "No way to guess at their security level. Here's what we do: We go back to the house and I gather a team of specialized aspects. Chin, Lua, Marci.

"We work some contacts, grab the architectural plans—and, if we're lucky, find out who installed this building's security. We might be able to find out who owned the building before this Kyle guy bought it, and—if they can be bribed—get an even better idea of what we're dealing with. We come back in two days' time, at three in the morning, when . . ."

I opened the door and stepped out into the night.

". . . or not," J.C. said, with a loud sigh.

I knocked on the driver's window, which Barb rolled down. "Go park the car someplace out of sight," I said, then started out toward the office building.

J.C., Ivy, Ngozi, and Jenny followed me. We crossed the dark lawn in a low run. Most parts of the building were floodlit, but on the east side the floodlight was flickering, mostly dark. So I approached from that side.

Jenny hung back the farthest, looking awkward as she tried to hide behind a tree. At least she was playing by the rules now. Ivy had done this sort of thing before, and crept beside J.C. and me with her shoes— not the most practical for an infiltration—held in her hand. I was worried most about Ngozi, but she was smiling as she settled in beside me near some shrubs.

"It's been a while," she whispered as we crouched down in the darkened shadow of the shrubbery. "I feel . . . I feel *good*. Like I can do this. Huh. Oh! Don't brush those leaves! Do you know what kinds of *chemicals* they spray on these things to keep them looking this green?"

J.C. scanned the side of the building. "You insist on doing this now?"

"If Sandra is in there, I want to know. We can't wait two days while they might move her."

He shared a look with Ivy, who shrugged, then nodded.

He breathed out. "You people are all crazy."

"Hey!" Ivy said. "I'm the psychologist here. I get to define who is crazy, and only four of us are."

J.C. counted the five of us. Then, hesitantly, pointed at himself.

"J.C.," she said flatly, "you're as crazy as they come. How many gun magazine subscriptions do you have?"

". . . All of them," he admitted.

"In how many languages?"

". . . All of them."

"And how many of those languages other than English do you read?"

". . . None of them." He peered through the bushes with his binoculars. "But I can read the pictures. Those aren't in Canadian or whatever, eh."

"Who's the sane one, then?" I asked Ivy. "Me?"

"Heavens no. It's Ngozi. Have you *seen* the chemicals they spray on these plants? You should really listen to her."

Ngozi nodded in agreement, but J.C. just chuckled. And I . . . I smiled a little. It was hard to feel any levity after what had happened, but I realized I still needed it.

Thank you, Ivy. "So how do we get in?" I asked.

"Air ducts?" Ngozi asked.

J.C. rolled his eyes. "Have you ever *actually* seen an air duct that a person could climb through? Like, one that was both big enough *and* wouldn't collapse from the weight of a person inside?"

"Sure," she said. "I've seen lots. On TV."

"Yeah, well, how about next time we're doing crime scene analysis, I yell 'enhance' like a billion times."

"Point taken."

"Fortunately," J.C. said, holding up the binoculars again, "this place doesn't look *too* secure. I don't see any external cameras—they could easily be hidden, mind you—and no lights in the windows indicates that if they're patrolling on foot, they're doing so rarely. Of course, these modern joints don't *need* patrols—everything is wired to go crazy the moment you breathe on the wrong door.

"Best way in is to do what Audrey always says—look for the human error, rather than trying to break the machines." He pointed, and I spotted a window on the first floor that had been propped open with a book, perhaps for fresh air.

"We go all at once," J.C. said. "If they're watching the area via camera, stringing it out is worse. This way, at least there's a chance the security guard will be looking away at the moment we run. Ready?"

We each nodded.

J.C. thumbed over his shoulder toward Jenny, who observed from farther back—perhaps not trusting herself to get close. "And her?"

"Ignore her," I said. "She . . . won't show up on their screens. She, um, has a stealth system."

"Not the writer chick," J.C. said, rolling his eyes. He pointed again. *"Her."*

I looked again. Barb was scuttling across the grass. She arrived, out of breath, and crouched next to me. "All right!" she said. "Sneaking in? I can dig that. What do you want me to do?"

"Go back to the car."

"But—"

"Go back to the car, drive off, and go to your uncle's birthday party. That's happening tonight, right? Grab some cake, Barb."

"You'll need—"

"I'll get a cab. Go."

Her face fell, then she nodded and slunk off. *If she exposed me to the security guards in there . . .* I shook my head, glancing back at the team—and was met with uniform looks of disapproval.

"What?" I said. "We don't need real people."

"There are things she could do that we can't," Ngozi said.

"I'm never one to turn away someone with a can-do attitude," J.C. said.

Ivy just squeezed my arm. "What if that's the problem, Steve? What if you *can't* just live with us? What if turning inward is what's causing all of this?"

"What? You're *that* offended because I turned my *chauffeur* away?" They *were* all crazy.

Besides. Maybe I didn't want someone watching as I went through . . . whatever was happening to me. Can't a man suffer a breakdown in private?

"Let's go," I said—then didn't give them a chance to object as I ran for the building. The others followed, even Jenny. I reached the side of the building, puffing, then approached the open window. It was the type that slid up and down, and through the glass I saw what looked like a service closet. There were buckets on the floor, and it smelled faintly of cleaning fluids. Perhaps they'd been airing it out.

I pulled up the window, then slipped through. I managed to do it without making any noise or knocking over the buckets on the ground, though I bumped my head on a shelf in the dark room as I stood up. I saw stars, and my vision flashed, but I managed to keep myself from shouting out.

I held open the window for the others, and J.C. gave me a thumbs-up as he climbed in. He probably hadn't seen me knock my head, but I figured I was doing better than I might once have. Our training sessions were proving good for something.

Ivy *did* knock over one of the buckets, but fortunately, the resulting clatter wouldn't be audible to anyone but me—though she shot me a chagrined look after doing it. J.C. helped Ngozi in, then Jenny came last.

I replaced the book, rested the window on it, then

moved to the door. I took a deep breath and cracked it open. If they had the doors alarmed, this would reveal me.

The light beyond the door was much brighter than I expected. I blinked against the garish, sterile glare. The hallway seemed empty, though J.C. pointed upward to a little knob on the ceiling, a hemisphere of reflective black glass. Security camera.

I pulled back into the room and closed the door with a click. After thinking a moment, I dialed Kalyani on the phone. "Grab Chin," I said softly.

A moment later, he was on the line. "Yeah, boss?"

"We're infiltrating the Detention Enterprises place," I said. "We've breached the perimeter, but the hallways have some surveillance cameras."

Chin chuckled softly. "You're surprised that a group that runs *prison facilities* has a basic level of security?"

"He's been reckless lately," J.C. said. "More so than usual."

"All right. Well, have a look at your phone, boss. You see an app called SAPE? That's your signal analysis booster. Give it a try, and set the thing to transmit data to my laptop."

"Done," I said, flicking a few buttons, watching data appear on my screen.

"Hm . . ." Chin said. "Visible guest wi-fi . . . hidden internal signals not broadcasting identities . . . Okay, cool. They're using AJ141 wireless cameras."

"That's good?"

"Kind of," Chin said. "So those little camera nodes broadcast signals back to a central watch station, right? And the night watchperson there cycles through the cameras."

"Can you hack it?"

"Nope," Chin said. "Not a chance. We'd need to

plug into the thing directly, which—if you hadn't guessed—would *kind of* involve going into its field of view. *However*, watch the signal on your phone. See that little blip?"

"Yeah. What is it?"

"That's a ping for data, which is causing the camera to reset briefly and start transmitting. Awkward. They probably configured new cameras to work with their older security setup. It means that while you can't hack the system . . ."

"We *can* see when one of the cameras is transmitting," I said, smiling. "Nice work, Chin."

"Yeah, well, don't get caught, all right? We've had enough bad news today."

"Speaking of that . . ." Kalyani said from near Chin, her voice timid. "Mr. Steve?"

"What?" I said, feeling cold.

"Lua is gone."

"I thought you said you had everyone!"

"We thought we had, but he ran out to grab something from his little survivor hut out back. And he didn't come back! We sent four people out together looking for him, but he's gone."

I leaned back against the wall, feeling sick. No. *Not again* . . .

"Hey Achmed?" J.C. said to Kalyani, leaning down to the phone.

"Please don't call me that."

"Yeah. Sorry. Trying to be funny, you know . . ." He took a deep breath. "There's a key hidden in a box under the third brick on the back path. Go grab it."

"For what?" Kalyani asked.

"It opens my gun locker, the one in the main hallway, where I keep the emergency shotguns in case of home invasion. Distribute them among the others, and you guys hole up in there, okay? Stay in one room, barricade the door . . . and be careful. If Lua goes nightmare, he might ignore things like locks and barricades. Guns should still work though."

"I . . ." Her voice trembled. "Okay. Okay, we'll do it."

"Good. Take care." He looked up at me, uncharacteristically reserved, then unholstered his sidearm. "Guess you were right, Skinny. Waiting two days to get in here wasn't an option."

"Do you want to tell me," Jenny said from right beside me, "how exactly this makes you feel?"

I jumped, and suddenly felt an irrational anger at her. She stood there, scribbling, like she didn't even *care* what was happening to everyone else.

"Either you are going to shut up," I said, "or we are going to come to blows."

"False dichotomy," she said. "There are more than two options. We could—"

"Go," I said, pointing back at the window.

"What?" she said, lowering her pad.

"Go. *Now.* Or I swear, J.C. will shoot you. Break the rules, get away, vanish—I don't care how. But *go away*!"

She vanished in a heartbeat.

I trembled inside, then felt sick. The other aspects stood silently. "Don't look so betrayed," I snarled. "I didn't ask for her. I didn't want her. I don't even know what kind of specialty she was supposed to represent."

I waited for the camera outside to go through a cycle, counting how long we had between its bursts. A minute and a half. Plenty of time.

J.C. led the way out into the hallway.

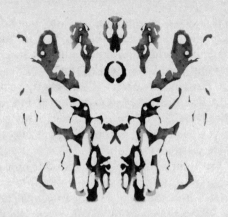

TEN

The cameras were spaced evenly through the hallways, but with my phone, I was able to pick out the closest signals. I got into a good rhythm, delaying underneath one camera while it was still offline, then quickly moving when the next one stopped transmitting. I tried doorknobs as I passed, hoping to find one unlocked that would provide computer access.

I didn't have luck at that, but Ngozi did spot something through the window into one office: a map of the facility on the back wall. I snapped a picture, then found my way to a spot around a corner and at the landing of a stairwell where we thought we'd be out of sight of the two nearest cameras.

Here, I took a breather while my aspects gathered around the phone to inspect the map. My heart was beating quickly, and my shirt was damp with nervous sweat. But so far, no alarm.

That doesn't mean anything, I reminded myself. *Any alarm would be silent, only alerting security*. Still, this entire place seemed eerily quiet. Empty, but bright, lit up white.

"There," J.C. said, pointing at the picture of the map, with its breakdown of four floors. One larger bit of text read: *Subject testing and holding cells.*

"What you want to bet she's in there?" J.C. asked.

I nodded. We went up the stairwell—dodging a camera in the middle of the next flight—and ended up on the top floor, near those holding cells. Here, unfortunately, we encountered our first live guards. I peeked around a corner, and found them right in the hallway. They leaned against the wall, tasers on their hips, chatting softly about football.

I backed away, looking down the corridor behind me, but the map said that direction only led to a dead end at a place labeled IMAGING CENTER.

I retreated to the top of the stairs, in a spot out of sight of the cameras. "Ideas?" I whispered to my aspects.

"You could take two guards," J.C. said.

Fat chance of that.

"I doubt we can talk past them," Ivy said, "considering the circumstances."

"Well," Ngozi said. "There's an air duct over there, down that hallway to the left."

"Not that again," J.C. said. He squinted. "We wouldn't fit."

"I wasn't thinking of going into it ourselves. . . ."

I waited, nervously, hidden on the steps and barely daring to breathe as kitten sounds echoed in the hallway above.

It took only a few minutes for the two men to approach, leaving their post. Confused, they passed right near my stairwell, then continued on down the hall-way, turning left. They probably shouldn't have left their posts, but it was perfectly natural. Who *wouldn't* be interested by the sounds of a lost kitten?

They'd find the sounds coming from the air duct where we'd hidden—around a corner and out of sight—Sandra's phone, playing the meowing kitten video that Audrey had been watching earlier. It had been danger-ous turning on Sandra's phone, but we'd put it into airplane mode and used a direct Bluetooth connection between my phone and it to load the cat video.

I heard the men in the corridor nearby, calling to the kitten in the air duct. I slipped past them, around the corner. Heart pounding, I walked underneath a sign that read, SECURE AREA—SUBJECT HOLDING. Just a little farther. Sandra. I heard . . . I heard her voice ahead. Singing. That old lullaby that she always—

Everything flashed white.

The hallway melted into light. I stumbled, and J.C. shouted, raising his gun and spinning around. For a moment, we were blinded.

The light vanished, and I found myself in a com-pletely different place. Instead of the hallway, I was lying on the floor in an unfamiliar room. It was a large, open chamber with concrete walls, a high ceiling, and industrial lighting.

What had happened? I'd . . . been teleported, some-how?

Kyle Walters stood before me: the balding, some-what buff man in the sport coat from earlier at the fairgrounds. I blinked, looking up at him, then at the small gathering of techy types behind him. Where had they come from? What was happening?

"Welcome, Mr. Leeds," he said, "to the future of hu-man incarceration."

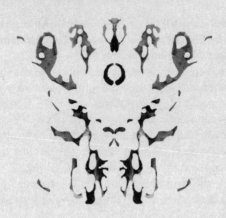

ELEVEN

Kyle offered a hand to help me to my feet. He had a false sort of friendliness about him, the smile of a man who would be your best friend for as long as it took to sell you a very nice pre-owned vehicle.

My surroundings had gone from a sterile hallway to an older warehouse. Not dingy, but *used*. Concrete floors with patches covered with chunks of carpet where computer stations had been set up. The scents were no longer of cleaning fluids, but of sawdust and someone's microwave dinner. It wasn't messy, it was just . . . real?

Real. That other building had been too perfect, maybe even too generic. The kind of tech office that you saw people infiltrate in films. A too-perfect, constructed world. Hadn't Chin said this man had bought a video game company?

But how had he made me feel like I was there? I wasn't wearing any equipment. "What did you do to me?" I asked.

"I took you to the *future*, Steve!" Kyle obviously wasn't the type of person who asked before using your first name. "You did pretty well."

"We haven't ever seen the trick with the cat sounds," said one of the techs behind him, a woman with her hair in a ponytail. "Innovative."

"You found the camera exploit as well," another one said. "So far, only security professionals have done that. Everyone else tries something cliché like taping a picture of the hallway in front of the camera."

"How did you do it, though?" I asked. "I'm not wearing a headset or anything. How did you put me into that virtual world?"

"We prefer the term 'holodeck,'" one of the techies said.

"No we don't," Kyle said quickly. "Ignore them. We prefer a proprietary term that carries no legal baggage or IP infringement." He slapped me on the shoulder, then put his arm around me.

Nearby, J.C. pointed out two men hanging back near a wall. One was the other guy from the hot dog stand, and both were packing nine-millimeters.

"I don't like this at all," Ivy said. "So everything we did . . . the incursion, dodging the cameras . . . it wasn't real?"

Neither are you, I thought. *Neither is most of my life.*

"You're turning VR into . . . prisons?" I asked Kyle.

"The natural response to current market incentives," Kyle said, steering me along as he started walking. "Here, let me unpack it for you. Do you know how much it costs to house an inmate in the United States for a year?"

"It's high," I said. "Like, twenty or thirty—"

"It costs an average of thirty thousand dollars!" Kyle said. "And can get as high as *sixty thousand* in some states. Per year, *per inmate*! And what do we, the taxpayers, gain from all of that? Are the inmates at least well cared for? No! Criminal-on-criminal violence is rampant. Living conditions are terrible. Prisons are overfilled, understaffed, and underfunded. In short, we're spending a ton for a cruddy product. How smart is that?"

"The solution seems to be to make sure fewer people go to prison."

"A wonderful ideal, Steve! I'm glad we have people like you to deep dive into the morality of situations. But for the real world, we also need people like me— and a little *practical* application."

"You still haven't told me how you immersed me in one without my knowledge."

Kyle led me to a window that looked in on a small room where a man lay in a bunk, peacefully asleep. Ivy and Ngozi crowded around. J.C. was playing it cool, standing back, glaring at those security guards.

"Emitters on the ceiling," Kyle said, pointing upward. "We can engage them without the subject knowing they're transitioning into a virtual world. That's the key; if they think it's real, all *kinds* of possibilities open up. This is the future, Steve. This changes the paradigm. It digs up the goalpost, and moves it to a completely different game."

I looked back through the window, feeling sick.

"Right now," Kyle said, "that man is working on an elaborate escape plan from the prison room he *thinks* he's in. We've offered carefully calculated goals— manageable hooks he can exploit to get him closer and closer to escaping. He's *engaged*, he's *excited*. He thinks he's going to do it—and in the meantime, we're paying the equivalent of less than *ten thousand* a year to keep him in there."

"Calculated goals," I said. "Like what?"

"Our basic prison plan will offer a multitude of potential escape routes," one of the techs said. "We're working on a tunneling quest line, a quest line involving the befriending of guards, and a third that involves escaping using the laundry bins. Or if the prisoner prefers, they will be able to become kingpin of the prisoners—gaining dominance over the various factions, and eventually moving into a suite within the facility to live like a king."

"What about muscle atrophy?" Ivy asked. "Bedsores? I can think of a dozen problems with this."

I repeated the objections, and Kyle just grinned. "You're a smart cookie, Steve," he said. "We're working on these issues—we have emitters that let the body move while the brain thinks it's in the real world. Ideally, we'll be able to use a mixture of idle and physical interaction to create a sustainable, perpetual, eco-friendly, and health-conscious incarceration solution."

"A video game for inmates."

"That and so much more! In our simulated routines, the prisoners have as much as a tenfold increase in satisfaction. Yes, game companies have been pioneering this technology—but nobody has been asking the most important question."

"Which is?"

"How can we get the government to sink a *ton* of money into this?" Kyle grinned. He seemed to do that a lot. "Incarceration is such a nasty business to the public. They don't want to think about it. They don't want to interact with it. Nobody wants a prison in their back yard, but everybody wants 'those people' to be taken care of. Well, we can take care of them."

Kyle rapped the window with the back of his hand. "For now, we can only simulate a simple prison facility, but we have plans. What if a prisoner could escape into the virtual world, but not know they're in a simulation? We could watch and see if they go back to a life of crime. If they do . . . well, we let them live in their own world of vice, hurting nobody. But if it turns out they have rehabilitated, or might have been innocent all along, we can just let them out. It's a *perfect* system."

"It's fake," I whispered.

"And which would you rather live in? The fake prison where you think you're free, or the real prison where you spend each day in drudgery? Honestly, when this project goes live, people will be *begging* to be let in."

"Yet something's wrong, isn't it?" Ivy said, narrowing her eyes and reading Kyle. "Ask him why he needs you."

"If it's so great, why kidnap Sandra?"

"Kidnap? Steve, Sandy came to us. And she suggested that we approach you."

"You could have sent me a letter."

"We sent seven."

I hesitated. Seven?

"Maybe we should answer our mail once in a while," J.C. said. "You know, for old times' sake."

Kyle cleared his throat. "We tried working through contacts to get your attention, we tried calling, we even sent Gerry by to knock on your door."

"You weren't 'taking new clients,'" the tech said. "I couldn't get past the gate."

It *had* been a while since I'd taken a case. The house staff had orders to turn away supplicants.

I stepped up close to the window, looking in at the prisoner. Lying there, eyes closed, asleep. But awake somewhere else. "Is Sandra in one of these rooms?"

"She is. But let's not get to that yet. You asked what's

wrong with our system—and well, there *are* a few bugs. Turns out, human brains are *very* good at picking out when things are wrong. There are so many details to get right—and the processing power needed to simulate reality is enormous. We do a poor job, and the imperfections build up. Normal people last maybe a few hours in the simulation, depending on their brain chemistry."

"The brain eventually rejects the reality," the woman tech said. "Much as it might reject a transplanted organ."

"The whole thing collapses," Kyle said. "They come out of it, and we can't get the simulation to take for them again until two or three days have passed." He paused. "Sandy's record in the simulation so far is eighty-seven consecutive days."

J.C. whistled softly.

"She got kicked out again this morning," one of the techs said, "and went on a little jaunt to the fairgrounds to contact you. Wanted to do it in person. Once she spoke to you earlier, she asked to go back in. It took for her immediately. It always does."

"Somehow," Kyle said, "her brain can make up for the gaps in our programming. We can transmit *concepts* to Sandy, and she makes up the rest, adding in the details. We need to figure out how she does this, because it could be the key. If we can get the brains of our subjects to construct their own reality, we don't need to re-create things exactly—we can just nudge them the direction we want, and let their minds do the hard work."

"You're the same way," a techie noted. "We turned on the simulation the moment you climbed in through the window, and your brain blurred the real reality into our fake one, filling in details that we got wrong, or that were too low resolution. Your brain, quite frankly, is *amazing*."

I rubbed my head, remembering when I'd bumped it into that shelf while climbing in the window. My vision had flashed white. Had that been the moment?

Ngozi had wandered over to the nearest of the computer stations, and was looking over the equipment—but I wasn't sure what we'd be able to tell without Chin here. Hell, this might be out of even his league. Wirelessly projecting global hallucinations directly into the brain? That was some Arnaud "theoretical physics" levels of science.

I looked to the side, to get Tobias's read on the situation. But there was no Tobias. Not anymore.

"So they need our brain," Ivy said. "You can make your own reality, Steve, and they want to know how."

"But they already have Sandra," I said. "Why do they need me?"

"Try understanding a disease with only one patient," Kyle said. "Or doing a drug test with only one subject. You're an incredibly rare find, Steve. Your mind is worth *millions*. All we want is for you to spend some time in the simulation. A few years at most."

A few *years*?

"No chance," I said. "I'm already wealthy. What could you possibly offer me to live in your box?"

"Sandra is free of her aspects," Kyle said.

Ivy looked at me sharply.

Kyle smiled. "You're interested, I see. Yes, she asked if we could stop the hallucinations. Construct a reality where she was free of them." He hesitated, and I caught what I thought was a sign of discomfort from him. "It . . . didn't work like we thought it would."

"When we put her into the simulation," a techie said, "she *added* to the programming, making her aspects

appear. And they interacted with the world we created—
Sandra layered another reality on top of our virtual reality, and adapted the code. But she wanted the aspects
gone . . . and turns out, we could help with that."

I shivered. Something about the tone in his voice.

"Anyway," Kyle said, "Sandy's been very helpful.
She's showing us how the brain alters its own reality.
We aren't really sure exactly why or how our programs
interact with her aspects, but they do—we're getting
all kinds of interesting interactions between our tech
and her brain. One thing is certain. We can help you
be free of them, like she is. No more aspects—no more
nightmares. No more voices."

Ivy looked aghast. J.C., though, met my eyes and
nodded. He'd never wanted to be an aspect. He could
understand how part of me just wanted things to
be . . . normal.

"Let me talk to Sandra," I said.

Kyle winced. "Now, see, here's the problem. She's
my only chip in this particular bet. Surely you see I
can't give her up without something in return? Look,
let's do a quick deal. Handshake. Give me a few days
of data, and let me prove to you that I can create a reality where you don't have aspects. In turn, I'll let you
talk to Sandra."

"He's a snake, Steve," Ivy said. "I can't believe you're
even *considering* this. Why are we listening?"

I closed my eyes. But it *was* strangely tempting. Last
time I'd tried to get away, Joyce had come complaining that I never took her on missions, Armando had
phoned me seventeen times, and I'd found Ivans in the
closet drinking the bottle of hotel wine. On top of it
all, J.C. had shown up "just in case."

My life was so stuffed full of fake people, I didn't
have room for anything or anyone else. But that look

in Ivy's eyes. And this offer . . . it would only give me another layer of fakeness. I wouldn't be normal, because none of it would be real.

"No deal," I said, turning to walk away. My three aspects joined me as I strode toward the front door of the large, hollow room.

"Very well," Kyle said with a sigh. "Gerry, try the isolation program on him."

I spun. "You can't—"

"Steve, *you* broke into *my* offices. *You're* the trespasser. I'm perfectly justified in holding you a little while, to be certain you aren't dangerous. Until the authorities arrive." He smiled. "Next time, maybe don't screw with the guy who literally owns the prison."

I lunged for him, but the room flashed white.

I stumbled over a rock and hit the ground. A sandy beach, with waves softly lapping to my right, a jungle to my left. My aspects stumbled around, J.C. with hand on gun, Ngozi gasping—horrified—to be suddenly outdoors someplace so wild.

A deserted island.

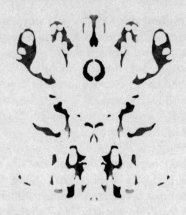

TWELVE

"That rat!" J.C. shouted. "That *slimeball*. He's getting free time studying us!"

Ivy helped me to my feet, but I had difficulty meeting her eyes. I sat down on a rock by the water, feeling exhausted. I was so *tired*. Tired of being a test subject. Tired of imagining a world where everyone lived—had friends, fell in love, visited family—except me.

Tired of being the middle manager of my own existence.

"I can't believe this!" J.C. shouted. "I can't . . . Yo, Ngozi. You okay?"

She shook her head. "No. This is *horrible*. Where are my gloves?" She fished in her pockets.

"Yeah," J.C. said, "but—like—there's no people, right? So no germs."

"Except for the fact that we're not really on a beach!" she said. "We're in that smelly warehouse, next to a table full of *six* old Chinese delivery containers. I'm going to end up touching one by accident."

"So what do we do?" Ivy looked toward J.C.

"Don't look at me," he said. "All I know how to do is shoot people and make clever wisecracks."

"Oh *please*," Ivy said. "Your wisecracks are *not* clever."

I put my head in my hands, looking at a wave roll in, feeling a pounding headache come on.

"I think Steve is going to be indisposed for a little while," Ivy said. "We might need to solve this ourselves. Ngozi, ideas?"

"Well, there are footprints in the sand over there," she said. "Might be one of those 'quest lines' the tech people were talking about."

I watched the wave roll in, deposit some sand, then die off. It would all just get sucked out again when the tide changed. Then return. A thousand little versions of Sisyphus, repeating until the sand wore away to nothing.

"Steve," Ivy said, stepping up. "We're going to follow those footprints. We'll be back in a minute. You'll be okay?"

I didn't reply.

"Just stay here, all right?"

They walked off. A part of me noticed that they were acting a little strange. They almost never left me. But now they went off exploring?

Maybe, I thought, *maybe they're excited to be able to actually interact with a world. In here, everything is fake. So maybe it's better for them.*

Or . . . was Kyle going to do something to them? To prove he could leave me here alone? How long would he hold me here? How long *could* he?

A strong hand gripped me on the shoulder. I jumped, turning, and found Lua standing behind me. Lua! He'd vanished from the mansion, becoming a nightmare.

I screamed and scrambled off the rock, pulling out of his grip and dropping into the rolling surf. I splashed, climbing to my feet, soaked wet and holding out my phone—for some reason I would never have been able to articulate—as if it were a weapon. Only then did I realize something was wrong. Lua didn't *look* like a nightmare—he didn't have the dead eyes or the sunken face. He looked just like his normal self.

"Sorry, boss. Didn't mean to sneak up on you." The large Samoan man folded his arms. He was wearing jeans and flannel, with the sleeves rolled up. He inspected the sky, then the woods, then the rock I'd been sitting on. "A deserted island. Of all the places for you to end up."

"It's . . . it's not real."

"What is?" he asked, then chuckled. He never laughed loudly, but I'd also never known him to be angry. In fact, it was hard for me to imagine him as a nightmare, like Armando had become.

"They got all the clichés at least," Lua said. "That bay is right out of a freaking Disney movie, complete with—yes—the mast of a sunken ship. Tribal drums in the background. Mysterious footprints. What you want to bet that if we start digging, we'll find a treasure chest somewhere on this beach?" He started toward the woods. "Well, let's get you out of here."

"Out?" I asked, scrambling across the beach behind him. "How?"

"They implied earlier they couldn't re-create more than a small space," he said. "A building at most. So I figure, if we get you out into the water—away from the actual island—the thing will fall apart." He started pulling at some vines dangling from a tree.

"Lua?" I said. "How do you know what they said to me earlier? You weren't there."

"I know what you know, boss. And you know what I know."

"It doesn't work that way."

"Why?"

"Because," I said. "Because that's the way I stay sane. That's the way Sandra set it up."

Lua grunted. "How did that work out for her?" He knelt down, twisting the vines to strengthen them, then wrapping them around the edge of a small fallen log.

"Lua, you're breaking the rules. I didn't bring you on this mission."

He kept wrapping the log, affixing it to another log he pulled from the underbrush. "Boss," he said softly, "you need to see what is real."

I stepped back; that was what Armando had said. I reached for a stick to use as a weapon, pulling at it, but it was stuck in the underbrush.

Lua went faintly transparent, as if he weren't all there. "I guess," he said as he worked, "we have different ways of trying to make you confront it. Armando, he always *was* a little loony. He had a loony solution."

I glanced in the direction the others had gone. I *really* didn't want to be alone with a possible nightmare.

"Don't mind them," Lua said. "They're getting pulled into the simulation, you know? Rolling with it." He yanked on his log and pulled—from the underbrush—a fully formed catamaran ship, made of logs and vines. "Not the best I've ever made," he noted, "but it's not bad, considering what I had to work with."

I gaped. That was a *serious* breaking of the rules.

"In here, you *are* the rules, boss." I could still see through him, and got the distinct impression that in his outline—as if he were a window—I could see a concrete floor, some desks with computers.

Voices.

He's up and walking. The brain has stopped suppressing his movement, even when we tell it to. That's new.

How are the readings?

Interesting. Completely different from Sandra—and completely different from when he broke in. These readings mean he's adding aspects into the simulation, though. The program should be able to interact with them, like we interacted with Sandra's aspects.

"I could live here," I said to Lua. "I could let them create my reality, and I could just . . . go with it."

"Isn't that what you do anyway?" He smiled, then turned and waved at the other three, who were walking back along the beach. He gestured toward the boat, looking very proud.

"Lua," I said. "What does it all mean? Why is this happening to me? How do I stop it?"

"You think I know? I'm what you made me to be— the guy who can get you off an island. In the end, we're all just trying to help." He got behind the boat and shoved his weight against it, pushing it along the sand toward the water.

J.C. and Ivy arrived to help push, while Ngozi complained that seawater was "full of animals." Finally she climbed aboard, then J.C. and Ivy joined her—with Lua ready to push the boat the rest of the way out into the water. He waved me toward the last seat in the catamaran.

I stepped into the warm water. "They can just stick me into another VR world if I escape this one."

"Nah," Lua said. "You can see through it."

"That's crazy," I said. "I can't even see what is real in my own *bedroom*."

"And tell me. Who is the strongest, boss? The guy who never goes to the gym, or the guy who tried—but failed—to bench his best yesterday?" He nudged me toward the boat, looking even more transparent than before.

I sat down, then realized there were only four seats. "You're not coming?"

"Gotta stay here now," he said, giving the boat a good shove. "Broke too many rules. But don't worry about me. I've got a day job." He winked. "Call center for an insurance company. Something boring. *Normal*."

He pushed us out into the water, then waved as we picked up oars and began to row. I watched him as he vanished, and I braced myself for the ripping sensation, the loss of knowledge and information. But this time it was more . . . more like a subtle *fade*. Like falling asleep.

The simulation barely lasted twenty feet beyond the small bay. One second we were rowing, and the next, the four of us were standing back in the warehouse. I reached up, wiping the tears from my eyes.

"That was awful," Gerry—the tech—complained from his seat at the computers. "He didn't follow any of the quest paths. He just broke the thing."

"A ton of hard work, flushed right down the drain," the female techie complained.

"It's the aspects," Kyle said. "They're letting him cheat. We're going to have to remove them. He'll be helpless without them."

"No," I said. "Listen. I—"

"Don't worry, Steve," Kyle said. "They aren't actually people. No loss. Mob scenario, Gerry."

The room flashed white, and we were standing in an old-time casino, next to a spinning roulette wheel.

A man burst through the door. "Big Salamander is here!" he shouted. "He's wise to—"

Gunfire blasted through the door, ripping through the man's body. He collapsed as men flooded into the room, then began shooting people indiscriminately.

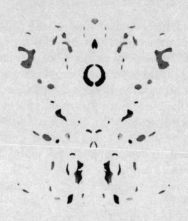

THIRTEEN

Ivy fell first. She clung to my arm as she looked at the bullet wound in her stomach. Then she began to slide down.

"No. No, no, no!" I screamed, kneeling beside her. Gunfire tore up the room. Ngozi dove for cover, but a bullet hit her in the forehead, and she collapsed. J.C. kicked over a table, then grabbed Ivy, hauling her behind cover.

I scrambled over beside them, bullets blasting wood chips from nearby tables. People screamed, but for once, J.C. didn't return fire. He pressed his hand against Ivy's wound. "Hey. Hey, stay with us. Ivy?"

"Steve," she whispered. "Steve!"

I huddled beside the overturned table.

"You need to promise," she said to me, "that you won't abandon the rest of them. That you won't let us end like this."

"I promise," I whispered.

She smiled, lips bloody. "That was a lie." She nodded toward J.C., and tried to sit up. He helped her, and then she kissed him. An intimate last kiss, amid a hail of gunfire. Our table wasn't doing much good. A shot went right through the wood and hit J.C. in the shoulder, but he lingered on the kiss until Ivy was gone.

He reverently lowered her body back down onto the floor. Then he looked at me, bleeding from one arm. "You're going to have to handle this alone, Skinny."

"I can't, J.C. I *can't*."

"Sure you can. You had an awesome teacher."

"Don't—"

"Why do you think I've been training you all this time? I knew." He tapped his head. "See what's real. You can do it."

"J.C. . . ."

He raised his fist toward me. "For good luck."

I raised my fist, then tapped his. He grinned, then pulled one gun from a holster under his arm and a second one from a hidden holster strapped to his right ankle. He stood up.

And was hit with about a hundred rounds at once. He collapsed back to the ground without getting off a single shot.

"No!" I screamed. "*NO!*"

I let out a ragged, raw screech, a moan of pain and frustration. Of *anger*. I rocked back and forth on my ankles as the bullets demolished the room. But they didn't hurt me. They weren't real.

Not . . . real.

The shooters grew faintly transparent. The splinters flying off the table, the spilled casino chips, the fallen corpses. It all . . . faded. The roar of the gunfire became a buzzing. In its place, I heard voices.

We need to learn why he's still up and moving.

We could tie him down maybe.

I could see them gathered around, watching me. Shadows looming, all save for one man at a desk of computers. *Chin,* I thought. *I need you.*

I stood up. Then, for effect, I ducked in a low run and scuttled across the casino room, as if trying to dodge bullets. That put me close to the computer desk in the real world.

To my eyes, the virtual casino faded further, and I could see real-world details. Kyle, grinning as if amused to see how helpless I was. The two guards approaching, perhaps worried that I'd hurt myself or ruin something in my thrashing.

The computer monitor.

"Yeah," Chin said in my ear. "That's easy. Not a bad UI, for what has to be an early build."

"Emitters are along the ceiling of this warehouse," Arnaud said. "In the whole room."

"Click that radio button," Chin said, "and change the target from 'single subject' to 'entire room.' See that checked box at the bottom? The one that says 'Debugging mode.' I suggest turning that off, as it might prevent them from using backdoors they've made to get themselves out of the simulation. Good luck."

I leaped for the computer, shoved Gerry aside, and clicked as Chin had instructed.

The guard from the hot dog stand rushed for me, but moved too slowly to stop me. Instantly, we were all there together. Kyle, the two guards, Gerry and the other techies. We stood in that casino, surrounded by dead people. The mobsters had stopped shooting, and were now picking through the wreckage.

"Oh, hell," Gerry said. He scrambled for the now-vanished computer controls, but just waved his hands through empty space. "Oh, *hell!*"

The hot dog guard grabbed me by the arm. "This won't accomplish anything. You're still in our prison."

I sagged in his grip, glancing toward J.C., dead on the floor. I muttered something softly.

"What's that?" the guard said, shaking me by the arm. "What did you say?"

"This isn't your prison," I muttered louder. "It's *mine*."

I bolted upright, slamming the back of my head into the guard's nose. As he shouted in pain I turned, grabbing him by the arm and flipping him over, then slammed him into the ground. I came up with his handgun, and held it out, sighting—flipping off the safety—just as J.C. had taught me.

Thank you.

I squeezed the trigger, firing off three quick shots, bringing down virtual mobsters who had been picking through the room. I wasn't really worried about them, but I wanted to get the others into firing mode. Indeed, the rest of the mobsters raised their weapons and started shooting again.

The other people—one more guard, Kyle, the four techs—screamed and dodged behind overturned tables. "It's not real!" Kyle shouted. "Remember, it's not real!"

It didn't matter. I'd been there so many times. What sounded real, what looked real, *was* real to you—even if you logically knew otherwise. Even Kyle ran for the doorway to a bathroom, where he could hide from the gunfire.

I stalked through the room. A pile of poker chips next to me exploded as a bullet hit. Shots passed right through me. I reached to my arm, where Armando had cut me, and found only smooth, unmarred skin. When had I started ignoring that wound?

A guard—one of the real people—pointed his gun toward me, so I was forced to shoot him in the shoulder. He screamed, and I casually stepped over and kicked his gun away from him. I pushed him down and took a second gun from his leg holster.

Thanks again, J.C.

I stood up and fired in two directions at once, simultaneously killing two mobsters. The techs were screaming somewhere nearby, but the only person I really cared about was hiding in the bathroom. I stepped up to the wall nearby, then pushed through. I didn't break through; I just shoved my way past it. As I did, the virtual world became even more flimsy to my eyes.

In the bathroom, Kyle spun on me, but I easily swept his feet out from under him, stepped on his wrist— getting him to drop the gun—then kicked his weapon away. I leaned down in a smooth motion and pressed two weapons to the sides of his head.

"Two guns, Kyle," I whispered. "One is real, one is fake. Can you tell which is which? Can you feel them, cold against your skin?"

He stared up at me, sweating.

"Death in one hand," I whispered, "a game in the other. Which should I fire? Right or left? Would you like to choose?"

He tried to stammer out some words, but couldn't even form a sentence. He lay there, trembling, until I stood up. Then I casually shot him in the side.

Kyle screamed, doubling over, blood leaking between his fingers.

"I lied, Kyle," I said, tossing the gun away. "Both guns are fake. I got them in the simulation. But you couldn't tell, could you?"

He continued to whimper at the pain.

"Don't worry," I said. "The wound isn't real. So no actual loss. Right?"

I dropped out of the simulation. The six people lay

unconscious on the floor, trapped in the simulation. Of my aspects—J.C., Ivy, Ngozi—there was no sign. Though I did feel a buzz from my phone. A call, from Kalyani.

I didn't answer. A moment later, a text came.

GOODBYE, MISTER STEVE.

Somehow I knew what was happening. Some of them had turned against the others, becoming nightmares. By ordering them all to congregate, I'd simply made the massacre easier. I tucked the phone away, and decided I didn't want to know which of them had chosen that path.

I just knew that when I returned, there wouldn't be any left. It was over.

Exhausted, I strode along the wall and looked into the windows here. Each was a cell, for testing patients.

Sandra was in the last one, seated on a short stool, eyes closed. I checked the wall monitor, tweaked a few settings, then opened the door.

I stepped into Sandra's world.

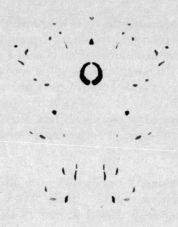

FOURTEEN

Her final hallucination took the form of a long pier at night, extending into a placid sea. Little paper boats with candles at the centers floated along, bobbing and bumping into one another.

They didn't do much to light the sea, but they did contrast with it. Fire upon the water. Frail lights one step from being snuffed out.

I walked along the pier, listening to quiet waves lap against the posts beneath, smelling brine and seaweed. Sandra was a silhouette sitting at the end of the pier. She didn't turn as I settled down next to her.

She was older than I remembered, of course. The older I grew, the more shocking it was to see weathering on the faces of people I'd once known. But she was still Sandra—same long face, same eyes that seemed to be always dreaming. A beautiful sense of control and serenity.

"Do you recognize it?" she asked.

"That place along the coast where we went," I said. "With the buskers on the dock." I could faintly hear jazz music in the distance. "You bought a necklace."

"A little chain. And you bought it for me." She put her hand to her neck, but she wasn't wearing it.

"Sandra . . ."

"It's falling apart, isn't it?" She continued to stare out across the ocean. "You're losing control of them too?"

"Yes."

"I was wrong. When I taught you all those years ago. I thought we could contain it, but we can't. I suppose . . . suppose it doesn't matter. It's all just in our heads."

"Who cares if it's all in our heads?"

Finally she looked at me, frowning.

"*Who cares?*" I said. "Yes, it's all in my head. But pain is 'all in my head' too. Love is 'all in my head.' All the things that matter in life are the things you can't measure! The things our brains make up! Being made-up doesn't make them *unimportant*."

"And if they control your life? Dominate it? Take you away from anything that could be real or lasting?"

I waved toward her simulated world. "This is better?"

"I'm at peace here. For the first time in my life." She hesitated, then met my eyes. "The second time."

"You told me I had to have purpose, Sandra. Is this purpose? Sitting here? Alone?"

"I have no choice," she said, then embraced me. "Oh, Rhone. I tried to leave again today. I visited the fairgrounds, to call you. They came back as whispers. It will happen to you too. They will steal your sanity. Unless you do . . . something . . . to contain them."

The tiny, paper-borne lights trembled on the ocean, and in a moment I caught a glimpse of the dark shallows underneath ... and dead eyes staring up out of the water.

Sandra held on tighter. I pulled her close as I picked out dozens upon dozens of corpses in the water, entombed in the depths. Her aspects.

"Oh, Sandra," I whispered.

"It is peace. The only peace I'll ever find."

I closed my eyes against that horror. Such loss ... the agony of feeling pieces inside of you being ripped away. I knew *exactly* what she'd gone through. Likely, I was the only living person who could fully empathize with what she felt.

"Mine are dead too," I whispered.

"Then you can escape."

"And if I don't want to? If I *want* them back?"

"It doesn't work that way. Once they die, they're gone for good. Even if you make new ones, the aspects you had can never return."

We embraced there for ... I don't know how long. It could have been hours. Finally, I pulled back from her and—looking into her eyes—knew that she didn't have any answers for me. At least not answers I wanted.

There was an indescribable hollowness behind her eyes. I'd heard it in her voice before, on the phone. She'd lost so much, she'd seen so many nightmares. It had led her to this. A terrible numbness. Like a real-life version of becoming a nightmare.

For a brief moment, I saw through the illusion, the hallucination. I was in a small room, and Sandra—it *was* her, alive and real—sat on a little stool on the floor beside me. Though our surroundings were a figment, she was real. She'd always been real. I knew that as well as I knew anything.

"Stay," Sandra said to me.

"All those years ago," I said softly, "when you left me . . . I tormented myself, Sandra. Yet my aspects were never able to solve this one most important mystery. Where had you gone? *Why* had you gone?"

"Rhone . . ." she said. "That doesn't matter now. *Stay.* If we have to be alone, let's be alone together."

"Do you know," I said, ignoring her plea, "a piece of me always suspected that I knew why you'd gone. I'd become too needy. That was the reason, wasn't it? You couldn't keep dealing both with your aspects *and* with my problems."

I stood up to leave, but let her hand linger in mine.

"I think I now understand your decision," I said. "Not why you left . . . but why you *had to* leave. Does that make sense?"

"It will happen faster next time, Rhone," she whispered. "If you go back out—if you claw your way through the whispers and nightmares again—the next set of aspects will degrade quickly. They'll die within months. It happened to me."

I winced, looking away, still holding her hand.

"It's either stay here in peace," Sandra said, "or go out there and suffer."

False dichotomy.

"And is there no third option? A path between the two?"

"No."

"You're wrong." I dropped her hand and turned to go.

"I didn't leave because you were too needy," she said. "Rhone? Stephen? I didn't find you too needy or anything of the sort. I left because I was starting to fall apart, and I worried that if I stayed, I would somehow infect you."

I turned back toward her, a woman sitting on the end of a wooden plank extending out into an endless ocean, corpses drifting lazily beneath her toes.

Then I stepped back up to her, leaned down, and . . . she kissed me. That old, familiar brush of the lips, followed by passion with her hand on my neck, pulling my face to hers. I let the emotion I'd guarded return, flood through me, the passion and even the pain. I pressed my lips to hers, let my skin touch hers, let my soul—briefly—touch hers.

I still loved her. That was real too.

She finally broke the kiss, pulling her head back an inch, staring into my eyes.

"You taught me," I said, "that I need to have purpose in life. I tried solving cases, but a part of me knew all along they wouldn't be enough." I took her hand. "But now, in this moment, I have a real purpose. A goal."

"What?"

"I'm going to find a way, Sandra. And when I do, I promise you, I'll come back. I'll do for you what you did for me. I'll bring you answers."

She shook her head. "Rhone . . ."

I squeezed her hand, then stood up and left her, taking the long walk back along the pier. It was so *strange* not to have a cluster of aspects around me, but I felt—already—the voices starting. The familiarity of the tones was fading away, becoming hisses and terrors.

I pushed back into the warehouse, feeling a dawning frustration and panic build inside me. How could I think to help her? I couldn't help myself.

I closed the door. Whispers hissed at me. For now I ignored them, returning to the fallen bodies of Kyle and his employees. I secured their guns—unloaded them and left them in one of the desk drawers—then I turned off the hallucination device.

Kyle immediately sat up, holding his side—poking it tenderly. He shot me a glare.

"You're going to leave me alone," I told him. "Don't contact me. Don't watch me." I walked toward the door. "But I intend to return, to visit a friend. When I do, you can study my brain—but only for the time I'm in the chamber with her. If you try to trap me again, there *will be consequences*."

Kyle nodded. "I'm glad you've seen the advantages offered by our revolutionary new—"

"Oh, shut up." I stepped out into the night, hands in my pockets, feeling wrung out. Most of me had died tonight. And I had no idea what to do with the parts that were left.

I was alone. Actually *alone*.

I found that I didn't care for it. I walked down to the shadowy parking lot, then hesitated as I saw something moving nearby, hiding behind a bush. It looked like . . . a person.

"Jenny?" I said, shocked.

The aspect vanished the moment I saw her.

I sighed, but was a little surprised that one was actually left. I stood there until—unexpectedly—my limo pulled up beside me. Barb rolled down the window, and looked out. "We done here, sir?"

"I told you to leave."

"Uncle Wilson warned me that you might occasionally be . . . difficult. I figured I couldn't exactly *abandon* you, even if you were annoying." She held up a thermos. "Lemonade?"

"I . . ." I wrapped my arms around myself. "Thank you."

She hopped out and opened the door for me, but the back of the limo looked cavernous without the aspects. Intimidating and cold.

"Could I sit up front?" I asked.

"Oh!" She opened the front passenger door. "Sure, I guess. But what about all the—"

"Don't worry about them," I said, settling into the seat. "Drive me . . . drive me to the corner of Fifty-Third and Adams."

"Isn't that where—"

"Yes."

I took the lemonade cup she poured, and it did taste a lot like Wilson's. She pulled the limo out onto the street, and we drove through a dark city; it was past eleven, approaching midnight. But it wasn't long before we pulled up beside the old building where I'd first met "Jenny" the reporter. I now saw it for what it was. An old abandoned building that might once have been an office structure.

"Park right there," I said, pointing to the curb. "A little farther forward . . ."

I climbed out and into the back of the hollow car, fishing in a bag on the floor. I finally came out with the camera. *Let's see . . . what time was it. . . .*

It took some fine-tuning to get it right. Barb had to pull the car forward a little, and I had to get the camera's timing dial just right. But eventually I snapped a photo, and it developed into a shot inside this very car from earlier in the day.

It showed me, Tobias, J.C., and Ivy. Laughing at something dumb J.C. had said, Ivy holding to his arm, Tobias grinning. I felt tears in the corners of my eyes.

Barb peeked in, looking over my shoulder.

"What do you see?" I asked.

"You, by yourself."

"I can still imagine them, in the right circumstances," I said, resting my fingers on the picture. "They're in my brain somewhere. How do I reach them?"

"You're asking me?" she asked. Then she perked up. "Oh! I totally forgot. Here, this is for you. He said to give it to you when you finished tonight." She reached into her pocket and took out a small envelope.

Inside was a small invitation to Wilson's birthday/ retirement party. At the bottom, it said, "Admits fifty-two." With a smiley face.

"He said there's no obligation," she said. "But he wanted you to know you were welcome."

I touched the tears on my cheeks, then checked the time. "Eleven forty-five? Will it even still be going?"

"I'll bet it is," she said. "You know Wilson and his fondness for nightcaps. He'll be sitting with the family around the hearth, telling stories." She eyed me. "Only a few are about you."

You know Wilson. Did I? He'd just always been there, with lemonade.

"I can't go," I said. "I just . . ."

The objection died on my lips. She must have sensed that I didn't mean it, because she went to the front, then drove to Wilson's house. He had spent many nights at my mansion, sleeping there, but did have his own home. Or at least a room in his brother's house where he stayed sometimes. I wasn't sure who actually owned the place.

Barb pulled us into the driveway—the limo barely fit—and then led me in through the garage of the modest home. She entered, and true to her word I heard laughter inside. Saw the warm light of a fireplace burning, with people sitting around and chatting, drinking cider and lemonade—which was apparently a thing for them too.

I lingered on the threshold as Barb got some cake from the kitchen table, then tossed her coachman's cap onto the counter and went over to the fireplace. She leaned down beside a chair there, and soon a familiar lanky figure unfolded itself from the seat.

Wilson seemed genuinely happy to see me. He rushed over. "Sir? Sir, please, come in! You remember Doris and Stanley? And little Bailey—well, not so little anymore, but we still say that. And . . ."

"I'm sorry," I said, turning to go. "I shouldn't be here, interrupting time with family."

"Sir," Wilson said, catching my arm. "Stephen? But you *are* family."

"I . . ."

"Don't worry about the others!" he said, gesturing toward what—he imagined—must have been my aspects. "We have plenty of seats! Just let me know how many. Please, you've been so good to me over the years. It would be a *pleasure* to host you."

"I'm alone tonight," I whispered, feeling at my jacket pocket where I'd put the photo. "Just me."

"Alone?" Wilson asked. "Sir, what happened?"

"Can we talk about it another time? I think . . . I think I might just want to have some cake."

Wilson smiled, and soon I was sitting by the fire with his siblings, nieces, and nephew. Listening to him tell *his* version of the teleporting cat case, which was admittedly one of the better ones. I didn't eat much cake, but I did enjoy the warmth, the laughter, and—well—the *reality* of it all.

All the things that matter in life are the things that you can't measure. . . .

I found that I'd inadvertently lied to Wilson, because I wasn't alone. I caught Jenny hovering in the kitchen, both my newest aspect and my last. She had her notepad out again, and was furiously writing.

EPILOGUE

I didn't go back to the mansion that night.

I couldn't go there and face that void. That . . . or worse. Madness, shadows coming to life to torment me. I just . . . I wanted a few more hours to recover.

Fortunately, Wilson's family had a guest room, which they let me have for the night. I retired there once the stories ended, and turned on the room's desktop computer. I did a little research, skimming pages on Wikipedia on basic topics I'd once known. To see if there was anything left in my brain.

I found the holes erratic. Most of it seemed to be gone, but then I'd touch on something online, and before I knew it my fingers would be typing out a string of words. When I sat back to study them, I couldn't find the information in my brain—but I'd obviously typed it, so I had it somehow.

That was how it had been for me when I was younger, before Sandra, and before the aspects. My brain tucked all of this knowledge away, but didn't know how to use it.

I slumped in the seat, overwhelmed and used up, frustrated and angry. "Is she right?" I said to the small, empty bedroom. "I promised to find a solution, but what hope do I have? Sandra knows way more than I do about this, and she couldn't find a solution."

No responses.

I took the photo from my pocket and propped it up on the computer keyboard. "Is this really it? I've lost them forever? Ivy, J.C., Tobias? Gone because my brain just doesn't feel up to the effort?"

"Not gone," Jenny said.

I spun my chair and found her standing in the shadows by the door. She held up her notepad. "I've got them right here."

"How are you still alive?" I said.

"You told me to go," she said. "You told me to go away, to break the rules. So I did. You preserved me."

"You're not a real aspect," I said. "I didn't summon you."

"Of course you did. The question is why." She stepped toward me, holding out the notepad. "What is it you wanted me to do? What's my expertise, Stephen Leeds?"

I looked away from the notepad. "I'll just end up repeating the cycle. It's either that or madness."

"False dichotomy," she whispered.

Pretending there were only two options, when there might be a third. Or more. I looked at the notepad, filled with scrawled notes. At the top of the page it read, *Tobias*.

She hadn't been taking notes on me, but on the aspects.

A third way out. A way to internalize the aspects, yet let them still live on? A way to be at peace with the voices, to give them an outlet other than to scream at me, ignored?

"I am an expert," Jenny said softly, "in them. In *you*. The sum expertise of a decade of living with them, and with this incredible, insane brain of yours." She proffered the notepad again. "Let them live again."

I took it, hesitantly. "It won't be the same."

"Make it the same."

"It won't be real."

"Make it real."

She faded. Leaving the notepad in my hand, filled with notes. Stories, lives. I didn't feel the sensation of ripping loss. The information was still there in my head. Her knowledge. My knowledge.

I looked at the glowing computer monitor. *This won't work,* I thought. *This can't work.*

. . . Can it?

I sat with the notepad under my hand, but I didn't need it. I just needed to know it was there. So I started typing.

My name is Stephen Leeds, I wrote, *and I am perfectly sane. My hallucinations, however, are all quite mad.*

I wrote for hours. Word after word after word. Somewhere near dawn, I saw a shadow reflected in the computer screen. When I turned, nobody was there, but when I looked back at the screen it was like I could see him behind me. I almost—but not quite—felt a hand rest on my shoulder. I didn't look away from the computer, but reached up, and touched the hand with mine. The hand of a man weathered with age.

Well done, Stephen, a familiar voice—not completely real—said in my mind. *Well done! Why don't*

you write about Ivy and J.C. going to Paris together?
She's always wanted to go. Something will go wrong,
of course. A diamond heist perhaps? The Regent Dia-
mond is there, on display at the Louvre. It's said to be
the clearest diamond in all the world....

I smiled. Sandra *was* wrong. It wasn't about con-
taining them. It was about letting them free.

I hurriedly continued typing. My adventures are
done. Finally, thankfully.

But my hallucinations ... well, they're *always* getting into trouble.